FOREVER CHAINED

by

ROXANE BEAUFORT

CW01019854

CHIMERA

Forever Chained first published in 2001 by
Chimera Publishing Ltd
PO Box 152
Waterlooville
Hants
PO8 9FS

Printed and bound in Great Britain by
Omnia Books Ltd, Glasgow.

FOREVER CHAINED

Roxane Beaufort

This novel is fiction – in real life practice safe sex

Prologue

'My queen is sad,' said the dark, saturnine being who lounged in a throne-like chair, watching his followers with heavy-lidded eyes. 'Bring a smile to her face. Entertain her.'

'Yes, master,' they cried, grovelling and squirming, on their knees – prostrating themselves, eager to please him. 'Whatever you say, master.'

Those who were mere hangers-on, not yet like him or those related to him, flaunted their sexuality, resplendent in leather. The women, every one a beauty, wore basques or tightly laced corsets over which their breasts bulged, nipples ripe as berries. Their skirts were so short they barely hid the apex of their thighs, affording glimpses of luxuriant floss, or denuded and jewel-pierced labia. The length of their legs was accentuated by black stockings and high-heeled shoes.

The men had also been selected for their good looks. Some were naked apart from straps that crossed their chests and banded their bellies, with thongs that ran down to lift their cocks and cradle their balls, then disappear into their bottom cracks. Others wore stylish suits, mostly black, and some had affected lavish costumes from earlier days; frock coats, breeches and top boots. Nearly all flourished an implement of some kind – a flail, a crop, a rattan cane or a flogger.

As for the rest? They were less substantial, weaving in and out of the shadows, sometimes solid, clad in clinging shrouds or robes with wimples, or priests' habits or old-fashioned mourning dress. They changed shape constantly, solid looking flesh becoming as frail as mist, not quite of the real world. Their faces became distorted, their bodies skeletal

5

– they whirled, transmogrified, human enough to dance with the rest, then as intangible as smoke.

Flares in wall-hanging braziers lit the vault. The walls were shiny, dripping with moisture. Lichen sprouted in masonry cracks. Stone coffins stood in gloomy alcoves, the lids open, the musty smell of damp earth hanging like a miasma over them. Tombs were used as tables, where candles dribbled wax down ornately decorated silver holders. The platters were silver, too, and heaped with party fare, cut glass goblets and bottles of vintage wine. The humans among them picked at the delicacies and washed them down with champagne. There was ample opportunity for the gratification of every appetite. An ugly manservant clad in rusty black was on call, his sunken eyes on his master, filled with dog-like devotion, ready to do his bidding, always.

One of the acolytes, a slim youth wearing nothing but a spiked collar, picked up a flute and started to play, the music enticing but eerie. He attracted the attention of a tall woman dressed like an Amazon, and she sidled up to him and wound one of her long legs around his thigh, rubbing her crotch against him with all the careless abandon of a whore. He ignored her, continuing to play.

The master glanced at his beloved, his bride and queen, concerned for her. She drooped at his side, so beautiful in her sorrow that his heart clenched and, had he been different, he was sure it might have broken for her. All he could do was send out waves of sympathy, his mind touching hers soothingly, and put his arm around her in an embrace that would become physical as dawn approached.

'Dearest,' he murmured, and licked a tear from her face. It tasted of salt, and blood. 'Be patient a little more. The time is rapidly approaching.'

'But I miss her so,' she whispered, that glorious mass of fair curls tumbling about her chalk-white face. 'She was my best friend. Leaving her was so hard to do.'

'Even for me?' His slanting green eyes held her misty azure ones, and he caressed her through the diaphanous robe that shrouded yet did not hide the perfection of her body and limbs. The flares struck sparks from the gems in her hair and ears, and on her neck and arms. Worth a king's ransom, they were an insignificant part of his fortune.

'I made my choice, and have never regretted it, but this doesn't mean that I lost all feeling for her,' she sighed, and it was like the wind stirring the treetops, or the merest whisper of wavelets running up the shore.

'I know, darling, I know,' he breathed, and bending his head he kissed her nipples through the silk, and passed a hand between her legs, the fabric parting like water. It was not yet that longed for moment when darkness began to yield to the sun as it appeared over the horizon, but her flesh already carried the illusion of warmth and heat, her secret folds wet for him.

He could feel his cock hardening in anticipation, the hunger in him almost as great as the craving he had satisfied earlier in the evening. His desire for her was insatiable, time of no meaning to either of them. She had not changed since that fateful night long ago when she became his, and he had been the same for far, far longer. There were definite advantages to being as they were.

'We'll provide amusement, brother,' cried a redheaded woman of bizarre, unearthly beauty. Her hair sprang from her head, coiling and twisting like snakes, then falling to her supple waist. 'My sisters and I have been clubbing. You should come. These places are for dancing, and filled nightly with nubile flesh, gorgeous girls and virile males, gyrating to a savage beat... like the drums we've heard in Africa. But more... much, much more besides. The air quivers with pheromones, and is spiced with the smell of sweat and sweet, fresh blood as adrenaline pumps through their veins. They start to lose control, obsessed by sex, blatant in their search for mates. Not long-term partners, but what they call "one night stands". These are the clothes the girls adopt. Immodest garments, expressive of their sexual freedom.'

She struck a pose in the shimmering sequinned slip she wore, low necked, sleeveless and with no back at all, stopping short where the V of her buttock divide showed, the whole kept up by shoestring straps. The skirt was brief and handkerchief pointed and her legs were bare, her shapely feet thrust into gilded sandals with high wedges.

'So, you've been mingling with the natives, have you?' he answered ironically.

'Oh, yes,' chimed in another, ebony-haired, dark-eyed, stately as an empress, wearing a pink chiffon blouse with nothing underneath, and a pair of tie-dye bootleg jeans. 'It's like taking candy from a baby. They are so susceptible to our wiles, such easy prey.'

'Be careful,' he warned, every line of his body proclaiming hauteur and leadership. 'We aren't in a war torn area now, where corpses pass almost unnoticed.'

'We're not stupid,' returned a third female, tossing back her braided and ornamented silvery-blonde hair. Younger than the others, she was as petite and charming as a fairy, yet he knew her to be the most vicious of the trio. Even though she was dressed in a silk skirt and matching brassière top, there was nothing of the ingénue about her.

Like those of her sisters, and him, her eyes held the darkness, wisdom and depravity of centuries.

'We've brought back some playmates,' said the redhead, her scarlet lips curved in a sly smile.

She clapped her hands imperiously, and a couple of young men appeared from the darkness near the bottom of the steps. They had their arms protectively around two girls, though all were making a brave attempt at appearing nonchalant.

'Cool,' one of the youths opined nervously, glancing round

at the vault and its unusual company. 'But the sounds are crap. We can't dance to that stuff.'

'Oh, darling, how remiss of us,' cooed the silvery-blonde. A snap of her fingers and rap blasted from unseen speakers. 'What did you say your name was?' she asked above the uproar.

'Lenny,' he answered guardedly, crop-headed, tattooed, and with rings in one eyebrow. A sweaty white T-shirt covered his well-muscled chest, and his lean hips were encased in denim, the bulge at his crotch emphasised. He jerked to the beat, unable to keep still.

'Well now, Lenny, you agreed to come with us,' the blonde went on, reaching out her long blue lacquered talons and tweaking his nipples through the cloth. 'What are the girls called? Danielle and Maxine, is it? Welcome aboard.'

'You said there was a party… plenty of booze and drugs,' objected the other man, a heavier type of Scottish extraction. He looked as if he could be trouble.

'It *is* a party, Robbie,' insisted the brunette, coming across without appearing to move, and winding her shapely, alabaster arms round his neck. 'And your little girlfriends will have a whale of a time, probably better than if they'd stayed with you. We know how to pleasure women, you see, and it's not all bang-bang-thank-you-mam.'

'Don't know what you're driving at,' Robbie snarled, looking like a thug with his shaven head and attitude. 'I've never had any complaints. They like a hot cock up 'em.'

'And do you?' the dainty blonde asked, reaching down and squeezing the packet behind his flies.

'Hey, what you getting at?!' he bellowed, torn between withdrawing and continuing to enjoy the pressure of her hand. 'We're not shirt-lifters, if that's what you mean.'

'Would I suggest such a thing?' she breathed coyly, batting her eyelids at him and increasing the grip on his cock. 'You're impudent. How dare you question my judgement? I think

9

you need to be punished.' She swung round to her sisters, saying, 'Don't you agree? This rude oaf will benefit from being chastised.'

'Indeed, and the other clod,' they cried contemptuously, and the arched roof echoed as their followers joined in, excitement running like wildfire among them.

'But first, we must attend to the girls,' the brunette reminded. 'Such feisty little darlings, who think they know everything there is to know about men, sex, and the universe. Time they were taken down a peg or two. This will amuse our queen, won't it, master?' and she turned her dark eyes to him enquiringly, red embers glowing in their depths.

'It may. But turn off that atrocious noise. Have you tasted them?' he asked, already weary of the show. The music ceased abruptly.

'Of course,' replied the three sisters in unison, nodding emphatically. '"Sweets for the sweet,"' added the blonde, licking her cushiony red lips. 'Try them, my lord.'

He shook his head, smiling ruefully. Was there nothing new under the sun? This was not a good metaphor for such as he, but his thoughts often lingered nostalgically on that majestic orb so long denied him. He was a creature of the night. Yet was he to be forever hassled by those who had followed him willy-nilly, those who were a long-time part of him, and those who had ambitions to become like him? Sometimes, weary of them, he would take his queen to some remote island where they could be quite alone. But by the very nature of their affliction, paradise such as this could not last long. Small animals, rodents and suchlike, would suffice for a short while, but then the wild craving would drive them back to civilisation in search of bigger game.

The sisters shrugged and beckoned their captives forward. Even the tough Robbie could not resist. In an instant their clothing had been whipped off, eager hands obeying the sisters' silent commands. Despite all their big talk, Robbie

10

and Lenny were hugely embarrassed, trying to hide their genitals with their hands. The girls, however, once over the shock, preened themselves before so many admiring eyes. The one called Maxine was coffee-coloured and leopard lean, and Danielle was plump, with a typical peaches-and-cream English complexion.

'On your knees, slaves,' the sisters commanded, and Lenny and Robbie were propelled forward and down by hands that could be felt but not seen.

With their shoulders pressed to the cold stone floor and their bottoms in the air, they presented a lively spectacle for the audience. Their testicles hung like ripe fruit between their thighs, their stubby pricks exposed and getting bigger, and their cracks in full view, with the tiny mouths of their arseholes pursed as if fearing invasion.

The master glanced at his queen. Not the ghost of a smile hovered over her lips. She looked as sorrowful as ever. 'Get on with it,' he shouted to his sisters.

The redhead took a flogger to Robbie's bare hinds. It had several thongs, each tipped with a knot. She raised her arm and it swished down in a direct line, landing across his rump. He jumped, grunted, then braced himself, taking it like the man he thought he was. He was rewarded by the brunette, who slithered beneath him and took his cock in her mouth. He yelped as she started to suck, then succumbed to the temptation of her experienced tongue. She milked him of his semen, swallowing it in great, greedy gulps, then writhed upwards and sank her sharp incisors into his neck. The creamy spunk that lingered round her mouth turned blood crimson.

Lenny, meanwhile, had been set upon by two women in leather who wound themselves around him, demanding that he lick their slits, the crops of their male escorts landing on his back and thighs. They allowed him to kneel up, in order that he might pleasure the women more fully. One at a time

11

they crouched over his face, held back their labial wings, exposed their engorged nubbins and had him lick them till they came. This didn't take long. Then they rolled him on his back and sat astride him, one over his face, the other impaled on his upward straining cock.

The remaining sisters attended to Maxine and Danielle. They were hauled to a double crosspiece centre floor, and iron cuffs clamped round their wrists. Maxine's breasts were pressed to the wood. Danielle faced outwards. Both had their arms strung above their heads by chains slipped through rings and bolts. Their legs were opened, spreaders thrust between them and manacles attached to their ankles. They did not struggle, though Danielle started to sob. Both had popped pills and consumed alcohol during the evening and the sisters had evoked strong magic. If anything, this resembled a drug-induced dream. Tomorrow they would wake with hangovers and no memory of their visit to the vault or anything that transpired there, not even the sisters' embraces that had drained them of their body fluids, just a little, nowhere near death.

'Such fun,' murmured the redhead, apropos of nothing in particular as she ran her hands over her victims' bodies, weighing their breasts, pinching the hardened nipples, running down their silken skinned bellies and dipping into their opened clefts.

She drove a finger into Danielle's pink hole, wetting it from the juice glistening there, then transferring this to the clit that protruded like a little penis between the girl's labia. She tickled the eager organ and Danielle cried out. The redhead immediately stopped all caresses and picked up a long, flexible cane. The air sang as she brought it down across Danielle's thighs. The girl screamed, and the audience roared.

The dainty blonde was examining Maxine's rear, smoothing her hands over the girl's muscle-packed buttocks and hollow flanks. 'You work out?' she asked.

'I do.'

'You prefer to make love to women than men?' The blonde trailed the tip of her whip around the lips of Maxine's sex as it pouted between her legs.

'You could say that.' Maxine's attitude was defiant.

'I do say it, and I say that you understand the paradox of pain and pleasure,' the blonde went on, wetting a finger in Maxine's vulva and applying it to her forbidden hole.

She strained against her bonds, muscles standing out under her shiny dark skin. 'Get off me,' she snarled.

For answer, the blonde gave her a taste of the lash, hard and fast and repeated several times. A lattice of stripes marked the brown backside. Maxine did not utter a sound or make any movement. The spectators murmured their approval, and each took a turn at beating the girl, till the blonde ordered them to stop and set her free, then lay with her on one of the divans, pleasuring her and taking her own pleasure in turn, though leaving some for her dark-haired sister who hung over them hungrily, her lips drawn back over her sharp white teeth.

'Come away,' the master urged his queen, wearied by a spectacle he had seen time and time again.

Soon his sisters would seek their coffins and the rest of the Undead slink into safe sleeping places, too. As for the humans who admired them and liked to play at being vampires, they would get into their cars and drive back to town, something deep within them satisfied by this brush with the mysterious, hellish and damned. They thrilled at the idea of the blood drinker, were probably toying with the fascinating notion of begging Dimitri to grant them eternal life, but were not quite sure. Not that he would do it. He chose with great care those to whom he offered the Dark Gift.

'Is it dawn?' the queen asked listlessly, staring at the breathtakingly handsome man who was her husband and lord.

She loved him, and was it possible for someone like her to say 'more than life', then this would have been her vow. He was so tall, so elegant, and had smooth pale skin, save for the flush on the prominent cheekbones and the crimson of his lips. He had fed not long before. Shoulder-length black hair and green eyes, an aristocratic, aquiline nose, and that arrogant, self-willed, sensual mouth completed his charismatic appearance.

'Almost,' he said, held out an arm and she slipped her hand into the crook of his elbow. Together, they left their riotous followers and retired to another, smaller vault.

The manservant preceded them, opening the heavy iron door and saying, 'Pleasant dreams, master... mistress.'

'Thank you, Carl,' she said. 'Don't forget to lock up when our guests have gone, and clear away the mess.'

'Yes, mistress,' Carl said, and backed out, closing the door carefully.

The vault was dark, save for a thin sliver of bluish light striking through a small aperture in the arched roof. There were no furnishings except a catafalque, draped in black and purple. Suddenly soul-weary, she sank into its velvety depths. He was there, holding her tightly against him, snatching at this moment that only happened at sunset or sunrise, when they could unite their bodies; human for a brief, heavenly while.

Their clothing had vanished and he ran his large hands over her perfect form, the hollows of her throat, the swell of her breasts, the tips of her nipples. She reached up and thrust her hands into his raven hair, pulling his face down.

His mouth joined hers, their saliva blending. She caught the aftertaste of blood, and this made her all the more lustful. Hot thrills seared her, and blinding visions of their encounters with those who had unwittingly supplied them with sustenance as darkness fell. Their unity, their separateness from mortals, their lawless, blasphemous existence, their utter loneliness and dependency on one another for any sort of comfort, made her cleave to him even more.

He covered her with his body as if enfolding her in giant wings, then entered her in one savage thrust. This was real. No phantom or astral congress, but a flesh and blood one. She gloried in his superhuman strength, his violence and need, the wildness of his nature, akin to the wolves with which he sometimes ran when it pleased him to shape-shift. She flung up her arms and gripped the carved bars at the head of the catafalque. It shook beneath his savage pounding. Her clitoris throbbed with need and he eased off, sensitive to her desires, slipping a hand between them and rubbing her till she was almost peaking. He pounded into her and she cried out as ecstasy took her and tossed her on high. He went in deeper, as if trying to become a part of her, and his growls grew louder as his frenzied invasion of her reached its height.

She felt the icy torrent of his semen as he released it inside her, and beat at his back and dragged her nails across his skin. He looked down at her and she drowned in the sea of his flaming eyes. She was drenched in human sweat and human love juices, remembering, just for an instant, what it had been like to walk in the sunshine, laugh and joke and enjoy the foods that nourished mortals.

Then the single bar of light became stronger and he reached up and pulled the curtains close around the funereal bed, making the darkness complete. She curled into his arms and lost consciousness, carried away on a whirlwind.

But, just before she was entirely absorbed in her strange, vampire dreams, she heard a woman's voice whispering plaintively, 'Don't forget me. Never forget. I loved you, too.'

Chapter One

A cold mist drifted in from the sea. Stella could smell it, salty and pungent and damp. The moon was full, hanging like a severed head, streaked with lines of thin black cloud. There was no shelter. The bushes were stunted and bent almost horizontal by the endless buffeting of the wind.

How did she get there? Was she dreaming?

She remembered going to bed in the house she shared with Kate. She had felt lonely and disgruntled, for the walls were thin and she had been unable to avoid hearing Kate shagging her latest boyfriend. Their moans and joyous exclamations and the creaking of springs had roused her to fever pitch. She had pushed open the neck of her knee-length T-shirt, smoothed the lush curves of her breasts and circled the tips of her nipples till they crimped. This was exciting and something she had not done in a while. After unsatisfactory experiences with a couple of fellow students, she had decided to give sex a miss till Mr Right turned up. Kate had laughed, said she was naïve and would never be able to stay the course. Listening to her yowling like a cat on heat, Stella thought she was probably right.

Still pleasuring her breasts with one hand, she let the other glide down across her belly and lift the hem of the T-shirt. Desire made her ache as she traced the mat of curly dark hair that covered her mound. Unable to stop herself, she let her favourite finger, the middle right one, slide across the closure of her outer lips. Her clitoris hardened, perking up beneath her touch. Within seconds she was rubbing herself frantically, legs spread, abandoning thought in the irresistible

16

desire to masturbate to orgasm.

She had fallen asleep as soon as she peaked, and now there was the sensation of flying that she associated with dreams. She could see clearly, every boulder of that rugged terrain starkly defined. There was a ruin below her. She looked down on its ragged, broken towers sticking up like dragon's teeth, and into its dark maw.

And then she saw him, standing there waiting for her.

His face was upturned, the most beautiful face she had ever seen, framed by a tumbling mass of inky hair – those ascetic features and that melancholy expression, and eyes of so dazzling a blue that they pierced her to the core. He held out his arms and she floated down into them. She was aware of the insubstantial nature of their embrace, yet of its curious flesh-like quality. Lust swept over her, a primordial passion unlike anything she had ever known. Strange, sensual music played somewhere – and ethereal voices ululated wordlessly, accompanied by the faint, faraway howling of wolves. It made her skin crawl, but aroused her to a frenzy. She wound herself deeper into the stranger's arms.

She wanted to tell him how beautiful he was, but no words would come out. He knew though, she could tell, nodding at her and smiling such a radiant smile, and such brilliant white teeth. Then he was gone and she was bereft, wondering if she had imagined him. Tears wetted her cheeks. He was so perfect a being, and she wanted him desperately.

His hand came to rest on her shoulder. She turned to see him bathed in a golden penumbra. She was naked and so was he. He was well built, with a broad chest punctuated by two wine-red discs, a flat belly, and a tangled bush of pubic hair from which sprang a large cock. The stem was thick, the luscious purple cap rising from the rolled back foreskin. It was wet and shiny, jism oozing from the little slit.

She stared down at it, riven with the longing to lap at it, then she tingled all over at the feather light sensation of his

17

fingers on her breast as he cupped it in his palm and thumbed the nipple. He was much taller than her, but she was aware of the effortless way in which his tongue flicked at her lips, entered her mouth, and savoured it. His breath was spiced with cinnamon, yet with an under-taste of iron – or blood. She was possessed of a dark, hungry need and lifted her hips and ground her pubis against the bulk of the engorged penis rising like a spear between them and pressing into her belly.

He grasped her and lifted her and held her for a moment, then lowered her onto his mighty phallus. She cried out with shock, for it was like a bar of solid ice. He was gentle, letting her take him inch by slow inch, till she was fully impaled, his helm nudging her cervix, her inner muscles gripping him like a velvet glove. Though his phallus was freezing it burned with a white heat, searing her vagina, stabbing her with the most intense sensations of pain and pleasure. She locked her ankles around his waist, his hands supporting her under the buttocks, and they were no longer on top of the tower but revolving in outer space, against a backdrop of indigo nothingness spangled with a multitude of stars. His mouth was on hers, his fingers finding her rampant clit, circling and frigging it.

A myriad images flashed across her vision – of deltas and cocks, semen and sexual juices – of men and women copulating – of deviants, too. Men with men and women with women, and threesomes, foursomes; any and every connotation. Lovely, bizarre, untamed women gorged on blood and spunk drawn from male partners. And there was a man; a large, powerful, awe-inspiring figure with a harsh face and green eyes with fire in their depths. Beside him, linked with him as if welded at the genitals, was a fair-haired woman of intense beauty, not wicked like the others who enjoyed cruelty for its own sake, but a sad creature.

And then the visions vanished and the universe turned from

indigo to pulsing crimson. She could hear the pounding of her heart as she watched the awesome spectacle of a torrent of blood pouring down like a waterfall over a precipice.

She wanted to scream, but was caught up in orgasm, no gentle climb or ecstatic plateau, just a terrifyingly fierce climax that wracked her from toes to cortex and stripped her of consciousness for a second. The pressure of his enormous cock intensified and she bucked against him, embracing him with arms and thighs, straining to make him a part of her as waves of blissful agony lit up her every nerve. And he was there, too, filling her with the sudden rush of his freezing libation, his face buried against her shoulder momentarily, as his hips continued to jerk.

Then suddenly, abruptly, she was alone. She lost all sense of direction, could not tell which was up and which down, tumbling into a black pit of oblivion, her last thought one of heartbreaking loss and terror.

Is it the singer, or the song? Stella wondered, staring into the dark hall, half blinded by the strobes.

She was the singer, playing the intro on the guitar. And the song had been composed by her and Kate, who extemporised on the keyboard. Jez added rhythm with a soft swish swish of snare drum, while Tommy's agile fingers worked magic on the violin.

The pub was crowded, a meeting place for students, many from the college Stella had attended until recently. But a career in computer science and business studies was not what she wanted. There was a drive within her impossible to control – the burning ambition to compose and perform. At moments like this she was in her element – on stage, leaning towards the microphone and launching into the lyrics.

'*And where is my darling now? She's lying in the cold ground, so fair and pale of brow.*'

'Jesus, that's bloody mournful,' Jez had complained at

rehearsal, running a puzzled hand through his hennaed dreadlocks. 'What's up, doc? You got PMT or something?'

'No, it just came to me in the night,' Stella replied. 'I woke up and made a note of it. And the music, too – leastways, the da-de-dah bit. Kate got it together. She knows about writing down notes and stuff.'

In the night? She remembered waking in need of the lavatory, then climbing back into bed and snatching vainly at fragments of her weird dream. Nothing would come to her, accept a feeling of cold that seemed to have penetrated her vitals, a certain soreness between her legs, and the song.

Kate had pronounced it to be brilliant, and immediately worked on it, then tried it out on the other members of *Zero700* and decided to launch it at the next gig.

This was it. Here they were, here *she* was, mouthing those oddly poignant lyrics. Who was it in the ground, and who the inconsolable mourner?

She suddenly noticed that it had happened; a hush that falls over drinkers and bar staff alike when a tune grabs their attention. She sang on and when she finished, was met by spontaneous applause. She bowed and took a break, wanting a drink and a cigarette.

'Hi there, sis.' It was the instantly recognisable voice of her brother, Stephen. She had not seen hide or hair of him for over six months and this suited her fine. They had never got on well, and since the funeral of their parents, tragically killed in a car accident two years before, the situation had worsened. Stella spent the time at university, and Stephen, older than her, dipped his fingers into any number of pies. He liked to think of himself as an entrepreneur, but his ventures were not successful. He usually managed to avoid trouble by the skin of his teeth, leaving his partners to face the music.

'What do you want?' Stella demanded offhandedly, refusing his proffered lighter and using her own.

20

It was the intermission and another band was setting up. Jez and Tommy had gone to the bar and Kate was holding court, surrounded by a gaggle of admirers. Stella wished she would join her. Stephen always made her uneasy. It was hard to believe they had been born to the same mother, fathered, presumably, by the same sire.

'That's not a very nice way to greet your only relative,' he said smoothly, and eased his leather-covered backside onto a stool, then snapped open a beer can. He was elegantly dressed, as always, a lean man of medium height, with a sharply featured face and short hair, cut and bleached by a top stylist in a prestigious salon. He always found the money for luxuries, no matter how deep in debt.

'I'd rather we didn't meet at all,' she said, puffing furiously at her cigarette; fat chance of kicking the habit with slime-balls like him about.

It was noisy at the side of the stage where the bar extended, enabling performers to get a drink, if they could make themselves heard above the hubbub. She caught the manager's eye, and ordered a lager. While she waited she spotted Kate's fiery hair and signalled urgently. Kate nodded and extricated herself from her fans, coming across, tall and slim and extremely attractive. Not for her tatty jeans and sloppy old sweaters when facing her public; she always dressed up to the nines. Tonight she wore a black, backless strappy top and a pink satin skirt split to the thigh. Her generous breasts were unfettered by a bra, her long legs alluring in fishnet hold-ups with lacy welts and the most outrageously expensive, spool-heeled shoes on her feet, yet she managed to get away with it. Worn by any one else, her clothing would have earned her the label of hooker.

Not Kate Barnes, however. She was a free spirit who just about managed to make a living with her music, but if times were hard, then she took any job available, never too proud to stack shelves or man tills in supermarkets. She carried her independence into her relationships, too. Most of the time she went to bed with men of her choice, but was not averse to the more gentle embraces of women.

Stella thought about this as her friend approached. Though they'd lived together for months, making love had not been part of the equation. She sometimes wondered how she would feel if they did. She envied Kate her experience and confidence, listened to her talking cynically about men, and often met her various studs strolling about the flat bollock-naked, on their way to the bathroom or kitchen. She'd learned to turn a blind eye, but lately had started to wish that she, too, might find a lover. This longing had grown since the night of her extraordinary and illusive dream. She found herself in an almost permanent state of arousal, her panties damp at the crotch, her labia super sensitive, her clitoris a swollen bud at the apex, no matter how often she played with it.

She felt like it now, leaning her elbows on the bar but wanting to finger herself, and when Kate came up and looped an arm affectionately over her shoulder, she said, a touch resentfully, 'Lucky you to have so many groupies.'

Kate grinned and hugged her. 'They're okay, but there's not much talent on offer tonight. They should be hanging round you. You're the singer... the front person. But you throw off the wrong sort of vibes, girl; too cool by half. It's fine to keep 'em dangling, but you've got to give 'em the come-on, too. Whether you follow through or not is down to you.

'The new song was a smash,' she went on breezily, 'just the sort of funky, folksy thing that's our trademark. We'll include it in the new demo tape.'

'You need a manager,' said Stephen, materialising beside her.

'And who the fuck are you?' Kate raised a haughty eyebrow and looked down her nose at him. She was slightly taller in her high heels.

'This is my brother, Stephen,' Stella said, simmering with rage. He was so damn pushy. She didn't want to introduce them, but couldn't very well avoid it, so she added, 'Steve, meet Kate.'

'I saw you on stage just now,' he said imperturbably. 'You're great. In fact the whole band has enormous potential. I can introduce you to someone who'll take you on and handle everything… knows everyone there is to know in the entertainment business. Why don't I take you to meet him?'

'Cool it,' Kate cautioned. 'There's Jez and Tommy. We don't do a thing without asking them.'

'Did I say you couldn't?' Stephen spread his hands apologetically and gave her the benefit of his most winning smile.

Stella hoped she would not be taken in by it. When he liked, her brother could charm the birds right down out of the trees, a well spoken, well educated product of the public school system. He was knowledgeable and bright, in with the right people, using his connections. The Kerricks had always been top drawer, until recent years when their fortunes had declined. There were not many of them left now; only Stephen and Stella in this particular branch of what had once been a thriving, influential, politically oriented family.

'Who is this guy?' Kate was in no way convinced.

'His name is Quincy Dubois.'

'I've heard of him,' she said, nodding her thanks when he placed a rum and coke in front of her. 'Doesn't he run a swingers club for liberated adults?'

'Among other things,' he said with a sly smile, and he was looking at her breasts that pressed so intimately against the jersey top, the nipples lifting the thin fabric.

He's disgusting, Stella thought, sick to the stomach to see

him leering at her friend. 'I don't think we need someone like him, do we, Kate?' she broke in.

Kate had that pensive look on her face, the one Stella always suspected, for it usually meant she was mulling over a scheme. Most times they worked, but there had been one or two failures. 'I'll see what Jez and Tommy have to say,' Kate replied, smiling at Stephen in a challenging way that few could resist.

'You do that,' he said, resting a hand on her thigh, 'and if they agree, I'll set up a meet.'

Kate did not move; she simply glanced down at his hand. He took it away and, 'How come I haven't seen you before?' she asked, sipping her drink.

'Stephen and I don't exactly gel,' Stella answered for him.

'I wouldn't say that,' he rejoined, his lips smiling but his eyes steely. 'However, I couldn't let my little sister's twenty-first birthday go by without getting in touch.'

'Oh, right,' Kate said. 'It's tomorrow, isn't it? We're throwing a party.'

'Am I invited? She has something to celebrate. It's not every day a girl inherits a property from a grandmother several times removed.'

Stella didn't miss the viciousness in his voice, though he covered it well. This bequest had always stuck in his craw. He considered that it should have come to him by rights, as he was the eldest. But no, Emma Kerrick had been adamant, clinging to life till she was over a hundred, remaining in her manor house in County Wicklow, and ensuring that no one robbed her of it. She eventually died in the year Stella was born. To the surprise and chagrin of all, her will stated that Stella Kerrick would have both Troon Hall and Emma's investments and savings on the day she reached her majority; not eighteen, but twenty-one as it had been in *her* day.

'You've mentioned this, haven't you, Stella?' Kate said, giving her a shrewd glance from sparkling brown eyes. 'You

24

lucky bugger! Wish I had a fairy godmother, or grandmother or whatever.'

'I've not thought about it much,' Stella admitted. 'In fact, ever since I was told the legacy was being held in trust for me, I've found it rather an embarrassment. I know dad was piqued because he hadn't been selected, but for some reason my ancestress wanted me to have Troon Hall and all it entails. I don't know what the hell I'm going to do with it.'

'You'll visit it; that's what you'll do, and I'll come with you,' Kate announced, downed her drink and stood up. 'Meanwhile, Posh Tart Lady of the Manor, the support band have finished, and we've punters out there and another set to get through.'

It was while Stella was into her second song, her mind focused on the words, the interpretation, the chords under her fingers, that she looked towards the bar. The pub was packed, the lights reduced to a glow. It was nearly impossible to distinguish a face in the crowd, but a pale oval drew her gaze, drew and fixed it and imprinted itself there forever.

He was wearing dark glasses. They obscured his eyes but reflected her, a tiny figure with a guitar. He was not drinking, just staring at her with relentless attention. She was sure it was him – her angelic/demonic lover, though his hair was slicked back and tied in a ponytail.

An incredibly strong feeling of arousal clutched at her pussy and gave it a squeeze. Could he feel it too? She knew who he was, recognised him as the entity who had been with her in her dream. Her nipples were hot against her crop-top and the seam of her jeans cut into her lower lips, tightening as they swelled. Her clit thrummed to the beat of the music, ready to hurl her into orgasm. She could feel his fingers on her breasts, his tongue at her epicentre, his ice-cold phallus in her body. Her training made her carry on with her performance, but passion was boiling inside her, rising, climbing. She gripped the neck of the guitar, longing to touch her clitoris and ease her aching need.

Her voice did not falter or her fingers stumble over the refrain, but it seemed he was on the stage, and there was someone else, too, overshadowing him. He was being manipulated by a menacing, majestic creature who was using them both, working their strings like a puppet master. She could hear laughter above the music, in and around it and deep in her soul; echoing, thundering – while slanting emerald eyes with red sparks in the pupils burned into her mercilessly, body, mind and spirit.

She and the beautiful young man came together, staring into each other's eyes, locked in a fierce embrace. Her fantasy closed in around her.

Then her eardrums were shattered by a storm of clapping and whistling. Kate was bowing and kissing her fingertips to the audience. A prod in the back told Stella to do the same. Jez and Tommy were acknowledging the applause, and the world righted itself as the lights came up. She looked towards the bar, but there was no sign of him. He had disappeared completely – if he had ever existed at all.

Amidst the cheers and encores, the exhilaration of success putting the rest of the band on a high, Stella experienced the deepest doubts, fearing for her sanity.

'I went to see her tonight,' Stephen said, lounging on the white leather settee in Quincy's luxurious riverside home. A leggy young woman was curled up beside him, her hand inside his flies, playing with his cock. Her hair fell in an unbroken sweep of gold almost to her waist. '*Zero700* are good; a bit rough round the edges but nothing a first-class manager couldn't improve.'

It was midday, and the view across the Thames was stunning, the City of London looking for all the world like a Canaletto watercolour of eighteenth century Venice. Towers and domes, spires and stacks, were all softened by distance, rendered light and buoyant. This spacious second floor apartment commanded a superb vista of river, shipping and buildings. From there Stephen could admire the capital without the inconvenience of air-pollution or road rage or beggars. Above all, he hated being inconvenienced.

Inevitably, an image of Stella flashed through his mind. Though of his blood she upset him more than most, an afterthought, born when their parents were in their forties. He had been ten at the time and away at boarding school. His jealousy of this little sister knew no bounds, especially when he learned of great-great-grandmother's will.

He had worked it out, studying family archives. Emma Kerrick, née Collingwood, was born in eighteen seventy-seven and married Clive, Viscount Kerrick, in the late eighteen-nineties. He had been the son of an earl with a large holding in Ireland, and their only child, a boy, was born in nineteen hundred. Several generations had passed; none of them prolific, and Emma outlived them all with a kind of grim determination, refusing to hand her property over to anyone. But it was as if, at one hundred and three, she at last relinquished her hold on life when hearing of Stella's birth. At the reading of the will, the astonishing information had been revealed that this child would inherit the entire estate.

Though young at the time, Stephen listened to the adults talking and understood the implications. As he grew older it galled him all the more, for he loved money and power above everything and fancied himself lording it as an Irish landowner. No chance of that, unless – and here the demon within him smirked and giggled – *unless* she met with an accident, or could be proved incapable. She wanted to be a pop star. Pop stars often adopted hedonistic lifestyles that led to an early demise. Sex and drugs and rock-n-roll. This was not so prevalent as in the seventies and eighties, but there, nonetheless. It was a life of enormous pressure and strain. Stephen had decided that Stella should be encouraged, and there was no one better fitted for the job of raising her to the heights and then destroying her than Quincy. He had no morals, no principles, and no milk of human kindness. Play their cards right, and in the not too distant future, Stephen might be the next in line for Troon Hall.

He gathered his wandering thoughts, aware of the mayhem in his trousers caused by the attentions of the girl. Quincy, who stood on the balcony with a pair of top-of-the-range binoculars focused on the passing water traffic, turned and trained them on him. He stared through the finely adjusted lenses for a long moment. Stephen began to feel distinctly uncomfortable, his dick so engorged it threatened to poke out of his trouser closure. The girl, he thought her name was Sherry, unbuttoned him completely and let that eager serpent escape through the gap. As Quincy subjected them to that blank, unnatural stare, she lowered her head and ran her tongue around Stephen's helm, dragging a sigh from his depths, then sucking him vigorously.

Quincy lowered the glasses and commenced to talk, fully expecting Stephen to keep it together and answer sensibly. 'Bring them to the office, and they'll need a demo. I'm looking for a new band to launch… that latest scam for deliberately creating a pop group has made a fortune for the promoters.' His voice was deep and cultured, though his background was obscure. If ever the sobriquet 'self made man' applied to anyone, then it was Quincy Dubois – and this was not his real name either. Few were party to that secret.

He strolled across and pushed up Shelley's tiger-print miniskirt. She wore no panties. Her bottom was raised as she bent over Stephen, torturing his cock with divine pleasure. Quincy looked down at her, bared from bum to clit, and smiled. He inserted a finger between the pursed, fair-fringed sex lips, exposing the wet pink flesh within. He wetted it with the juices already gathering there and massaged her nubbin lightly. She wriggled her bottom appreciatively, but did not stop sucking Stephen's cock.

Though heterosexual, Stephen's loins responded to the sheer bulk and personality of the man. He was in his late thirties, and his thick hair was touched with grey, only a sprinkling that had been exaggerated by his hairdresser and would be controlled. It was styled like that of a roman emperor, brushed forward to curl on his forehead. It gave him a distinguished look that, coupled with his straight-backed stance and proud posture, made the whole aura surrounding him forceful, powerful and irresistible.

Wanting to please him, Stephen managed to say, 'I've told you about Stella's inheritance. Well, she'll get it today. She went to see the solicitor this morning, but wouldn't let me go with her, the bitch.'

'I don't blame her,' Quincy remarked, placing his hands each side of Sherry's buttocks and spreading them wide. 'You're a turd, Stephen, and I wouldn't trust you further than I could fling you.'

'I can do you a bit of good,' he answered sulkily.

'So you will, dear boy,' Quincy went on, unzipping his trousers and producing a large, well-formed cock that he rubbed carefully, making it grow, the reddish glans naked of foreskin. 'But this doesn't make you any the less a turd.'

He brought his hand down across Sherry's rump in a hard, stinging slap. She reacted by biting Stephen's tool, almost precipitating ejaculation. He didn't want to come yet, didn't want it to be over, that glorious sensation as her red lips caressed his knob and her tongue sucked and slurped on it, each stroke one of bliss. He suspected that Quincy had plans for her, and didn't intend to miss a minute of it.

Quincy slapped her four more times, then slipped a hand between her legs and gentled her pouting lower lips, rubbing her ardent little bud till she shuddered and bucked, losing her hold on Stephen's prick as she came, shrieking. Quincy smacked her again, growling, 'Don't let go of him. I want to see him spurt all over your face.'

As he spoke he anointed the tiny crimped mouth of her anus and pushed two fingers inside. She squealed, but continued to suck Stephen. He loved what she was doing to him, but she blocked his view of Quincy, her hair steaming down. It was only by her jerks and sighs and expression of downright pain that he knew Quincy had thrust his huge appendage into her forbidden hole and was arse-fucking her. This excited Stephen so much that his balls contracted and semen shot out of his cock-tip, spraying Sherry's face, hair and breasts. She tried to move but Quincy's hand came down on the back of her neck, holding her in place as the final inches of his cock shunted into her with a force that shook all three of them.

She yelped, Stephen grunted, squashed at the bottom of the heap, and Quincy gave a great bark as he spent into the condom buried deep within Sherry.

He withdrew almost immediately, rolled down the rubber and tossed it from the balcony into the fast flowing river. Then he wiped his cock on a tissue, tucked it into his trousers and zipped up. Sherry rose, about to go to the bathroom to wash off Stephen's spunk.

'Leave it,' Quincy commanded, and caressed her backside through her little skirt. 'I like to see you smeared with his come. It makes you look what you are… a whore.'

'Yes, master,' she said obediently.

'And pull up your skirt. You know I want you accessible at all times.'

'Yes, master.' She did so, and stood beside him as he idled through her crisp bush, exploring the damp folds, then lifting his fingers to his nostrils and sniffing her fragrance.

'And *Zero700*?' Stephen ventured.

It was almost impossible to gauge Quincy's moods. They swung violently, depending on business deals, sexual proclivities, or the availability of a certain white substance from South America. He sold more cocaine than he took, but there were usually lines available for him and his cronies. But Stephen wasn't one of the chosen few.

Quincy handed him the cordless phone. 'Call them,' he said.

Stephen dialled the number of Stella's flat. After a few rings someone picked up the other end and a female voice said, 'Hello, Kate speaking.'

'Hello there, this is Stephen… Stella's brother.'

'She's not here,' Kate replied, so cool that he felt icy fingers touching his cock, making it quiver.

'That's all right. I really wanted to talk to you anyway, about the band. I'm phoning from Quincy's apartment… he wants to meet you and the rest of the gang. Have you a demo tape?'

'Better than that – we've just cut a CD. I've talked to the boys and they're into it. Why don't you bring him to Stella's party this evening? Jez and Tommy are coming, and we'll be jamming. I'm sure she won't mind Quincy listening.'

Stephen wished he had her faith in his sister's welcome when he turned up at the door, but he said, 'I like it. Wait while I ask him.' He covered the mouthpiece and turned to Quincy. 'We can go to Stella's party,' he informed him. 'The band will do a session. Are you up for it?'

Quincy pulled a bored face and shrugged his heavy shoulders. 'Will there be any tasty pussy? Are you going to get heavy if I pull your sister?'

The idea made Stephen glow. That would teach the stuck-up, selfish cow. God, she must be smug as fuck after her talk with Mr Jarvis, the family lawyer. How much had they stashed in her bank account? How many investments was her financial adviser wet-nursing through the stock market? Damn and bugger it! He'd like to get his hands round the throat of that silly old mare, Emma, and wring the life out of her, if it wasn't for the fact that she was already dead, had

31

been for over twenty years. Well then, her skull. Perhaps he could get hold of that and smash it to smithereens. Was she in a vault somewhere in the grounds of Troon Hall?

'Of course I won't mind, Quincy,' he replied, coming back to the matter in hand. He lifted the phone and said to Kate, 'Is there going to be lots of crumpet?'

'Crumpets?' she answered dryly. 'We hadn't planned to include them on the menu.'

'Not *crumpets*—'

'I suppose you mean girls.' Her voice sounded as brittle as crystals tinkling in a cave miles underground. 'There will be, but I don't advise you call them that to their faces. They're likely to go ballistic. The last time some guy tried they blew the pub apart and he got glassed.'

'Oh, I see, a bunch of cold, ball-cracking feminists,' Stephen answered, hating the type, or what he imagined to be the type, having never bothered to have a serious conversation with a woman.

'Not at all; more like a bunch of lookers who know their own worth. Do you still want to come?'

'Yes. What time?' Apart from other considerations, he was keen to find out how Stella had got on with Jarvis.

'Around nine. Do you know the address?'

'Yes, it's near Highgate Cemetery, isn't it?'

'That's right. Bring a bottle. Oh, and Stephen...'

She was using that bossy tone that made his cock sit up and beg. 'What?' he replied unsteadily.

'How about giving her something really classy for a present? I think you owe her.'

Chapter Two

'I like this place,' said Prince Dimitri, seated cross-legged on the flat top of a monument.

The moonlight glistened on austere white marble, and touched the bowed head of the stone angel with a broken harp standing behind him. 'It's full of the most amusing Victoriana,' he continued. 'How they loved death in those times; the crosses, the statues of weeping cherubs, the waxen lilies, the jet beads, the widow's weeds and mourning black. They cut hair from the heads of the departed and had it woven into ornamental brooches, accustomed to visits from the Grim Reaper. These days it shocks people, no matter how much they read about it in the newspapers or see it on television. It's still not taken into the home; the corpses sanitised and kept in refrigerators, not laid out in the parlour for friends and relatives to view. Former generations saw it as a daily occurrence. Couples had many children, but only a few survived. To reach a ripe old age was rare. They were used to death, just like us, my dear Lazio.'

'I find it gloomy and overdone and not at all artistic,' his young companion replied, glancing disparagingly at the avenues of stately mausoleums, hedged by ancient yews. 'I prefer the graveyards of Italy, or New Orleans.'

Dimitri was beside him, staring into his face with a trace of anxiety. 'You are depressed, my friend. What is it? You've made contact with her. All is as it should be, isn't it?'

'I've found her, for *you*, if that's what you mean,' Lazio said ungraciously, behaving in that loutish way he had observed in young adults of the so-called civilised human race. Once he too had been among their number, but had respected his elders and never answered back. One did not if one was born into the upper classes as the Honourable Jeremy Farquarson, late in the reign of Queen Victoria.

'I know and I'm so pleased,' Dimitri replied. 'Candice is delighted.'

Lazio shrugged and moved out of his reach, bewildered by his own strong emotions concerning Stella. He revered Dimitri and looked upon him as a father, for he was the one who had made him and changed his name to a more appropriate one – Lazio. He and his wife taught him everything he needed to know in order to exist among the *nosferatu*. They had protected him from harpies like those ghastly yet wonderful women who claimed to be Dimitri's sisters – the ebony-haired temptress, Medea, the silvery-blonde, fairylike Madelon, and the Titian-headed vixen, Allegra. All were outstandingly lovely, but vicious and depraved.

Then there was Belphegor, who took an avuncular interest in him, but was never quite to be trusted. Handsome, dandyish, he liked to flip backwards and forwards in time, a dilettante vampire. Whether attired in a toga, or flaunting himself as a Restoration rake, complete with rapier, peruke, petticoat breeches and a wide-brimmed, feathered hat, or driving a two-wheeled phaeton in the Regency period, attired in buckskins so tight that he might as well be naked, he was always a figure of fashion. Even when he ventured into the future he managed to find the most elegant, all-in-one garments in silver manmade fibres, and his space helmets had to be seen to be believed.

Summoned by thought, he appeared between two magnificent but decaying tombs, placed an arm round the shoulders of Dimitri and Lazio, and gazed at them fondly, his eyes smiling, his lips drawn back over canines that grew longer and sharper than normal after dark. He was wearing pastel pink chinos and a draped jacket over a polo-necked sweater. His bare feet were thrust into loafers from a top Milanese designer.

'You have need of me, my prince?' he said, his voice carrying a trace of that Eastern European accent he had never quite lost.

'I think not,' Dimitri answered coldly.

'But Candice…?'

'I am taking care of the matter. Keep out of it.'

Lazio was familiar with the story of how Belphegor had saved Dimitri during the witch-hunts in Paris in the sixteen-seventies, transforming him into a being like himself. He had drained him of blood to the point of death, and then made him drink deeply of his own. This was the traditional way of making a vampire. Lazio had gone through the painful process himself, after Dimitri offered him the Dark Gift in exchange for death on the battlefield. But whereas he did not resent his maker, it seemed that Dimitri did. There was no love lost between these centuries old vampires, and Belphegor was forever sniping at Candice, jealous of her influence over the prince.

'Oh, but my dear, I'm offering my help to solve the little problem that is worrying your bride,' Belphegor said blandly and insincerely. 'You know I hold her in high regard.'

Lazio sometimes cursed the ability to pick up on present thoughts and mental images of past events. This, along with an extraordinary keenness of vision and hearing, of being able to shape-shift, travel great distances in a flash, and use hypnotic powers, had been revealed when he woke from that trancelike death of the human body and found himself to be what he had become – a thing unable to die.

Now he experienced Belphegor's lust and unrequited love for Dimitri, his own body warming into pleasure as one of the dandy's slim pale hands caressed the prince's buttocks. Now they were not in Highgate Cemetery in the twenty-first century, but in France during the time of Louis XIV, the Sun King. It was a period when great wealth and luxury contrasted with the direst poverty. Dimitri had been studying medicine in Paris and inadvertently become involved with witchcraft. Belphegor had arrived in the nick of time; ready to save him from being burned at the stake, in return for his acceptance of a new existence.

And Dimitri had acquiesced, rather than face torture and a horrible public execution. Lazio watched with his magical eyes, seeing a panelled room where firelight dance, and experiencing Dimitri's feelings as Belphegor possessed him, slipping his cock into his arse and bringing him to a frenzy of pleasure. At the very moment when the creature's cold semen jetted into the depths of the prince's forbidden place, so his fangs sliced through his neck and found an artery. When he had fed, he flicked back the lace ruffle at his wrist and bit into the flesh, and blood freshly pumped from his heart spurted into Dimitri's mouth.

'Drink of me,' Belphegor muttered urgently, and Lazio remembered Dimitri saying the same to him on the night of his regeneration in a muddy trench after a battle.

The feelings pouring through Dimitri and himself were almost indescribable. There is nothing on earth, in heaven or in hell that comes anywhere near that of the transference of the soul to a body which has been subtly changed by the infusion of the blood of a vampire.

Lazio felt a powerful force in his genitals. His cock swelled and his balls ached, and an enormous orgasm took him a roller-coaster ride to the ends of the universe. He shared this with Dimitri, while Belphegor mentally fucked both of them.

In reality neither had moved, the moonlight shining down serenely, the black shadows of the trees and tombs inhabited by ghosts. 'Go away, you poor lost things,' Dimitri said, and the apparitions halted and listened. 'Go towards the light. Use the stars if you want, but leave here. You're fortunate.

You can move on to other incarnations. Accept that you are now spirits, and go.'

'Oh, leave them be,' Belphegor snapped impatiently. 'They enjoy moping and mowing, I'm sure of it. It gives them the chance to frighten people. Not all, of course,' and he nodded to where a couple lay on the grass between graves. 'Some are impervious, lost in rutting heat.'

The woman was stretched on her back, her generous breasts exposed, her skirt hitched up, her knickers discarded. Her lover covered her, the white globes of his buttocks gleaming as he pumped away between her legs, his balls tapping lightly against her perineum. The vampires drew closer, watching them, nostrils quivering at the smell of sex juice and the blood streaming hot and fast through the hearts, veins and arteries of the fornicating pair. Flesh or clothing proved no barrier to their super keen sight and they looked into the crack between her sturdy, wide-stretched thighs. The wrinkled mouth of her anus was displayed to them, the black furred lips of her outer labia, the pink, wet membrane of the inner ones, and the glistening, swollen, needy pearl that crowned her slit.

'She's married, but not to him,' Belphegor observed, his invisible hand penetrating her lover's body and touching her clit. 'She's feeling so deliciously guilty, and it's adding to her excitement. That's it, darling, keep thinking of the word "adultery", and you'll come. Can you feel me tickling your cunny? It's me bringing you to bliss, not that clumsy ass. Go on, you sluggard. Call yourself a stud!' he shouted at the man.

A whip appeared like a black snake in his hand and he slashed it down across the man's quivering bottom. Each tip was clad in steel, and marks appeared, long scarlet lines crossing and criss-crossing as he yelped and plunged and never stopped fucking, goaded by the slave-driving Belphegor.

'That'll make you work, donkey-dick!' the vampire shouted and the whip whistled and cut, biting deep into the flabby male flesh.

'Oh… oh… what the hell's happening? Who are you? Let us alone. Where's your mobile, Janice? We're being attacked by a pervert. I'm going to call the police.'

'No, you mustn't,' Janice cried. 'If Jim finds out he'll kill me! Ah… that's it! Go on. Go *on*! Oh, bloody hell… I'm coming!'

Belphegor smiled benignly, and put the full force of his vampire strength behind the final blow. The whip cracked. The woman screeched, and the man yelped with agony and ecstasy as he emptied his tribute into her.

'Jesus Christ!' he mumbled, his face buried in her ample bosom, his lips seeking her nipple and sucking with the avidity of an infant. 'What was that?'

'You were great, tiger,' Janice answered, a happy smile on her face, her hands running up and down his rump.

The skin was smooth and unblemished. Belphegor's whip marks had faded completely. He grinned at Dimitri and Lazio and said, 'That prat won't recall a thing. A pity, really, for he needs a sharp lesson in how to treat a lady. He thinks that cock in cunt is the be all and end all.'

'Drop him in some sex manuals when you're passing,' Dimitri remarked acidly, then wrapped himself in his long black cloak and added, 'I'm hungry. The snack I had earlier has worn off.'

'Why don't we troll along to Stella's party?' Belphegor suggested, cocking an impish eyebrow at his darkly handsome, aristocratic creation.

'What do you know about that?' Dimitri returned, scowling.

'My dear, I know *everything*. Have you forgotten?'

'I've not forgotten that you like to meddle,' he snapped back.

'Unfair,' Belphegor said. 'I'm merely offering my help.'

'Lazio is in charge.'

'All right, I know. Shall we go, Lazio, and leave this sullen prince to his own devices? He loves playing Hamlet.'

'I shall go alone,' Lazio said firmly. He had already impinged on Stella's thought patterns and did not want to frighten her. Besides, he wanted time with her, fascinated by her beauty, her talent, her singing voice and bright, imaginative mind.

'Oh, very well, have it your own way,' Belphegor said huffily. 'I'll see you two later. I'm going to a rave where the flesh is delectable and the blood delightfully strong. Bye, bye.' And with a twirl, he disappeared.

Dimitri vanished too, continuing his nightly task of replenishing his strength. Lazio had already imbibed, finding a young woman crying in her bedroom. She had just been jilted, her fiancé confessing that he had been sleeping with her sister. Lazio kissed her eyelids so that she was unaware of him, yet soothed as he encouraged her to masturbate, bringing comfort to her body and solace to her bruised feelings.

As she reached completion he had drunk at the wellspring of her throat, then left her dreaming that she had found a man who would love her sincerely and never betray her. She deserved it.

Stella sat in the kitchen, showing Kate the photographs of her house that Mr Jarvis had given her. She was sure there must be others among the cases and boxes filled with papers left by her parents, but she could not recall seeing one.

Kate took the faded picture from her and studied it closely, then said, 'Blimey! So that's Troon Hall.'

'What d'you think?' Stella's head was still buzzing from her meeting with Mr Jarvis, that balding, elderly solicitor of the old school, very much concerned with protocol.

'Wicked. When can you take over?'

'Any time. Look, I've got the keys,' and she took the

rusted bunch from her bag and rattled them dramatically.

'Money?' Kate queried, ever blunt.

'Invested. Mr Jarvis had a financier take care of this years ago and a tidy sum has accrued. So it's goodbye to worrying about the bills. They've given me a monthly allowance, and left the rest where it is.'

'How much?' Kate went on making sandwiches which, when ready, were wrapped in cling-film and placed on the units along with all the other food they had prepared for the party.

'Five hundred a week,' Stella said, smiling widely. 'I can't believe it. I've been scrimping and struggling for so long.'

'It's not a huge sum,' Kate reminded. 'But you'll manage.'

'Manage? It's like winning the Lottery. No more being late with your rent, or my half of the expenses. And Mr Jarvis said he'll make arrangements for further sums if I need them to go to Ireland. Troon Hall has been kept up to scratch, apparently. Looked after by caretakers, a Caley Rogan and his wife. All I've got to do is ring them saying when I'm arriving, and they'll do the rest.'

'What about *Zero700*?' Kate asked, piling salad into a large earthenware bowl.

'More money,' Stella announced, coming out of her traumatised state and daring to believe her luck. 'We'll get a new van. Well, not brand new, but better than Tommy's old crate that keeps breaking down. And, for starters, this is for you,' and she dragged a bundle of notes from her wallet, passing them across the table.

'I can't say it isn't welcome,' Kate commented. 'Things have been a tad bleak lately.'

'That's over. What's mine is yours. You've looked after me, letting me share this marvellous house, which I could never have afforded in the normal way.'

'Neither could I,' Kate said with a laugh, pushing a stray red curl back under her bandana. 'It's only that it belongs to an aunt who is abroad and let me have it at a nominal rent till she gets back. This won't be soon, maybe never, for she hates the English winters.'

'We'll be able to do that when the band makes it,' Stella said, filled with optimism. 'Money breeds money, so they say. All we need is to be top of the charts.'

'And this is where we're going to get. Your brother Stephen rang and asked to bring Quincy Dubois to the party.'

'Oh, Kate,' Stella wailed, slumping at the table. 'I don't want Stephen to come. You've no idea what he's like… nothing but a weasel.'

'I don't care about him. It's Quincy we need to impress. We planned a jam anyway, so he may as well hear us. Look, you're tired. You've had a day of it. Off you go and put on your glad rags. I'll finish here. You're the party girl after all.'

Without needing a second bidding, Stella commandeered the bathroom and took a shower, massaging creamy lather over her skin, then luxuriating in the feel of the spray on her breasts, the foaming suds dangling from her nipples. The pale young man in the pub sprang to mind, and she let her fingers cruise down over her slippery wet belly to the soaking curls on her pubis, made darker by the water. It was impossible to resist, and she eased her feet slightly apart, her lower lips parting over the nubbin that crowned her avenue. The warm, scented water coursed round it, teasing as it ran, like a long, playful tongue.

His tongue? What would it feel like if he went down on her? Was he the man who hovered on the periphery of her dream? When she first saw him she had been sure, with lightning bolt certainty. But now? She was almost convinced; it seemed highly improbable. How could she dream about someone she had never met? Or had she subconsciously registered him in the pub before and that clever-than-any-computer brain of hers had got him out of her eligible men

41

memory bank and dusted him off.

Real or unreal? It was nothing compared to the hunger gnawing at her. She touched her clit with a soapy fingertip and shivered at the intensity of feeling this invoked. Her nipples were already standing up from the shower's ministrations, and now they stiffened even more, their colour turning from pinkish brown to umber. Stella unhooked the showerhead and trained it between her labial lips. She gasped at the explosion of pleasure as the hot water jetted against her exposed and ravenous bud.

She wanted to orgasm at once, yet wanted to delay the lovely sensation. Holding the jet in place she lifted a hand to her nipples, bringing her breasts together by hunching her shoulders and drawing in her elbows, then palming one nipple and rubbing the other. The pleasure was all consuming. She leaned back against the floral tiled wall of the shower stall. Trickles of water streamed from her wet hair, running over her arms and breasts, cooling as it went and stippling her skin with goose bumps, making her aware of every inch of exposed flesh. Her juices were mingling with the water cascading down her thighs as she moved the jet slowly and languidly over the hard little gem of her clitoris.

She closed her eyes and opened her legs wider, feet braced against the shower tray.

The pale young man! Where had he come from? She wanted him there, filling her hot love-channel with his cold, cold cock.

She thought about past lovers. There had only been two. Rob, a computer nerd from college, who had been an eager beaver but clueless – and Chris, who treated her like he did his own cock when jacking off; no gentleness, no finesse. Neither had brought her to orgasm. But her dream man had, and would do again if, in truth, she had found him on the physical plane.

Meanwhile there was her watery lover, the shower. She

moved it with increasing speed, and the jets flicked over her clitoris like countless tiny needle-sharp teeth. She felt she was floating on a great lake of pleasure, communing with the deepest regions of herself, her astral body and her immortal soul. As she climbed towards ecstasy she felt, for a fleeting instant, that she was being observed by an invisible presence. Then writhing and moaning she reached an orgasm that left her shaking. Her head spun as she put out a hand to steady herself. The last delirious spasms died away and she washed her pussy clean of her abundant juice, then turned the shower tap and stepped out, wrapping herself in a fluffy bath towel.

She padded into the passage and returned to her bedroom. She glanced at her watch as she rummaged for a garter belt, bra and panty set and stockings to go with them. The drawers in the tallboy were chaotic, but she tracked down the articles she sought. They were new, bought in anticipation of her birthday celebrations, expensive rose-pink lace over paler chiffon, the panties cut high at the sides, bikini style. Tingling with excitement, she fastened the suspender belt round her slim waist and then sat on the dressing table stool and carefully extracted the stockings from their cellophane wrapper. They were flesh-coloured, the pink heels, toes and welts so fragile that she feared to snag it as she rolled one up her leg and fastened the front clip. The other followed, and then she stood, squirming round to secure the tops at the back.

The sensual sight in the mirror arrested her momentarily. Her hips and bottom looked inviting, lewdly displayed between the suspenders and the stockings. She bent at the waist and her buttocks parted, displaying the dark crease between and the fluffy, purse-like mound of her pudenda. Greatly daring, she slipped her feet into a pair of high-heeled court shoes, also new and rose-coloured. Then she squiggled round and stared at her image again. This was even better, the heels bunching her calves, extending her thighs and making her buttocks protrude even more.

'Yummy,' she heard a voice whisper, and was not sure if it was in her ear or in her brain. 'Splendid buttocks. They'd look even better if flushed and reddened by a crop or whip. You need a master to chastise you, my dear. Myself, to be exact; Belphegor.'

She stared wide-eyed in the mirror. Only she was reflected. She turned and looked round the room. It was as innocent as always, furnished in that rather out-dated style favoured by Kate's aunt, a double divan bed, built-in wardrobes, a radiator under the window, flowery curtains on a track, fitted carpet, and a unit housing a portable telly, video and Stella's hi-fi system. There were her books and CDs and personal possessions, as normal as could be. No one else was there. She was quite alone.

Feeling uneasy and guilty, as if she had been caught playing with herself, she pulled on her panties and bra. But they were too pretty to ignore and she posed in front of the mirror, admiring them, thankful that she had retained her size ten figure. She dropped her skirt over her head and zipped the placket, then put on the top that went with it. Both were made of flimsy material, patterned with delicate leaves and flowers, the skirt swirling out round her legs, the top sleeveless and wrap-over and tying at the front, the new bra lifting and separating her breasts. Though double layered, her legs could be glimpsed through the skirt, and her nipples showed, two dark points lifting the blouson.

She switched on the hairdryer and, head down, ran the diffuser over her damp hair. Shaking it from side to side she seized handfuls and scrunched them, reforming the natural curl under the heat. She righted herself, turned off the machine and fluffed up her dark gypsy mane. She applied more make-up than normal, emphasising her green-brown eyes with kohl and mascara, and taking a pencil to her wing-shaped brows. Blusher and a vivid shade of lipstick completed her new look – that of a woman of substance – the Mistress of Troon Hall.

However, she found herself hurrying, no longer easy with her own company – wondering about the voice she was sure she'd heard.

From somewhere in the outer regions of the house the doorbell rang. The guests were starting to arrive and Stella left her bedroom to welcome them.

Everyone said it was a great party. There was plenty of food, plenty of drinks, and a cross-section of people, mostly unemployed or students, and mostly young. They sat on the floor, on couches, chairs, or beanbags. Some propped themselves against the walls. Jeans were the order of the day, and a herd of hooded fleeces.

The females had gone for glamour on the whole, adopting that film star and model almost nudity look. Strapless bodices, floppy lurex ones that offered no support to the bosoms beneath, leather bras decorated with chains, á la the fetish scene but not quite, and a selection of tiny skirts that barely covered their modesty. Stack-heeled shoes or sandals completed their bizarre outfits. They posed like tarts on parade before clients, yet thought themselves independent and sexually liberated, shot the men down in flames with their one-liners and generally treated them with contempt.

'Silly mares,' Quincy commented as he and Stephen walked into the sitting room. They were late, though only a little, not to be confused with the pub-crawlers who would be trying to gatecrash after eleven-thirty. 'They all want a good seeing-to. Which one is your sister?'

Stella saw her brother leading over a commanding bull of a man. He was thickset, big and brawny, handsome in a rugged way, older than Stephen by ten years, his hair closely curling round his well-shaped head.

'Stella, this is Quincy Dubois,' she heard Stephen say, and felt her hand engulfed in a large one with a warm, dry palm. This was no flabby handshake, but confident and masterful. His touch reverberated down to her pussy and lingered there.

'Happy birthday, Stella,' he said, the deep cadences of his voice penetrating her depths as surely as if he had already inserted his cock in her.

'Thank you,' she stammered, completely nonplussed. He was not what she had expected.

'Stephen tells me you sing. He says you're good, and so is your band. I manage bands. I want to hear yours.'

Kate came over, resplendent in a black velvet nothing of a dress with scintillating diamond motifs placed strategically here and there. She looked impressive, with her russet hair piled up and her legs covered in high leather boots with silver imprints.

'Quincy Dubois,' she said, in a thrillingly husky voice. 'I'm Kate Barnes. *Zero700* will be playing shortly. Can I get you a drink?'

'Thank you,' he replied, exuding considerable charm.

Stella then found herself trapped in a corner with him; Stephen had vanished and Kate not yet returned with his drink. She could feel perspiration trickling down her back and was annoyed with herself. She wasn't a virgin who didn't know one end of a man from the other, but even so he made her feel gauche and inexperienced, yet not unpleasantly so. She had already drunk two Margaritas, her favourite cocktail, and it *was* her birthday after all, but she was not used to alcohol and they had gone to her head.

Quincy had her cornered, hands flat on the wall each side of her, his arms braced. 'Stephen didn't tell me his sister was so beautiful,' he gushed.

'Come off it!' Stella recovered enough to laugh. 'What a chat up line.'

He dropped his arms and shrugged, still smiling at her engagingly. 'I never chat up women. It's not my style. But if I find one attractive, then I let her know. I find you very attractive. You want proof?' and he seized her hand and pressed it to the hard bough tenting the front of his expensive silk and wool trousers.

She started, her fingers involuntarily closing over the hot flesh concealed within. Quincy traced over her nipples, and passion darted through her. Her clitoris thickened and she could feel dew wetting the gusset of her new knickers. She snatched her hand away from his bulge as if scalded.

'Stop it,' she gasped, her face flaming. 'Someone may see us.'

'And if we were alone?' he said, his steel-blue eyes mocking her. 'What would happen then?'

'I-I don't know,' she stammered. 'Nothing. Why should it?'

He laughed and moved away a little, leaving her feeling cheap. 'My dear, I can see that you need coaching,' he chided.

She was rescued by Kate. 'Here's your beer, Quincy,' she said, not in the least abashed by him. 'And the band are setting up. Won't be long now.'

Stella escaped, hot, bothered and aroused. Quincy made her afraid, and his overbearing manner angered her, but above all, she found him the most exciting man she had ever met. There was a sense of danger about him that made her tremble with delicious anticipation. She knew she should avoid him like the plague, but felt incapable of doing so. She was relieved when she could lift her guitar from its stand and tune it, while Kate stood at the keyboard, Jez did a few practise rolls on the drums and Tommy plinked the violin's strings.

This was better; she need not think about the disturbing Quincy or the pale, elusive young man.

As always, as soon as they started to play she forgot

everything else. She lost herself in the harmonies, the chords, the lyrics that had sprung from somewhere inside her – poetry set to music. *Zero700* played for half an hour with hardly a break, and the audience was quiet from the onset, sitting around drinking, smoking and appreciating songs that spoke of their youth, optimism and ambitions, their disappointments, their love affairs and secret desires.

And Quincy was at Stella's side when she took her final bow. 'That was splendid,' he said, and addressed the other band members who were watching him, guarded but hopeful. They were all aware that they needed *that* break, that single stroke of luck necessary to launch them into fame and fortune. Without it, they would probably never make the big time, no matter how talented.

'I want you to go to a studio my groups sometimes use, and do a recording there,' Quincy said. 'Meanwhile, let me have your demo and leave the rest to me.'

'You want to manage us?' Jez asked, squinting at him suspiciously. 'And why should you want to do that, man?'

'Because I've a hunch you're going to make it. And I always follow my hunches.'

'But I've heard of you – you're big time,' said Tommy, a streetwise lad, with short sandy hair and muscles developed in the local gym, who played the violin like a virtuoso. He had wanted to go to music college but it hadn't worked out. 'What d'you want with a little outfit like ours?'

Quincy eyed him speculatively and said, 'Believe in me. Trust me. I know about these things. What say you, Kate and Stella?'

'We'll give it a shot,' Kate said, looking him straight in the eye. 'But don't give us any bullshit.'

'How about you, Stella?' He was awaiting her answer, and she knew he wanted much more from her than a session in his recording studio. She was out of her depth, and aware of it. Unable to flirt and lead men on, like Kate, Stella wore her heart on her sleeve, and this ruined her defences. Wondering what to say in reply, her attention was drawn towards the latecomer who had just caught her eye.

It was the pale young man.

Chapter Three

'My name is Lazio,' he said, materialising in front of her, as if spawned by the night.

Though she had been hot, Stella was now freezing cold. This time there could be no mistake; it was him! The dream lover who had thrust his icy phallus into her. Like called to like, darkness answered darkness. She who had thought herself to be normal, straightforward, even innocent, now recognised another part of her psyche, something wild and abandoned that yearned for adventures beyond Planet Earth, among the stars, in the depths of hellish universes and black holes that defied imagination.

Lazio! The name rang in her ears like a clarion, challenging her, daring her to risk all for him, even her immortal soul.

He was wearing jeans and a sweater, like any other there, but no – not like any other she had ever met. His hungry eyes were incandescent – blue, mauve, the metallic pewter of mercury, she wasn't sure which. They changed, even as she stared into them. She was paralysed, and he lifted his hand and gently stroked down the side of her cheek with one of his beautifully manicured, almond-shaped nails. It left a long scratch behind. She felt blood trickling, but when she touched the spot her fingers came away unmarked.

Disjointed thoughts teemed in her brain, and vivid images. She saw mountainous wastes and heard the swish of snow as it fell from gaunt pines. The moon hung, a sombre reddish ball, over their tops, and sleek grey shapes padded beneath the branches. More and more gathered, and one huge, magnificent beast stood facing her. He raised his muzzle and howled, and the other wolves took it up.

The silver-furred leader of the pack was joined by his mate. He mounted her and, as he did so, she stared fixedly at Stella with bright eyes, her red tongue lolling. Stella started, her pussy heating as she felt every inch of his prick entering her and locking there, driving his seed deep within her, unable to break free until he had discharged his semen. The rest sought out partners, each taking their pleasure in the snowy night. When he had finished, the alpha male licked his bitch's hindquarters and then loped to a rise and stood there proudly, feet planted in the snow. He threw back his handsome head, stared up at the moon and bayed again, long and loud.

With a whoosh she transcended time and space, and was now above a grim, turreted castle perched on an escarpment. Water thundered down a ravine into the river far below. Lazio was holding her in his arms, and they were hanging in air. The courtyard was full of carriages, wagons and people, as exotic music, excited voices and bursts of laughter came from within.

There were men-at-arms guarding the battlements, but Lazio and Stella passed unnoticed, as if they were ghosts. They stood in the arched alcove of a window ledge, his arm round her as they gazed into a great hall. The leaping flames from log fires at either end augmented the light from torches set in cressets along the stone walls and that of thick, cream, ecclesiastical candles in wrought-iron holders.

The hall was crowded with peasants in traditional costume and jet-haired gypsies. The women were in brilliant shawls, the men in dark clothing, collarless shirts, and gold-hooped earrings, their swarthy faces rendered villainous by rat-tailed moustaches. There were other people too, gentry by the richness of their garments and the sparkle of jewels, orders and gem encrusted sword hilts. The oak refectory table was laden with food, every taste catered for – meat in abundance, salmon and fruit, dairy products and crusty loaves, but not everyone ate. Some sat there without a morsel passing their lips, neither did they imbibe of the golden wine from Tokay or the plum coloured vintage pressed from grapes grown in vineyards below the castle. They occupied places of privilege at the top end of the table, while the lower orders ate below.

They were watched indulgently by their feudal lord seated at the head. He reminded Stella of the wolf – the green eyes that refracted red – the feral strength – the hubris.

She trembled. Who was this ruler? He embodied enormous power. It was neither good nor evil, but could be used for either purpose with equal, devastating effect.

'That's my maker, Prince Dimitri,' Lazio said, and it was only the second time he had spoken to her.

'I don't understand. Who is he and why are we here? It's my party – I should be in London.'

'You are,' Lazio replied. 'Look,' and scooped up a ball of snow and held it out. It changed into a mirror, and within it she saw Kate's house and the partygoers. Oddly, she saw herself, talking to Stephen and Quincy.

'But…' she began.

'Later all will become clear to you, but for now simply watch,' and his fingers were on her lips, stopping further questions.

There was a woman at the prince's side. She was gorgeously gowned in purple velvet and her gems were superb, a tiara sparkling amidst her tumbling mane of blonde curls. Dimitri had his arm round her shoulders, one hand reaching down to cup her breast, while the other rested in her lap, pressing against her hidden pubis. Stella felt the caress; in the same way she had experienced the pack leader's spiky cock jabbing into the she-wolf.

At the same moment that Lazio touched her body, the material of her dress melted like mist. 'Yes, oh yes, I want you so badly,' she moaned, feeling her nipples responding to his fingers, lifting her leg and hooking it round his hip, grinding her pubis against the hard, chilly baton of his phallus.

It was as if they were both entirely naked, clothing no barrier, and she flung back her head and stared up into his eyes, anticipating a glorious union. It was dark where they stood, but the pale wedge of his face was of an unearthly beauty, white as a corpse, except for the hectic colour flushing his cheeks and full, sensual lips. He lowered his head and kissed her throat, lingering there, his teeth grazing the skin. At that touch a strange lassitude swept over her. She wanted more, yearned to feel his incisors lacerating her, his soft mouth sucking, soothing, taking her into darkness.

'Patience,' he whispered, lifting his head to look down at her, and her clitoris stirred under the pressure of his invisible finger. 'We shall be lovers, never fear, but not yet.'

'Why? What is it? Can't you tell me?' She was crying, or thought she was, aware of a tear coursing down her cheek.

He caught it and it turned into a crystal. He placed it in her palm and closed her fingers over it. Then with a sigh that contained sorrow, anger and frustration, he was moving down her body, around the dimple of her navel and into her bush. He thrust his tongue into the hidden folds of her labia, dipped into the nectar seeping from her vulva and covered the hidden entrance to her anus.

She writhed and gave a long wailing cry as he moved back to the dark curls and found her clitoris, lapping over it, circling it, then settling into a steady rhythm. She shook, wracked with pleasure, and an awesome bubble of exquisite sensation burst as she abandoned herself to his lips, his tongue, his gnawing teeth. It was awesome, wonderful, unendurable, and she needed his cock inside her to assuage the savage anguish.

'For God's sake, fuck me!' she screamed.

Instantly, she was back at the party. The relentless desire inside her was still there, but Lazio had gone. So had the castle, the wolves, and Prince Dimitri. Even as she struggled

53

to remember, the visions faded like a hypnologic dream. No time had passed at all since Lazio first appeared.

The party was going with a swing, music thumping from the stereo, every room crammed with people. Kate appeared from the kitchen.

'Time to bring in the birthday cake, before everyone's too pissed to notice,' she announced.

Someone cheered.

Quincy's face swam into focus through the smoke haze. 'So will you come?' he asked, raising a quizzical eyebrow at Stella.

'Er… what? Come where?' She was recovering quickly, though still confused. Someone should be there with her. Who? Then his image dropped into her mind. Lazio! Where was he? She was aware of something in her palm, and there lay a single, sparkling diamond, her tear transformed by his magic. She drew in a sharp breath and closed her fist round it. This was their secret, the living proof that he existed.

'I've just invited you round to my place,' Quincy said, and moved nearer, a sleek predator closing in on his prey. His hand cupped her bottom, fondling its roundness through her skirt.

'I can't leave my guests. Did you see a dark-haired man come in just now? Lean face. Striking eyes. I must find him.' This was of earth-shaking importance, not the fact that Quincy was touching her up, even though her wayward flesh was responding.

'I didn't see anyone of that description,' Quincy said, his deep voice and gentle fingers on her rear undeniably persuasive. 'Your guests are enjoying themselves just fine. The party's bound to end with people passed out on the floor, or balling in the garden or bedrooms. You won't be missed if we slip away for an hour or so.'

'Come on, Stella – blow out the candles, and don't forget to wish,' Kate insisted, and those who could squeeze into the room shouted encouragement.

Stella always found this an embarrassing moment, had done so from a child, but was duty bound to please Kate, who had organised the cake, and those who had come to drink her booze and sing a raucous, 'Happy Birthday to you'.

She screwed her eyes tight shut, but what should she wish? She remembered the old adage, 'Be careful what you ask for. The gods may be listening and give it to you.'

Fame and fortune? Or love? Maybe all three? I want to see Lazio again, was her final choice.

The ritual was performed, the candles extinguished, leaving a little puff of smoke and a waxy stink behind them. There was the briefest of weird atmospheres, a second's silence, all movement suspended, frozen in time like an enchantment in a fairy story. Then it was over; noise returning and people jostling, dancing, drinking and passing round joints.

'Thank you, Kate,' Stella said and hugged her, glad of someone real to grab hold of.

'You're welcome,' Kate replied, always the mother hen. 'Are you okay?'

'Too many drinks, I expect. I need some air.'

Stella was still very aroused and though warmed within as if she had just climaxed, her pussy hungered for a cock. She wondered if she was losing her mind. Too much stress, perhaps, though she had not been aware of being under pressure lately. She should be on top of the world. Troon Hall was hers and she was planning to visit it very soon. She had money for the first time in her life.

Her parents had never been very good with finance and, when they died, Stephen and she had discovered that the family home had been mortgaged to the hilt and by the time this had been paid off and the funeral expenses met, there was precious little left for them. She used her portion to complete her education, and Stephen had, as usual, invested his share unwisely. No wonder he was so miffed by her inheritance.

That's the only reason he's turned up for my birthday, ferreting around, trying to rob me, she thought crossly, and he hasn't even brought me a present. I never expected anything other years, but this *is* my twenty-first.

It was all too bothering, and she needed to clear her head. She turned to Kate who was in deep conversation with Jez, making her wonder if there was anything going on between them, apart from both being musicians.

'What's up?' Kate asked.

'Nothing's up. I just want to pop out for a bit. Quincy's got something he wants to show me.'

'I'll bet he has,' Kate quipped, her eyes sharpening as they searched his face. 'Just you look after her,' she added firmly. 'I don't want my best friend upset.'

'Trust me,' he replied, hand on his heart. 'Would I harm such a singer, to say nothing of such a lovely girl? We'll be back. Don't worry.'

Stella stashed the diamond in her handbag, fetched a ruby-red pashmina and he held it out for her, draping it round her shoulders in a gesture guaranteed to make her feel special and cherished. He's charming, she thought, so why do I have this uneasy feeling? At least he's solid, flesh, bone and muscle, not some will-o'-the-wisp who keeps appearing and disappearing.

Stella opened the door and stepped out into the starry night. The party hubbub faded, and she looked back once to see figures silhouetted against the bay windows, then hurried down the path and through the gate. Quincy's car was at the kerb, and she heard the click as he demobilised the locking system, then they were inside and gliding through the London streets to his Camden Lock apartment.

'Birthday or no, that girl's upset,' commented Conlan Henny to his date for the evening.

'I'll bet she's had a row with her boyfriend,' she opined sagely, sitting opposite him at a table pushed up against a wall and toying with the sliver of lemon and ice cubes in her gin and tonic. 'Men are the root cause of most women's problems.'

'Maybe she has,' he agreed. 'Something's rattled her cage.'

As usual the kitchen was the focal point of party activity. They had been lucky to find seats and refused to budge, unless forced to in order to queue up at the bathroom door, bursting to use the toilet.

Student parties were not usually Conlan's choice, but he had bumped into Kate in the supermarket and she invited him along to her friend's twenty-first. He could not very well refuse, for he hadn't seen Kate since they left university, he to pursue his ambition to study classical music, and she to follow an entirely different bent.

He was pleasantly surprised when *Zero700* played. It was not what he expected – badly put together and banal junk. And the singer had caught his attention, something sad about her pulling at his susceptible heartstrings. He watched her blowing out the birthday cake candles, and deep inside he wept for her. Just for a moment she stared straight at him, though he could see she was probably too distressed to register his presence. But maybe not.

For a fraction of a second something had flashed between them, igniting a spark. Then she looked away. Even so, his instinct told him that the shared glance had special significance. So that was Stella Kerrick. Her dark hair, slim body and heart-shaped face had instant appeal.

Then she spoke earnestly to Kate and left with a thickset, casually but expensively dressed man. Watching her leave, Conlan fished a used envelope from the pocket of his denim jacket, slit it open, drew curly clefs down the left margin and added staves across. Then he began to place notes on this improvised manuscript.

He could hear the sounds as if on another plane, divorced from the party uproar. The black notes hovered in the air like bats. He was puzzled. Normally he saw birds, but tonight it was definitely bats, just waiting to be put down – sharps, flats, quavers and semi-quavers – for soloists and orchestra, clear as a bell. These were themes for *Persephone*, his latest brainchild, a music drama that was causing him untold birth pangs and demanding his undivided attention twenty-four hours a day.

Now fresh harmonies flowed from the ether, into his brain, through his fingers and the ballpoint and onto the paper. He struggled to grasp them, the music rising, falling, sinuous and sensual. It excited him physically, sent the blood pounding to his loins and made his cock stir behind the faded fly fastening of his weather-beaten jeans.

'Don't you ever stop working?' complained Alithea Carpenter, his date who was a junior chorus member of a prestigious opera company. She flicked her toffee-coloured bob, and added, 'Are you writing a part for me?'

'Who knows?' he smiled, pushing back a lock of unruly brown hair that had fallen forward over his brow. 'I haven't got that far yet. Maybe I'll audition you for the heroine, Persephone.'

'Would you really?' she said softly, slipping off one shoe, stretching out a leg and rubbing her naked foot across his bare instep under the table. 'I'd appreciate that, Conlan. How about if we leave the party early and go to your place? You can play it for me.'

The ethereal music vanished. Reality kicked in. Conlan was conscious of the suggestive movements of her toes, which she was using like little fingers to make the pressure build up in his testicles. He had not fucked her yet. In fact, he was not sure he wanted to become entangled with her, though his prick was responding as if it had a life of its own, rising urgently in the confines of his jeans.

He knew, too, that she was an ambitious women who probably thought it a useful career move to seduce a young composer who'd already had a symphony performed that had earned praise from fastidious and difficult to please music critics.

'Tell me about the opera,' she urged, running the tip of her tongue round the rim of her glass in a way suggestive of lapping at his cock-head.

Her wide, seemingly guileless eyes studied him as she continued to play footsie, but now those impudent toes were travelling upwards, edging towards his crotch. Conlan's belly muscles clenched in anticipation and his swollen member jerked.

'It's to be entirely new, uninhibited and explicit, an *avante garde* production with singers who can act and dancers with the bodies of Olympic gold medalists,' he began, warming to Alithea and her naughty foot. 'I visualise huge scenery and daring costumes, a Greek legend set in modern times. It's based on the legend of Persephone who was abducted and raped by the king of the underworld, Pluto. He took her to Hades as his bride, robbing the world of spring and summer and rousing the wrath of her mother, Demeter, the powerful nature goddess. That's a contralto role, by the way.'

'And Pluto must be a baritone, as he's the villain,' Alithea suggested, leaning forward so Conlan could see down her cleavage. 'Personally, I prefer them to tenors. They make me horny, off stage and on.'

'Right,' Conlan went on, wondering if she was wearing a push up bra or if that mouth-wateringly firm bust-line was unsupported. 'The tenor part is Mercury, who rescues Persephone.'

'It sounds great,' Alithea murmured, gazing at him dreamily and continuing to walk her foot up his thigh.

Conlan lost concentration. All he was aware of was her

toes nudging between his legs. They worked gently round his stiff organ and the swelling balls beneath. His chest was tight, his breathing ragged, and he became very still, staring down at the stripped pine table surface ringed with beer stains.

She smiled slyly, letting him know that she was aware of the tumult in his cock, and her big toe hitched round the button at the top of his flies. Conlan gasped, his trapped penis throbbing. He was afraid he would come, right there in the middle of the party, darkening his denims with his sticky tribute. Alithea twiddled her toes in an intimate gesture that was almost his undoing.

Just for an instant it was as if another face was superimposed over hers – that of one of the devil women who inhabited Pluto's kingdom. He had written some of his most powerful music for them. They trapped his imagination and refused to let go. Neither did Alithea.

He shrank away from her seductive foot and tried to think of anything rather than orgasm – the stern face of his professor at the Milan conservatoire where he had studied – the dour countenance of his bank manager on his last, unsuccessful attempt to raise a loan – the lecherous glances delivered by his middle-aged landlady. He achieved mastery over his rebellious phallus and it gradually subsided, though a dull ache in his balls remained.

Alithea grinned unrepentantly and said, 'Way to go. You know you want to shaft me, and I want it, too. If you were to feel me right now, you'd find I'm very, very wet.'

He was excited, yet vaguely repulsed by her boldness, but no gentleman worth his salt could refuse such an invitation. Before long they were walking through the streets towards his flat on the ground floor of a tall eighteenth century house facing a tree-shaded square.

'I hope my landlady isn't about,' he said, as he fumbled for his key.

'Is she that much of a dragon?' Alithea giggled, and slipped into the hall behind him. 'Doesn't she approve of you bringing girls back?'

'It's not that,' he whispered, ears cocked for any sound from the basement as they tiptoed across the terrazzo-tiled floor. 'She's divorced. The house is hers and she had it divided into apartments. Unfortunately, she lives downstairs. Too close for comfort. She insists that I call her Avril, instead of Mrs Loftus. I think she wants to get into my pants.'

'You sound terrified,' Alithea chuckled, as he stood back so that she might precede him into the large studio-cum-living room.

'I am,' he confessed. 'She likes men half her age and lures them into her clutches by throwing barbecues in the garden, or giving the most horrendous parties where everyone gets drunk and randy and maudlin.'

'Never mind, it's a lovely flat,' Alithea said, strolling behind him as he walked through the magnificent, cluttered room that might have once been the scene of elegant soirées.

Now it was filled with the accoutrements of a musician; busts of the great composers; shelves lined with books and CDs and recording equipment; prints and posters and programmes of concerts and, most important of all, a stately black grand piano.

'It's a good place to work,' he agreed, taking her into the well-appointed kitchen and spooning instant coffee into two mugs. 'The rent's high; I can just about meet it. But it's perfect for being at the hub of things, and Mrs L lets me keep my old banger in the garage round the back.'

'Because she wants to shag you legless,' Alithea said, and Conlan grew hot under the gaze of this lovely, big-breasted young woman.

Her waist was narrow, her hips broad, the generous bottom concealed by an Indian cotton skirt. She was infinitely touchable. He wondered about her buttocks. They were white, no doubt, she was so fair and didn't look the sunbathing type. He visualised them turning pink if he spanked her. He looked down at her feet in their little, spike-heeled shoes, and remembered the sensation of her toes fondling his genitals. His cock became erect on cue.

Alithea saw it and reached out to cup the fullness he could not control. She stepped closer, her breasts lifted, the nipples pebble-hard under the silk blouse. She was almost as tall as him, and her lips were parted, her eyes half closed. Conlan could feel her breath on his mouth and taste the faint flavour of gin. He capitulated, slid his hands round the pliable waist and drew her against him forcibly, omitting a stifled groan as his penis made contact with her pubic bone.

'Conlan...' she murmured, and wound her arms around his neck.

He sank into the warmth of her mouth, feeling her tongue twisting against his in a dance of desire. He was immersed in her, absorbed in the soft, wet cavern and that active, fleshy tongue. He probed her, explored her, as he would later explore the velvety lips of her sex, and baptise his swollen cock in the slippery haven of her pussy.

Fully aroused, he wanted to do it now, at once, without delay, but Alithea, assured of the outcome, was prepared to linger over the foreplay, piling up sensations, leading them gradually to the peak.

'I haven't come here for a quick bonk,' she said, holding back even as she took his hands and placed them over her breasts.

He immediately felt guilty, the most tactless and coarse of boors, the kind of man he most despised who could think of nothing but poking his dick into the nearest orifice in order to empty himself of spunk.

'Of course, not,' he stammered, though could not resist brushing his thumb pads over her nipples. 'I'm sorry, Alithea. Let's go into the studio. I'll bring the coffee. You wanted to hear excerpts from the opera, didn't you?'

'I did,' she replied with a catch in her voice, arching her spine to add to the enjoyment radiating through her breasts. 'Play to me, and then we'll see what happens, shall we? Bugger baritones; I find you most terribly attractive.'

With his erection jouncing with every step he took, Conlan led her back into the area where he felt most at home. It was the place where he sat alone for hours, far into the night sometimes, in the throes of creation. Then, fired by his muse, he forgot to eat or sleep, coming back to the world as dawn crept between the curtains. Only then would he stagger into the adjoining room and fling himself across the bed, too exhausted to undress, plunging into oblivion.

And this was when it was going well. The worst time was when it wasn't, refusing to gel – that dreaded time of composer's block. But this hadn't happened lately. Inspiration was running high, almost too fast, too intense, his ears ringing with the siren song of the vampiric demon women who inhabited Pluto's hellish domain. They were beautiful, daunting, daring him to write them exquisite music – he saw them every time he closed his eyes. One was blonde and petite, another was a black-haired houri and the third was statuesque, her flaming hair writhing round her head like Medusa's serpents. He could not shake off these images. They were there all the time, just on the edge of his retina, their Lorelei song reverberating through his brain.

He put the mugs down on a low brass table and sat at the piano, running his strong fingers over the keys in a series of warm-up chords. Alithea was behind him, her breasts pressing against his shoulder, her aroma wafting into his nostrils, the scent of aroused female, crossed with expensive French perfume.

'Is that the score?' she whispered reverently.

'Some of it,' he said, opening the dog-eared, stained and scribbled over manuscript, though he did not need to sight read; it was all there, branded on his memory, 'act two.'

'You don't compose on a computer?' Her question was muted, her voice expressing the respect she had for those blessed with the gift to invent glorious music for singers like herself.

'Sometimes, but not at this stage,' he said, and struck a series of discords, sombre and menacing. 'The opening of the second act. This is where Persephone is first taken to Pluto's gloomy realms in the bowels of the earth.'

His hands tingled as he spread them wide to reach those atonal sounds. He saw the scene clearly; the frightened goddess snatched from sunlight and flowers, the throne room of her new lord, barbaric and strange, filled with cohorts of fierce warriors and wild women, with a wailing background chorus of tortured souls.

'This is Persephone's leitmotif,' he explained, his fingers wringing heart-rending music from the piano. 'It recurs throughout the work. Listen to her pleas for mercy when she's strapped to a crosspiece and whipped into submission.'

'I hear it. God, it makes me go cold! Would you whip me like that, Conlan?'

'I might,' he said, and played on, wanting to stop and undress her and rub himself all over her body, but condemned to go on like the girl in the story of the red shoes, who had to dance without stopping till she dropped dead. He felt as haunted, and every bit as driven.

It was Alithea who finally interrupted, flinging her arms round him and pulling him back against her, almost toppling him from the piano stool. 'Enough,' she muttered thickly. 'Play more later, but now… fuck me!'

She unbuttoned her blouse, unclipped the front of her white lace bra and her breasts spilled out. She held them in both hands, lifting them to his mouth. He took one of them between his teeth, nibbling the tip until it was twice its normal size. It tasted nutty and sweet, and Alithea shuddered and pressed closer, gripping him firmly round the arse. He stood up and was pulled off balance, stumbling against her, and her own bottom landed in the ivory keys with an inharmonious clash.

'Over there,' he muttered, and half pulled, half carried her to the buttoned Chesterfield, then fell with her into its sagging depths.

In an instant her skirt was up around her waist. His heart beat a frantic tattoo. There was something so tarty about a woman with her clothing awry, and Alithea wore no knickers. His penis released a trickle of dew against his navel as he saw her widespread legs, her mound forming a luscious triangle of damp hair several shades darker than that on her head. Her knees drifted apart and her labial wings unfurled, displaying the pink inner lining. Conlan experienced that feeling akin to awe that always consumed him when he gazed at a woman's secrets, humbled in the presence of such mystery and promise.

He'd not had many partners, but since being schooled in the art of love as well as that of the pianoforte by a mature female professor at university, he had become so skilled that every lady he'd serviced remembered him with warmth and gratitude.

Now he could see the flush spreading up over Alithea's breasts and into her throat and cheeks, a glazed look in her eyes as her fingers massaged each side of her clitoris.

'Let me,' he murmured, propping himself up and bending over her so he would not miss a moment of that climb to orgasm she would reach under his touch.

'I will, but first I want a feel…' Alithea said in an unsteady voice. She found his zip and ran it down swiftly.

Conlan was more than ready for her when she thrust her hand inside the gap, closed round his cock and drew it out, long, thick and upward curving, with a shining cap. He gritted his teeth as she grasped the hot bar of flesh and stroked it. She stretched the foreskin away from the bulging head, then pushed it up again – up and down in a tantalising frottage that brought him ever nearer to eruption.

For a moment, he was tempted to yield to his basic instincts that were urging him to hold her down and simply go for the kill. He would sheath himself deep inside her with one brutal thrust, unprotected, spilling his seed in her, risking impregnation. How easy it would be to slip into the role of an uncaring, unthinking, irresponsible brute – like the god, Pluto.

But that was not Conlan's way. He liked women, admired their minds and adored their bodies. He respected them, though his mother had never given him cause, with her selfish absorption in her acting career and a succession of lovers. But that was long ago and far away. A lot of water had flowed under the bridge since then.

'Hush, take it steady,' he cautioned Alithea softly.

'Yes, I will, I want to…' she panted, moving her hand, squeezing his rod, reaching beneath to feel the tautness of his balls, kneading them gently and then returning to his cock. It twitched between her fingers.

He spread her out beneath him, gazing enrapt at the map of her body, her lovely breasts crowned with stiffening nipples, her flat belly, the luxuriant floss and swollen avenue all longing for his caresses. He accepted the challenge of this waiting flesh, determined to show her that he knew what he was doing. He sucked at one teat while rubbing the other. Alithea moaned and trembled and lifted her pubis.

He looked into her lust-drugged eyes, ran a hand over the rounded stomach and buried a finger in her dewy folds. Just as he had coaxed the most poignant music from the piano, so he now worked his finger round her clitoris. It gave him tremendous joy to be able to pleasure her. He wanted to give and give – to raise her to the greatest, most explosive climax she had ever enjoyed.

One of the most important lessons his teacher had taught

him was to prolong the moment. So he roused Alithea in peaks and troughs, gradually increasing, letting the feeling die away, building it up again until at last she splintered into orgasm. He kept his hand round her spasming sex, helping her prolong the ecstasy. At last the wildness faded from her eyes and she purred like a cat, and grabbed his cock, pulling him over her.

'One moment,' he had sense enough to say, and reached for a condom, rolling it on.

'Now,' she demanded, her legs round his body and guiding him into her. 'Do it to me... hard! I want to feel you right in there.'

Hampered by his jeans he succeeded in clenching his buttocks and thrusting into her. First the head of his cock entered that hot, slippery channel, and then the length of the shaft till the whole of his member had disappeared and his pubic hair butted against hers. He closed his eyes, reduced to jelly as his glans touched Alithea's cervix and pleasurable spasms spiralled through him, along his spine and into his brain. He wanted nothing but to repeat it, to go on and on.

'Oh yes...' he panted, unable to prevent his hips pistoning, driving his cock.

'Come on,' Alithea groaned, working her pelvis in time with his. 'Fuck me hard. That's it...'

He was taken by an invincible storm, lifted high, whirled in a vortex of rainbow hues as his semen erupted from him in blissful release.

'Wow!' Alithea exclaimed as he slumped on her.

He could feel her fingers smoothing the back of his neck, coiling in his hair. For his part he would go through the motions of tenderness, while all he really wanted to do was turn on his side and sleep. Alithea was a nice girl, but now they had finished he wished she would leave. It was more important that he be fresh for composing in the morning.

It seemed that she read his mind, for she shifted his weight and rolled from under him, saying matter-of-factly, 'Thanks for letting me hear your music. I must go now... have an early rehearsal tomorrow. *Madame Butterfly*, you know.'

He lay on the couch, missing the warmth of her body, watching her sleepily as she dressed and ran a comb through her hair.

'Shall I ring for a taxi?' he offered, ashamed of his feeling of relief that she was being so sensible and not demanding any commitment.

'I'll do it,' she said blithely and dialled a number. Someone answered and she gave the address, then replaced the receiver in its cradle.

'Shall I see you soon?' he said, sitting up, feeling obliged to make some gesture of continuation. 'What about lunch one day?'

She smiled and leaned over to kiss him. 'Perhaps. Don't worry about it. You're a great screw.' The bell rang and, 'There's my cab,' she added. 'Goodnight, Conlan.'

'Goodnight, Alithea,' he said, and accompanied her to the door, tucking his shirt into his jeans and zipping up as he went.

She reached up and placed a kiss on his lips, then said, 'By the way, about that girl whose party it was, the one you were lusting after.'

'I wasn't—'

'You were,' she continued. 'Go for it, my dear.'

And with that, she disappeared into the black maw of the taxi.

Belphegor followed, and when Alithea let herself into her house, he slipped inside too, though she was unaware of him. He watched as she undressed, showered and finally sank naked into bed. The room was dark, save for an imitation art nouveau lamp. The vampire crept under the covers beside her, and let his hand drift over her face and close her eyelids.

He had observed her with Conlan, who was one of his protégés, though he did not know it; so talented. He deserved supernatural assistance. The sight of her ripe, robust body had made Belphegor's mouth water. The hour was late and soon he must slumber, but just one more for the road, he decided.

She was far gone when he took her arm, turned it over and placed his lips where the vein throbbed inside the elbow. He used her carefully, his teeth so sharp she did not even stir in her sleep, but she smiled and sighed, and enjoyed orgasmic sensations far sweeter than normal sex as he sucked his fill, then lapped over the wound so that it healed at once. She would never know what it was that had been pleasuring her, the revenant who had stolen into her bed in the deep shadows of the night. It wouldn't be the last time, he vowed. She was so juicy a morsel.

Chapter Four

It's so clean and uncluttered, Stella thought, almost afraid to walk on the pristine rugs scattered across the shining teak floor of Quincy's entrance hall.

She had often gazed admiringly at the recently built, riverside condominiums owned by high-flyers. Viewing them from a distance, it had never crossed her mind that one day she might be a guest in one. People who could afford such places were outside her social circle. She had been impressed when the car paused at the sensor operated security gates. These had rolled apart to let them through and closed firmly behind them. Imprisoning them, or keeping out undesirables? It had to be the latter, surely? she mused, with a little flutter of uneasiness.

Quincy had driven into an underground parking bay, leapt out to open the passenger door for her, then left the luxury sports car, confident it would not be vandalised. An elevator whisked them up to the second floor and his stunning apartment.

Subdued lighting radiated from overhead spots, and the airy living space was furnished with leather couches and armchairs, sleek steel units containing books, discs, a DVD and stereo. In complete contrast to this almost aggressive modernity was an antique desk, its brass finials bearing Egyptian motifs. It stood at an angle near the window, its smooth calfskin surface broken by the latest in computer technology and a compact white telephone.

Quincy snapped his fingers and steel bars slid back from the wall-length French windows. They parted noiselessly and the silk curtains billowed slightly as he conducted her to the balcony that ran the width of his property. An orange neon glow lit the sky over London. The glass façades of office blocks glittered like the stars, and the river reflected the lamps on bridges and waterfronts. At first Stella was aware of the buzz of a city that never sleeps, but soon she became acclimatised, it became part of her existence.

'It's breathtaking,' she gasped, leaning her elbows on the rail.

'The only place to live in London,' he answered, and he was behind her, his hands on her shoulders, warm through the thin blouse. She resisted the urge to lean back into him. It was too soon. She mustn't blow this opportunity. Quincy could be more than just useful to *Zero700*.

He sensed her resistance and released her with a smile. 'Would you like a drink?' he asked.

Would she? She didn't know. Her head was already muddled. So much had happened that day, a momentous birthday on several counts. She shook her head. 'No, thank you. I'm not a big drinker. It usually gives me a headache.'

'That's good to hear; band members who go on the piss are a pain, ' he said, and pressed a button on the DVD player. The forty-eight inch screen fastened flat to one wall lit up. 'This is the latest from my stable: *Wild Dogs*. It was released concurrently with their new single, just before they went on tour in Japan. That's the place to go. We'll have your band out there before you know it.'

The video was violent, ear-splittingly loud and bordering on pornographic. Stella had heard of *Wild Dogs* and seen them interviewed on television. No boy-band, they were raw and brash. Three pouting, strutting, laddish girls and two tough, lithe, crop-headed guys. The choreography was brilliant, but the content alarmed her. The words of the song were suggestive to the extreme and the actions of the participants as near to copulation as could be squeezed past the censor.

Though alarmed, even a tad shocked, Stella was undeniably aroused. The sexual fires smouldering at the base of her spine had been fanned but not entirely satisfied. Now her nipples chafed against the delicate lacy bra and it was as if a dozen tiny, impudent creatures were playing with her pussy, dragging her panties into the narrow, vertical line and coaxing forth her juices. Her clitoris thrummed with the memory of her own fingers when she showered and, later, those of the shadowy figure who continued to haunt her.

She stared at the brazen female singers. Professionals to the fingertips, they managed to maintain a performance while capturing their partners in leg locks, all bare thighs and flashes of crotch that begged the question of whether or not they were wearing panties under those minute skirts. The artful photographic angles were obtuse, the film skilfully edited, but even so, there was the hint of pubic floss, the suggestion of a cock entering a vulva, and the clever simulation of defiant nipples bare for sucking. Or was it faked? The intriguing thing about the video was that one could not be quite sure.

Quincy edged closer to Stella on the deeply cushioned couch in front of the screen, his arm resting along her shoulders. His body was solid, warming her all down one side. She inhaled the musky odour of a healthy male, overlaid with costly aftershave. There was a lot about him that appealed to her, not the least of which was the power he exhaled through his pores. It acted on her like an aphrodisiac. If only she had met him a short while ago, before her demonic angel appeared, then she might have thought him the answer to all her prayers.

'You like the video?' he asked quietly, and his hand descended from her neck to the upper curve of her breast. He took his time, every inch he covered making her shiver, and when he reached the nipple it was as if an electric charge shot right down to her clitoris.

'It's well done,' she conceded, struggling to keep her voice steady. 'But *Zero700* could never do anything like that. We're not that sort of band... more folk, if you know what I mean.'

He chuckled deep in his chest, and his other hand came to rest on her thigh. 'You'd be surprised what I can make you do,' he said confidently. 'Anyway, what you're seeing here is the cut version, cleaned up for the general public. This is the original one,' and he got up and slid a disc into the machine, then resumed his place, but this time his hand advanced a shade higher up her thigh.

She did not attempt to stop him. In fact, she was hardly aware of it, so absorbed in the DVD. The same music, and some of the same action, followed by scenes that shocked her profoundly. She was viewing a church, richly decorated – candles glowing, brass chalices wafting incense, statues of saints and a naked girl spread-eagled in front of the altar. A man stood over her, his head hooded, face masked, his torso naked, his brief leather shorts just about containing the bulky package between his thighs. Dancers swayed in the background, all leather clad, wearing masks and skullcaps.

The beat pounded, the music grew louder. The girl on the floor was seized and bent over the back of a pew. Her legs were kicked apart and tethered by the ankles, held taught and supported by her high-heeled shoes. Her wrists were manacled to iron rings hammered into the wooden seat. Her full, creamy-white breasts swayed on the far side. The camera panned in on her rump. It was forced into the air, and the cameraman concentrated on her crinkled anal mouth and her glistening wet vulva. Her pussy lips were swollen, poking between her crease, hairy and lewd looking.

The muscular bullyboy flourished a belt in his right hand, the end wound firmly round his fist. The singers wailed, the air cracked as he brought the strap down with a thwack across the girl's buttocks. The belt whistled again, slicing through the ether like a sword. It hit her another savage blow. Her bottom clenched and wobbled convulsively. She tugged at her restraints, her screams becoming a part of the music.

Stella could not drag her eyes away. Every time the girl received another lash she felt it in her own body, as if it was she being chastised. She leaned against Quincy, and he ran his hand under her skirt, lifting it to reveal her panties. He pushed them aside and combed his fingers through her bush.

'You wish it was you, not her being punished,' he stated arrogantly, and touched the tip of her throbbing bud.

'No… I mean… of course not,' she stammered, her hips writhing against that tempting touch. 'It must be horrible. I'd hate it.'

'Would you, my dear?' he goaded, and his finger wormed its way into her cleft, anointing it and then returning to spread the fluid where she needed it most. 'You'd be surprised how many women, and men for that matter, enjoy handing over their will to someone stronger. It frees them from responsibility. They can do things they only dreamed of in their most debauched fantasies, liberated from responsibility. "He made me do it", they can say. Someone as sexy and beautiful as you would blossom under the dominance of a master.'

She shivered; someone else said that to her while she was preparing for the party. Or had it been a figment of her imagination?

Quincy's words thrilled her to the core. She rejected the idea of subservience as archaic, yet something primitive buried deep inside her welcomed it, the primitive part that exists in all human beings, simply veiled by a thin veneer of civilisation. Her eyes were fixed on the screen, even as she arched against his finger, chasing the promised orgasm. She could feel the long hot shape of his cock pressing close, and she wanted him with a fierce need that beggared belief. She

74

was alarmed. What was happening to her lately? She was rapidly turning into a rampant nymphet.

Even as the girl's eyes watered from the repeated blows, Stella felt herself getting more and more aroused. The sight of that bottom, bright red from the lash and quivering as it received yet another, excited Stella in a way she had never believed possible. She could feel her face flushing and could not control her gasps as the tingling in her pussy increased.

The man flung aside the belt and released his penis. It uncoiled from the leather shorts like a hungry snake. *Wild Dogs* sang louder, the beat frenetic. He moved into position between the girl's thighs and ran his hands over the angry stripes scoring her buttocks. Then he angled his helm against her slippery opening and pushed. Her squeals rose above the music as he rammed home, buried to the hilt inside her. The girl stopped struggling, and her cries changed to ones of animal enjoyment.

He withdrew, then propelled himself forward again, plunging into her wetness. Out again, in time to the rhythm, then slamming into her, his hairy belly slapping against her raw skin, one hand beneath her, rubbing her clitoris. He pistoned ever faster as the beat speeded up, working himself towards orgasm, and the singers shouted and gyrated, rubbing their own genitals or those of their partners, the whole scene degenerating into an orgy.

'I'll re-run it,' Quincy said, licking the rim of Stella's ear. 'We'll be able to hear it from speakers in the bedroom.'

'But I don't… I ought to be getting back,' she began in protest, then stopped as he seized her.

'The most boring words in the English language; don't, ought not, and shouldn't,' he laughed. 'I never, ever use them. Come along,' and he drew her to her feet.

Her panties were uncomfortable; the gusset wet and dragged tight into her slit. She stumbled along with him as he led her down a wide hall, thickly carpeted and hung with modern paintings. His bedroom was at the end, an even more luxurious place dominated by a huge bed. She wondered if he used it for group sex – she wouldn't put anything past him.

There was a Jacuzzi sunk into the floor of the en suite bathroom, the décor like something from a nineteen-thirties movie extravaganza. Just for a moment she longed to immerse herself in the square black tub, and feel the bubbles caressing her. Quincy, it seemed, had other ideas.

'Lift your skirt and bend over,' he said crisply, and there was something in his eyes and his steady voice that made her obey. 'Now bend properly, over the bed.'

'Like the girl in the video?' she quavered, trepidation implementing desire and curiosity, unable to shake off the images created by *Wild Dogs*, their song playing in the background.

'Something like that,' he said.

She lifted her skirt and rested her forearms on the quilted satin bedcover. The cool air wafted over her, and she could smell her own arousal. Her position raised her buttocks, her panties cut high at the sides, running into her crease and leaving her bottom entirely exposed.

'Give me your bum, Stella,' Quincy whispered, and she could feel him close. 'Tell me, my dear, have you ever been taken up the arse?'

'No, never,' she replied nervously, conscious of her vulnerability. The angle of her body effectively pushed the suspenders attached to her garter belt and stocking tops out of the way. Her hindquarters and thighs were totally exposed.

Not daring to look round, Stella felt his hands at each side, pulling her knickers down and off. Then he started to finger her, ringing her anus and attempting penetration. She flinched away. 'No, please,' she begged.

'No? To me?' he mocked, and slid into her vagina instead, working his finger in and around, aping the motion of coition.

76

It was wonderful and she could not help thrusting her bottom against the deliciously competent finger. But it was not enough, and she awaited his blow with tingling anticipation.

It did not come. He took his finger from her and picked up her panties, burying his nose in the damp, silky bundle. Stella waited, willing him to do almost anything if he would only bring her to completion.

'Get up,' he said, and laid her knickers on the bedside table, almost reverently.

She did so, relieved to move from that uncomfortably exposed position, and when she looked round at him it was to see that he had taken off his designer jacket and stood there in his shirt-sleeves, the neck unbuttoned. Crisp dark hair curled at the opening, and beneath his waistband, his trousers were distorted by the large erection concealed within.

'You need training,' he said, softly and seductively. 'There are so many pleasures I can teach you, if you place yourself in my hands. Will you do that?'

'I'll try,' she whispered.

'Then lie down,' he said, and with lithe grace, he swung her up and deposited her on the bed. 'I promise I won't do anything you don't like.'

Still wary, though her scruples had succumbed to lust, Stella sank into the softness of the duvet. Quincy knelt above her, holding her arms apart over her head. He stared down into her eyes, his own blade-sharp, and then, before she could stop him, slipped a cord over each wrist and fastened it to the ornamental bars of the headboard. His sensual lips parted, and for an instant he delayed there, poised over her breasts. Then he untied the wrap-over front and lowered his head, his tongue flickering across the hard points of her nipples poking through the pink lace bra. Pleasure saturated her, pooling in her sex, and she was silently begging him.

'Not quite yet,' he said. 'You must wait,' and he straddled her, pressing down to make her aware of the rock hard cock swelling against his flies.

'You bastard…' she moaned, ashamed of the ease with which she succumbed to his teasing.

He changed, eyes flinty, raised a hand and struck her across the cheek. 'Be silent, slave,' he growled. 'You'll be punished for that.'

'I'm not your slave,' she whispered, shocked by his reaction. 'Let me go at once.'

Quincy ignored her, reaching for a flexible paddle on the nightstand. It was a small, whippy object covered in white leather and, without hesitation, he applied it to her thighs, belly and breasts. It stung and she yelped, tugging fruitlessly on her bonds and kicking out with her legs till he used more cords to tie her ankles to the foot-posts. Now she was completely helpless, hating and loving it, totally confused by the opposing emotions sweeping through her with every swipe of the paddle. Pre-orgasmic waves rippled down her spine and into her loins, but they were not enough to bring her to the peak.

He sniggered and put the paddle down, as if she was a thing existing entirely for his amusement, he unzipped his trousers and exposed a large stiff cock. As she watched he rubbed it slowly, fondling the thick, dark-skinned shaft and smearing the glans with pre-come juice. Leaving it standing proud, he unbuttoned his skirt and shrugged his shoulders out of it, and she admired his tanned, muscular body.

He unbuckled his belt and his trousers slid down, his impressive cock swaying as he moved, jutting above his large balls swinging in their sac. Stella licked her lips, wanting to take that circumcised knob in her mouth and milk him of his spunk. He grinned and knelt astride her face, then used his cock like a paintbrush, trailing his jism over her forehead, her eyelids, cheeks, mouth and throat. Finally, he pushed down the bra cups and her breasts popped out. He squeezed them together, forming a deep cleavage into which he inserted his cock, rubbing it up and down between her breasts as if the cleft were a vagina. His expression became intense, and his jaw set as he struggled to hold back the ejaculation threatening to engulf him.

'Ah!' he exclaimed, and pulled away sharply. 'Not yet... not yet. We must make this last.'

He rested beside her and tormented her nipples. When she was almost at screaming pitch he pulled open a drawer and produced a large, lifelike vibrator, switched it on and applied it to her inner thighs. He moved it slowly, tauntingly, lasciviously towards her sex, and then allowed it to flirt with her clitoris. He teased her, running the rubber glans round her opening, then pushed the whole of it inside her, the vibrations pulsing against her G-spot, but not relieving her aching clit. Slowly, Quincy withdrew the dildo, then pushed it back in again.

'Oh, rub my clit with it,' she pleaded, close to tears. 'More, please give me more.' She thought he was about to answer her prayers when he eased the dildo out, but instead of applying it to her nubbin, he let it glide over her perineum and nudge against her anus. He pressed and the buzzing object, slippery with her dew, penetrated her rectum, inch by slow inch. With his free hand he deftly stimulated her bud. She was so anxious to come before he stopped that it inhibited her pleasure. She strained, but was stuck on that pre-orgasmic plateau, unable to ascend to bliss.

As if taking pity on her he abandoned the vibrator, sheathed his cock in a condom and wormed his way down her body. She waited in an agony of suspense. What was he going to do? Take his own pleasure and leave her unfulfilled? Beat her with the paddle again? Postpone her orgasm till she was way beyond caring?

Instead, she felt his warm breath on her pubis and his fingers holding her lips back so that her engorged button swelled shamelessly from its cowl. She felt his mouth on it,

79

sucking and lapping, and almost at once a shuddering, mind-blowing climax surged through her.

His control snapped and he covered her savagely, his penis plunging into her, working furiously till he came with a roar, then collapsed across her, his face buried in her hair.

'You see what a willing little thing she is, my boy?' said Belphegor, peering through the plate-glass windows into the bedroom. 'I particularly enjoyed the bit when he took the paddle to her bare bottom. Did you see those gorgeous crimson roses springing into being on her flesh?'

Lazio glowered, his ice-blue eyes flashing dangerously. 'But with him? That depraved beast? How could she?' he demanded, and there was an air of the jealous, outraged lover about him that amused Belphegor enormously.

'Calm down,' he advised, patting him on the shoulder. 'Just wait till we get them to Ireland. Then the fun will begin. It's all coming together… how I love some of these modern phrases, so concise… each player in our little production ready to take his or her part.'

'Why did you bring me here? Why can't I tell her who I am and what is expected of her? Dimitri will be furious if he suspects that you've been interfering.'

'Interfering?' Belphegor said, the picture of injured innocence. '*Moi*?'

'Why do you torment him so? And why are you so bitchy to Candice?'

'Bitchy?' Belphegor scoffed, tossing his hair back petulantly. 'I'm sweetness and light, compared to how I could be. We were so happy until she came along, Dimitri and I and the witch sisters. We had such fun, and then he has to go and find Candice, a reincarnation of the love he lost back in the seventeenth century. She couldn't hack him becoming a vampire and shut herself up in a convent, the silly girl.'

80

Belphegor was worried about Lazio; he didn't want history repeating itself. Vampires were supposed to be horrible and frightening and gruesome, not sentimental and capable of falling in love. He knew Dimitri was fond of the boy, looking upon him as a son. Though the nosferatu had many miraculous powers that some humans envied, they could not produce children. It wasn't necessary for them to do so. If they selected someone special and worthy of the gift of immortality, then they sucked their blood and, in return, gave them the option of drinking their own. The person they chose had to have sterling qualities that appealed to the Undead. They despised and spurned the pathetic wannabes, vain fantasists who had watched too many horror films.

Thus Belphegor had chosen Dimitri, coming across him in Paris where he was studying medicine and offering him eternal life – because he fancied him, and to save him from being tried for witchcraft. And Dimitri, likewise, had rescued Lazio from a battlefield in Belgium during the Great War.

'The Angel of Mons, August twenty-eighth, nineteen-fourteen,' Belphegor said aloud, resting elegantly against the stone rail of the balcony and gazing into space. 'It was at dusk on a hot clear evening, about nine o'clock.'

'What are you on about?' Lazio's blue eyes were like shards of ice that pierced Belphegor's defences.

He deflected them, saying, 'I was thinking about the night you were reborn. The Angel of Mons got a lot of press, and many soldiers swore that the Divine intervention of an angelic host saved a British Expeditionary Force from being destroyed, when they were fighting a desperate rearguard action against enormous odds. It wasn't angels, of course, but Dimitri, Candice and yours truly. I organised it, had us dressed in flowing golden robes and with Dimitri in the centre as he's the tallest, wearing huge outspread wings. I stage-managed the whole thing, always knew I should be in the theatre, and it was most impressive, with us hovering in mid-air and seemingly standing on a star. It proved effective and the enemy, that was the Germans, reported that they found themselves absolutely powerless to proceed, and that their horses turned sharply round and fled and nothing could stop them.'

'I remember,' Lazio said slowly, and there was pain in his voice. 'Dimitri found me in a water-logged trench.'

'You were shot to pieces, dear boy, and he saved you.'

'I was twenty and fresh from Sandhurst. My name was Captain Farquarson, and this was my first battle. I was leading my men…'

'You'll always find vampires hanging around war zones,' Belphegor went on. 'Nothing altruistic about it. There are rich pickings, though as you know, we can't feed on corpses. The heart has to be beating. Medea, Allegra and Madelon would appear at night in field hospitals, dressed as nurses. Sisters of Mercy. Call me old-fashioned if you like, but I believe they did a good job, helping those poor boys pass over more easily. They showed them a glimpse of paradise as they drained them, giving them enchanted, sensual dreams.'

'Very noble, I'm sure,' Lazio said cuttingly, his face gloomy as he watched Quincy mount Stella for the second time.

'Oh, don't be such a misery,' Belphegor snarled, and his fingertips shot out flames. 'There's absolutely nothing you can do to alter fate. This drama is destined to take place. Wait till you meet Conlan Henny. He'll put your nose out of joint, I can tell you. But it won't make any difference to the final outcome. Trust me, I know.'

'No more shelf-stacking,' said Kate, gleefully, seated on a stool, her skirt rising above her knees, rounded and glossy and inviting the touch. The kitchen was old-fashioned enough to be the very last word in retro design and, as it was at the rear of the ground floor, it looked out over the back garden.

'Don't give up the day job,' reminded Jez, smiling at her, his hand coming to rest on her thigh. 'I'll continue being a car mechanic till I see that contract in black and white.' She reached out and ruffled his hennaed locks, clicking the colourful beads threaded through them.

'Yeah, Quincy may be all mouth and trousers,' added Tommy. 'I'm not giving up bar work just yet.'

'He likes the demo tape,' Stella put in quietly, slicing a wickedly sticky and calorie stuffed Lardy cake she had bought to celebrate.

Her money from the solicitor had not yet appeared in her bank. These things took time and she could not yet afford to be extravagant, though she had discussed the purchase of a van with Jez and Tommy. One thing she had done was resign from teaching PC skills to a bunch of middle-aged housewives who wanted to go back to work but didn't stand a hope in hell of employment unless they were computer literate.

When the cake was quartered, she handed it round. This, along with numerous cups of coffee, would keep them going while they mulled over their first meeting in the Wardour Street office Quincy rented in the heart of London's theatre land. A week had flown by since her party, and though disappointed, she pretended she was unmoved because he had not contacted her with a view to another date. He had phoned Kate, however, very businesslike as he organised their session in the recording studio.

He didn't invite Stella to stay with him that first night in his apartment, but then, she told herself sensibly, he had expected her to return to her guests. Indeed, he hadn't even driven her back to Highgate but phoned for a cab. She felt dismissed, as if of no further interest once he'd screwed her. That was all right for tough girls like Kate, but Stella's feelings had been as bruised as her bottom. The marks left by the paddle faded after a few days, while those imprinted on her ego were still red-raw.

His office had been bustling, and she noticed his secretary, Sherry, of the straight blonde hair, big tits and curvaceous figure. She gazed at him adoringly and Stella sensed an intimacy between them that put her hackles up. He had paid *Zero700* a lot of attention and had Sherry rushing about, fetching drinks, getting people on the phone, while he behaved in an entrepreneurial manner calculated to impress. It may have worked on Stella, but Kate was scathing afterwards, agreeing with Jez and Tommy who classified him as an arsehole.

Much to his annoyance, Stephen had not been invited along, so he kept ringing Stella and hassling.

'When is he organising a gig for you, and when are you going to Troon Hall?' he demanded.

'I don't know,' she had answered to both questions. 'Leave me alone.'

'Selfish bitch,' he rejoined, then his voice lowered menacingly. 'I'll find out. Quincy will tell me and I'll be right on your tail.'

'Drop dead,' was all she could think to retort.

Sipping her coffee, elbows resting on the table, she now concentrated on the talk rattling round the kitchen. Despite their attempts to play it cool, the band was in a lather of excitement. This was every group's dream. There was so much talent out there in the marketplace that it needed a Quincy Dubois to get them noticed.

Stella was torn, wanting to be a part of *Zero700*'s success, yet itching to go to Ireland and see her property. She had thought a lot about Lazio, but so much was happening. She felt herself being swept along by an inexorable tide of events that gave her no time to ponder anything other than reality. But she was plagued by the strong feeling that he was in the vicinity somewhere, and she kept getting pictures of Troon Hall flashing across her inner eye.

'So, is it okay to start looking for a van?' Tommy asked,

rousing her from miles away.

'Sure, no prob,' she replied. 'From what Quincy said we're going to need one, pronto. He's lining up gigs in Bristol, Manchester and Leeds, and when I mentioned that I needed to visit Ireland on business, he was enthusiastic about doing Dublin. Advanced publicity and all that, and he's got a record producer interested in us and a slot on daytime TV.'

The doorbell rang and Kate went to answer it, returning with a lanky, rather rumpled young man with floppy brown hair. 'This is Conlan – Conlan Henny, one of my mates from college,' she announced.

'I was at your birthday party, Stella,' he began, stumbling slightly over the words.

'Ah yes, there were so many people,' she said. 'I do remember you though. I saw you just as I was leaving with Quincy. You were with a girl with sandy hair.'

'That's right,' he acknowledged, hands thrust into trouser pockets, and she registered broad shoulders under the blue denim shirt, a narrow waist, baggy beige chinos and chunky sports sandals. 'I had to come round and thank you.'

'Are you still composing?' Kate asked, sitting him down and putting a mug in front of him.

'Oh yes, I'm working on something big. That's another reason why I've called in. I was impressed by *Zero700*, and would like to write a song or two for you. Any chance you might be interested?'

Kate glanced across at Stella and the others. 'What do you think?' she asked.

'Are you any good?' Jez asked him bluntly.

'Who can tell? Was Beethoven rated before his death?'

'I wouldn't know. If it was John Lennon now, I'd be on the same wavelength.'

'I haven't written anything for pop, but I'd like to give it a go,' Conlan confessed, and his brown eyes shone with enthusiasm. 'I've written a symphony and a requiem mass and there's a record company dithering, almost but not quite, signing up an orchestra and conductor to perform a suite I wrote for The Northern Company of Contemporary Dance.'

'That's impressive,' commented Tommy.

'Highbrow stuff,' put in Jez, disparagingly.

'Back off, give him a break,' Kate ordered sharply. 'I heard some of the folk songs he wrote at college and they weren't bad.'

'I'd like to listen to them,' Stella said hurriedly, wanting to learn more about the young composer. He really was attractive and she felt they might have a lot in common. He was neither a sophisticated seducer nor a shadowy, ghostlike person who had left neither address nor phone number.

'The piano is in the sitting room, Conlan,' Kate said. 'Help yourself.'

'We're off van hunting, ' said Jez, lounging to his feet, his scruffy jeans and torn T-shirt all part of his image. 'You coming, Kate?'

She was considering Stella and Conlan, her brows lifted in an enquiring way, a little smile curving her poppy-red lips. Picking up her short leather jacket she flung it over her skimpy top, pulled down her little silver skirt and accompanied the men to the door. 'Will you be all right for an hour, Stella? See what Conlan has on offer and we'll listen to it later, okay?'

'Okay,' she replied, and was glad to be alone with him. Somehow she felt sure she would understand him better than her friends. She liked orchestral music, whereas Jez did not give it a chance. Tommy was an ally, however, teetering between serious violin study and the more lucrative popular scene.

As Stella took Conlan to the upright piano in the lounge, left behind by Kate's aunt, she saw herself in the mirror over the mantelpiece, and narrowed her eyes thoughtfully. Quincy said she was beautiful and sexy, she thought, warmed by his remembered words. She lifted her head proudly, firm breasts rising and falling with her breathing. Would Conlan think her beautiful and sexy too?

'Nice room,' he said, looking round. 'I couldn't really see it the other night; too crowded. Did you have a good time?'

Stella could feel her cheeks turning pink, but hoped he would think she had been sitting in the warm April sunshine. After a diabolical winter, the weathermen had predicted a fine spring and hot summer, and so far they were right. 'Yes, thank you,' she replied, wondering what he would think of her if he knew the truth, and the undeniable fact that she had enjoyed herself as never before. 'Quincy promotes bands, you see,' she stumbled on. 'He wants to manage *Zero700*.'

'That's good.' Conlan smiled, and she thought how infectious it was, making her lips curve in response.

I want to make love with you, she decided, and the sensuality of this notion tingled down her spine. She fidgeted a little, shifting from one foot to the other, feeling the dampness of her panties, her pussy warm and eager. 'Have you brought any of your music along?' she asked, just for something to say.

'No, it's all in my head,' he said, then added, faltering a little, 'You look great... that's why I came here really, to see you again.'

'But the songs you want to write for us?'

'Those too, but they are really for you.'

If it had been anyone else Stella might have thought he was bullshitting her, but not Conlan. If ever there was a sincere man, it was he. She had looked at him on her birthday night, seen his open expression, his serious face, and it felt so right. Although she went off with Quincy, who was trouble incarnate, Conlan had lingered in her mind.

'Thank you,' she murmured, suddenly shy.

'Well, anyway, here goes,' he said, somewhat bashfully,

stretching his arms in front of him and flexing his fingers.

He started to play and Stella was intrigued by the soft, lilting, rather forlorn refrain. Words drifted into her head; it would not be hard to compose lyrics for the haunting music. 'Ah, here's where Tommy could come in on his violin,' she said at one point, when Conlan stopped.

She saw he was looking at her breasts, his lips slightly parted, and he did not seem to hear her. Then he pushed back a lock of unruly brown hair and said huskily, 'Right, yes, that would be good. It's based on an Irish folksong, and there are existing words, if you want them.'

'Let's give it a go,' she said, and took up the piece of crumpled paper he handed her. She leant against the piano, an arm resting on the top, watching his slim fingers moving over the keys. He kept his eyes firmly on them as she sang. It seemed she already knew the tune, as if it had been locked in her subconscious and now released. Where had she heard it before? Ireland again. It seemed as if everything was leading her there these days.

When the final chords drifted into infinity he sat for a moment with his hands on his knees, then said, 'That's very good. I think we may have a hit here. You learn remarkably quickly.'

The room still echoed with those plaintive notes, and it was so quiet now that they could have been in the Wicklow Hills, miles away from civilisation. 'Are you Irish?' she asked.

He nodded. 'Sort of, way back. My grandparents came from Kildare. Why?'

'I've inherited a property there, and I'll be visiting shortly. Why don't you come along?' she suggested, and immediately could not believe what she'd said.

'I'd love to,' he replied, and his eyes lit up, his hands leaving his knees to clasp her hands. 'I want to write for *Zero700*,' he added, 'but I must admit I was using it as an excuse to meet you again.'

Stella stood back a little and stared into his face. They were at the crossroads. She either put up demarcation lines, or she didn't. She wanted him to respect her, both as an artiste and a woman, and he wouldn't if she proved to be an easy lay.

'What about your girlfriend?' she prevaricated, knowing he wanted to kiss her. 'The one you were with the other night.'

'Alithea Carpenter. She's not my girlfriend – more of a colleague.'

'I see. So you're foot loose and fancy free.'

'Yes. And you?'

Quincy and Lazio appeared in her mind, but neither had asked her for commitment. 'I'm free, too,' she insisted.

His face cleared and he stood up, caught her by her thick curly mane and kissed her. It was a brief kiss, but it excited her and had a feel good factor that was heart-warming. His cock was hardening in his trousers, but she stood quite still and refrained from pressing against it.

He let her go and though still holding her lightly by her upper arms, grinned and said, 'I'm glad no one has laid claim to you. I want to get to know you, Stella, to work with you and play with you. We don't have to rush things.'

It was dark in the coffin, a deep, black Stygian darkness where no single ray of light penetrated. Lazio slept, the profound, mystical sleep of the vampire, but in his sleep he dreamed that he saw Stella with another man. Not Quincy, that might have been tolerable, but a fresh complexioned, brown-haired young man, and Lazio knew who it was. Belphegor had told him. This was his protégé, the young genuis, Conlan Henny. Belphegor liked musicians and composers. It was he who had been the driving force behind Niccolo Paganini and Franz Liszt, both of whom had earned the reputation of being in league with the devil.

Lazio struggled to wake, but could not. Anger churned within him, flowing in blood-red waves, beating against his active brain and inert flesh. Stella was his. No wily schemer like Belphegor was going to steal her from him.

But it was too much, and too early. Dusk was hours away. There was nothing he could do, that weighty lassitude stealing over him once more. Lazio slipped into the deep, catatonic trance of the Undead.

Chapter Five

They hardly had time to look round Dublin, arriving at six o'clock in the evening, with a sound check to organise and no chance to get their bearings.

'We're always rushing, these days,' Kate complained, helping to hump gear from the van into the back of *O'Donoghue's*, one of the most popular of the many 'singing' pubs. It was hosting their first appearance on Irish soil.

Quincy had promised that soon he would hire a coach so they could travel in comparative comfort, but just for now they had covered miles up and down the English motorways in Stella's new vehicle along with the equipment, leaving their mark on clubs, halls, and open-air festivals. He had carried out his intention of exposing them to publicity and *Zero700* was becoming, if not a household name, something very close. Experience counted for an awful lot, and they were nothing if not experienced. For months before they met him they had played in skittle alleys, trendy jazz clubs, and at student union gigs and parties, and were better off for this baptism of fire.

He was pleased with the result of his input. Already it was showing a profit, and this would escalate now that the first CD had hit the record stores. He strolled into the pub as if he owned it, the public bar already occupied by drinkers and pool players, the tables at the back filled with people waiting for the entertainment to start. Stephen and Sherry accompanied him. He brought her along in her secretarial and sometime shag capacity, and Stephen because he might prove useful when it came to squeezing money out of the

Troon Hall equity. *Zero700* might be up and coming, but one could never have too much cash. Stella's house was to be invaded tomorrow, when they drove to County Wicklow, lock, stock and barrel.

Quincy could hardly wait, going along with Stephen's tale of the mismanagement of Emma Kerrick's will, but inwardly vowing to use his influence over Stella in order to grab the lion's share. It was obvious that she was besotted with him, and he had deliberately kept her dangling by ignoring her. He smiled darkly, recalling her hunger for carnal knowledge. She was so green it had been rather like a deflowering. He wanted to repeat his assault on her untried flesh, his loins lurching as he thought of the marks left by the paddle. Get her down to Troon Hall and there would be ample opportunity for him to fulfil his burning ambition to bugger her, maybe Kate as well, though he doubted that her arse was virgin territory. He looked forward to subduing and humiliating Stella, certain that Sherry and Stephen would be willing participants.

Meanwhile, there was that certain stir in the atmosphere that heralds a gig. He nodded to a couple of reporters and a photographer from the local newspaper to whom he had sent free tickets. The roadies were setting up on the low stage of the function room. Jez was liasing with the sound engineer, and Tommy tuning his violin and making adjustments to the amplifier. The genial bartender was swapping gossip with some of the regulars, but keeping an eye on what was taking place. The pub was already full, a young crowd in the main, lured by *Zero700*, whose reputation had preceded them.

And then there was Stella, and Quincy felt that familiar movement in his groin. Jesus, but she was horny in her short black skirt and sexy high heels. Her T-shirt bore the band's logo, and over it she had slung an ethnic jacket, in crushed mulberry velvet. Her hair was teased out and gelled;

two hectic spots of blusher underscored her cheeks, and her mouth was painted with red lipstick that held the purple hue of blood. She had outlined her eyes with kohl and thickened her lashes. She was feisty, thrilling, slightly weird, and the older domino playing patrons of the bar, Guinness drinkers who loved to yarn, stopped dead in their tracks when she appeared, glancing at her somewhat askew.

Quincy liked the atmosphere in *O'Donoghue's*, a dimly lit, back-to-the-womb sort of place, the air redolent of cigarette smoke, hops and malt and whatever secret ingredient, some said the waters of the River Liffey, that fortified the dark, creamy stout. It was rich with mahogany panelling, brass, cut glass and mirrors, and reminded him of certain watering holes he frequented in London's Soho.

Yes, he thought, slipping along one of the wooden benches behind a square table, he could settle down rather well here, or at Troon Hall; his Irish residence. That had a fine ring to it – he wouldn't give up the town one – but this could prove a useful retreat. No questions asked, as long as one was generous with handouts. He might even marry Stella to insure his right to such an estate.

Steady on, his alter ego cautioned. Marriage? That had never before been a part of any agenda. Quincy slouched low, long legs stretched out under the table, and took the dumpy glass of whisky that Stephen brought across. Sherry was sulking; she always did when Stella was in the vicinity. He gave a sardonic smile. Women were so predictable. They thought themselves liberated, but introduce them to a man who they both desired and all this went to the wall. Under cover of the table he slid his hand over Sherry's knee, lifted the hem of her miniskirt and found the little triangle of silk that covered her mons. She wriggled appreciatively. Then a voice announced the band, and Quincy lost interest in Sherry's pussy.

Kate stood at the keyboards and Stella prowled around the

stage, mike in hand, guitar put aside temporarily. Though the crowd waving their arms appreciatively would sometimes blot her out, nothing could prevent him hearing the sound. These were new songs written by Conlan Henny, who had begged for the chance. Quincy wasn't quite sure about them, for they opened wounds in his heart he had thought long healed.

His troubled childhood came back to him, those times of poverty and want and danger. The songs weren't about this, of course, but they spoke of unhappy things, and not only to him, judging by the faces of the audience. They played for half an hour, dance tunes and ballads full of eldritch harmonies, ragged and uncanny. A storm of cheering and stamping greeted their first break.

'Didn't she do well?' asked Conlan, appearing out of the crowd, full of what Quincy decided was puppyish enthusiasm. He could almost see him wagging his tail.

'Yes, I think we've several hits here, to be included on the next CD. Don't worry, there'll be something in it for you. A large amount, I shouldn't wonder. Sit down, have a drink. Stephen, will you do the honours? Sherry, this is Conlan, by the way. See that he has everything he needs.'

'Yes, Quincy,' she said meekly, and simpered a little, making an attempt to flirt with Conlan, who did not seem interested.

'You like the music?' he asked her.

'It's a bit like a dirge,' she opined. 'I go for something livelier.'

'It's a lament for lost love,' Conlan explained patiently, and Quincy wondered why he bothered. Sherry was not the brightest of girls.

It was while they were waiting for the band to reappear for the second and final set, that his attention became riveted on the group who had just arrived. They were led by a tall, exceedingly distinguished looked man, his black hair curling to his shoulders, his thin, almost regal face turned towards

Stella. His eyes glowed green, with little crimson sparks in their depths. With him was a stunning woman, as perfectly attired as he was. It was almost as if they had dropped in on their way to the theatre, both dressed in a formal way, fifty years out of date. Her shining golden hair was piled up and adorned with a tiara, her simple black cocktail dress with its flowing taffeta coat, livened by the addition of more flashing diamonds at her ears and throat. The crowd parted to let them through, silently, respectfully, as if they were visiting royalty. The woman stood still, gazing at Stella intently, a look of yearning and sadness on her classically lovely face.

With them was a younger man, equally striking and handsome, and as well dressed though in a casual fashion, and three glamorous women. They glowed like dark comets in the bar, and Quincy felt superstitious fear trace ice down his spine. Memory flared suddenly and he had the urge to cross himself.

He was boy again at his grandmother's knee in a village in Rumania. He called her *babushka*, in those distant days before his world collapsed and he was brought to England as a refugee.

'Beware, my child,' she would say. 'Beware the dreaded erl-king who lurks in the forests and will lure you away to play with his lovely daughters. You will never return. But most of all, watch out for the *nosferatu*, the Undead, the vampires that suck the blood of mortals in order to survive. Like the Wandering Jew and the Flying Dutchman, they are condemned to roam the earth for ever, unable to die and seek God's forgiveness.'

He had not thought of her for years or the legends of his country, but now it all came flooding back. Who the hell were these newcomers, and was 'hell' the operative word?

'My name is Dimitri,' the tall man said and, though Quincy had not seen him move he was right by his side. 'Allow me to present my wife, Candice, and these are my sisters, Allegra,

95

Medea and Madelon, and this is our young friend, Lazio.'

Quincy gulped. It was as if his tongue was suddenly several sizes too big for his mouth. 'Pleased to meet you,' he lied, and introduced himself and his companions.

'Charmed, I'm sure,' said Dimitri with a slight bow and his accent, though similar to Quincy's, was much more pronounced. But then, Quincy had worked so hard to lose his, taking elocution lessons and aping the intonations of his schoolfellows and later, business associates.

Candice had a rare, cool beauty, an ice-queen with lustrous azure eyes. She did not speak, her slender white hand tucked into the bend in her husband's arm. The one called Lazio was of poetic appearance, with a pale, raven-haired intensity, but the sisters were spectacular, and the lust Quincy had been bottling up all evening now swept over him like a tidal wave.

He could feel his balls tightening, and his cock swelled to full propensity, its tip wetting his silk boxer shorts under the customised jeans. What use *babushka's* warnings now? Even as Quincy had listened to her, a little boy of five who had been christened Costache Giugaru, he had thought that playing with the erl-king's daughters sounded fun. But vampires were a different kettle of fish. He remembered panic sweeping the village when a woman died under mysterious circumstances. She had been a cleaner up at the castle, an ancient, gloomy pile that was unoccupied for most of the year, but the owners had returned for a while, an unsociable lot, so rumour had it. After a while she started to sicken, shrinking from a busty, wide-hipped, apple-cheeked woman to a thin, wan thing with no energy. She took to her bed and died shortly after.

Hysteria swept through the territory with the uncontrollable fury of a forest fire. The doctor said he could find no cause of death, save for two tiny punctures at the side of her throat that might have been caused by an insect or small rodent.

The priest, when consulted, was non-committal and shifty. This was enough for the villagers. They became convinced that she was the victim of a vampire. There was a violent clash between them and the gypsies who worked for the palace owners. The woman was eventually buried, after her husband insisted that a stake was driven through her heart and her head severed from her body. It was the twentieth-century, an era of cars and air travel, the telephone, cinema and television, yet their behaviour was straight from the middle ages.

Sitting in the pub in Dublin over thirty years later and into the new millennium, surrounded by noise and music, Quincy watched this incident replaying on the screen of his brain, and looked at Dimitri's sisters and desired them and was petrified. They dazzled the eye and bewitched the senses. Every man present was ogling them, and a few women, too.

The linten-haired one dimpled at Quincy as innocent as the rosebud pinned to her corsage, yet as he looked closer he saw a maggot squirming at its heart. She wore a floral tulle dress in a pale shade of gold, with green appliquéd leaves and flowers. It was a wonder she had not been arrested; wearing such a revealing garment, the bodice as scanty as a harlot's nightgown, her nipples exposed between the embroidery, and the flaring skirt so transparent that all could see she was not wearing knickers. Even the belt drew attention to her supple body and the deeply indented navel. It was made of denim and looked like the waistband of a pair of jeans, studded and jewelled, an absurd and costly fashion accessory.

Quincy had seen the dress or something very like it in a Sunday supplement. Made by a leading French couturier, it was priced at over two thousand pounds. Whoever this woman was, money or modesty seemed to be of no consequence.

'I'm Madelon,' she lisped, with another intriguing foreign intonation – French, he thought. 'Isn't Ireland picturesque, and its inhabitants, too? So fey. I really believe in their stories of leprechauns and fairy rings. Are you staying here long?'

'I don't know yet,' he replied. 'We'll be making a trip to Wicklow tomorrow.'

Her sisters were staring at him, their wide scarlet mouths curved into smiles. Allegra had Titian hair that tumbled to her waist, and Medea's head was crowned with a coronet of blue-black tresses. The redhead wore low-slung, hipster jeans and a halter-neck top cut from the same material. It was held in place by two thin straps that tied at the back. The outline of her nipples poked through the thin fabric. The denims were so tight that the gusset seam separated her sex lips, the cleft strongly defined. The dark Medea had on a turquoise satin dress, the skirt slit to the thigh, the top kept together, back and front, by beaded thongs. All three fulfilled every man's dream of exotic women – sex incarnate.

'What a coincidence!' Medea exclaimed, her eyes inky pools in which he could feel himself drowning. 'We are staying in that area. Aren't we, Dimitri?'

'Indeed we are,' he responded, and pulled out a chair so that Candice could sit. 'Where did you say you were lodging?'

'I didn't, but it's Troon Hall, recently willed to our singer, Stella Kerrick,' Quincy answered, though he did not much care for the predatory glint in Dimitri's eyes, or the sudden interest flaring in Lazio's. As for Candice? She sat there like a graven image, displaying no emotion, but concentrating on Stella.

The set was drawing to a conclusion, but even when it finished the audience would not let them go, clamouring for encore after encore. When they finally escaped the stage the crowd surged to where merchandise was on sale: T-shirts, mugs, posters, CDs and tapes. Oh yes, Quincy left nothing to chance, milking his latest prize cow for all it was worth.

He rescued the band from autograph hunters and shepherded them to his table, and was astonished when Stella slewed to a halt, gazing blankly at Lazio. She was trembling. Kate eyed him up and down boldly, and then turned her attention to Dimitri, giving the women a cursory glance.

'Your neighbours, or so it seems, Stella,' Quincy began, and made the introductions.

'How come?' she asked, her voice shaking.

'We are living in the old monastery, not far from Troon Hall,' Dimitri replied. 'Quincy tells me that you are now the owner. It's a marvellous house and has been kept in remarkable repair. Built around seventeen-sixty, I believe, in true Palladian style.'

'I have seen photographs,' she replied stiffly.

'We would like you and your friends to visit us, for dinner perhaps,' Dimitri continued.

'Thank you, we'd be happy to accept, wouldn't we, Stella?' Quincy said, caught her eye, and was horrified to see an echo of his own fear reflected there.

'Yes, of course,' she responded, her voice that of an automaton, her eyes switching back to Lazio. 'So kind of you to invite us.'

'I'm looking forward to visiting Wicklow,' put in Conlan, though he seemed distracted, as if listening to elfin music from another realm.

'Stunning scenery, so I've heard.' Quincy was struggling to contain the wayward erection that seemed to swell further under the alluring influence of the sisters. Was it their fingers he could feel, fondling his tool? It was impossible. Their hands were visible, gesturing as they spoke, in true Continental style. 'This is a country of horses,' he went on. 'I wonder if it's possible to go riding – even hunting.'

'We love hunting, don't we, girls?' Allegra said, and her tongue-tip ran over her lips. Her sisters laughed, and it was a brittle sound, like breaking glass.

'Nothing beats it,' they chorused, arms slung around one another's shoulders, their lithe bodies undulating, their eyes, teeth and talons gleaming in the dusky pub light.

'The selection of the quarry,' said Madelon, and her hands seemed to appear at the front of Allegra's waist, apparently passing through her body.

'The chase,' added Medea.

'The kill!' said Allegra.

'Time to go home,' Dimitri cut in, and his eyes flashed angrily.

The sisters cringed, stopped flirting and retreated to the door. Dimitri stood back, waiting for Candice to precede him, but she hesitated, smiling at Stella. 'I hope you will visit us,' she said silkily.

'I will,' Stella responded. 'Goodbye till then.'

'Goodbye, Stella Kerrick,' Candice said, and took Lazio by the arm.

'But can't I stay?' he protested, dragging back and looking longingly at Stella.

'Lazio, don't keep me waiting,' thundered Dimitri.

The next time Quincy looked for the strangers they had gone. It was as if they had never been there. He had the paralysing feeling that if he asked Kate, Stella or any of the others, they would look at him as if he was crazy and deny any knowledge of them.

'Who d'you suppose they are, these rather pushy neighbours?' Conlan asked, bringing over a tray of drinks.

Quincy was so relieved not to be alone on this one he could have flung his arms round his neck and kissed him. But he covered it well, shrugging. 'Who knows? They seem prosperous, and the women are fit. What more could one ask?'

'So are the men,' Kate beamed, taking no notice of Jez's annoyed expression. 'I wouldn't mind getting in the sack with either of them.'

'I'll visit them,' Stella said determinedly, momentarily knocking Quincy off kilter. 'I want to.'

'Me too,' agreed Conlan, settling beside her, resting his elbows on the table and pushing his hands through his tousled mop of hair. 'Fascinating foreigners. Hungarian or some such, the birthplace of Bela Bartok, one of my idols. I'll bet Dimitri knows his music. He strikes me as the type.'

'Candice isn't foreign,' Stella said firmly. 'I think she's English to the bone.'

'We don't want to waste time socialising,' Stephen interrupted. 'There'll be a lot of sorting out to do at Troon Hall.'

Stella rounded on him, and Quincy saw another side of her – a termagant it was wiser not to cross. 'Who said anything about you coming? And as for the house and its contents that you can't wait to get your greedy hands on? It's strictly my business, not yours. I intend to stay a while, and Kate, too. She can help me if need be, so why don't you piss off?'

Whoops, Quincy thought, then relaxed, aware of Sherry's hand creeping like a little mouse towards the packet between his thighs. She found it and fastened her paw over it. The soft pressure and the excitement of having her masturbate him under the table while people surrounded them made him forget the prickling unease he had suffered in the presence of Dimitri and company.

Stella walked into the courtyard and headed towards the van, carrying her hand luggage and expecting to travel with the band, as usual.

She had breakfasted with them and Conlan, while her brother shared a table with Quincy and Sherry, and was now eager to get on the road and cover the fifty miles or so that separated her from her house. She hardly slept last night, hyped up from performing and seeing Lazio again, more

101

real than ever before. It had been a tremendous shock to find him in conversation with Quincy. Was he, too, staying at the monastery? Would they be likely to meet? And what was the link between him and the lovely, sorrowful Candice?

Nerves as taut as bowstrings, she had lain in bed and brushed her pubes with her fingertips, then parted her moist delta, dreaming of Lazio all the while and pretending it was his fingers, insistent and wicked. With quickening breath and a thumping heart she had parted the folds and exposed the moisture within, then wetted the little sphere, hard as a pearl.

In the comfortable hotel bedroom she had stared into the darkness, her clitoris the centre of her universe. She stroked it, circled it, teased it and roused it, reaching orgasm several times, moaning and gasping. Then she thought she heard a voice, could feel hands fondling her breasts, and hot, bittersweet breath on her skin. Fiery eyes burned into hers and a seductive, obscene and melodious voice whispered of terror, shame, racking pleasure and tingling anticipation.

'You're a dirty little whore, and we shall have you, all of us… soon, very soon… you will belong to us and never be alone again.'

'Lazio?' she cried, but knew it was not him; he wouldn't frighten her like that. Another entity was mocking her, using her for his diabolical amusement. Maybe it was the one who had spoken to her before. He had a strange name – Belphegor.

Eventually she fell into a troubled sleep, her fingers sticky with love-juice, her hand still clasped over her pudenda.

Stella saw Quincy leaning against his car, nonchalant in jogging pants, fleece and trainers. 'Travel with me,' he said, detaining her, his hand on her arm as she went to pass.

'I'm going in the van,' she said, though the idea of riding in the luxury car was appealing.

'Get in,' he insisted, and opened the rear door. She slipped across the tan leather bench seat and he got in beside her.

One of his heavies was at the wheel, a hard-faced individual who leered at her in the driving mirror, his bullet head covered by a baseball cap, his broad shoulders and powerful arms emphasised by his sweatshirt.

As soon as the door closed the car purred into life and swung out onto the road. A quick glance round told Stella that the van and Conlan's beat-up old car were following. She caught a glimpse of a furious Sherry in the passenger seat, and an ignoble satisfaction sparked in Stella's gut. Sherry was jealous, and Stella had suffered throughout the journey, wondering if she was giving Quincy what she wanted. Now the boot was on the other foot.

'Take off your knickers,' Quincy suddenly ordered.

'What?' Stella was dumbfounded.

'Your knickers,' he repeated without looking at her, lounging back and watching the road unfold before them. 'Take them off.'

'You've got a nerve,' she said, but he did not seem to hear and neither did the driver, though she met his narrowed eyes in the mirror and saw the lust glinting in them.

'Do as I say.' Quincy's hand swept down on her thigh, slapping it hard, then gripping it painfully.

'Ouch – I don't have to,' she quavered indignantly, and began to struggle in earnest, filled with anger that she had allowed herself to be trapped.

'I told you in my apartment, I can make you do anything. Don't waste time fighting me, Stella. It's my whim to have you sitting on the leather bare-bottomed, so do it.'

A naked bum sinking into the smooth upholstery of his top quality car did not sound such a bad idea, really, but she refused to lose face and continued to resist, until Quincy succeeded in clamping a hand round her wrists. He reached under her skirt, lifted her hips and pushed it up to her waist, then hauled down her knickers. He tossed them to the driver who held them to his face, while continuing to handle the car with one hand.

Stella felt the sensual sensation as the yielding leather caressed her rump with a chill that rapidly turned warm. She slumped back and he toyed with her, and secretly she wanted more, willing his fingers to enter her, helpless to resist. Their touch was impersonal, but she liked having no control over them. They caressed her bud until the sensation was too great and she shuddered into a lovely orgasm.

'Good,' he murmured, gripping her thighs and spreading them wide. 'You really are a lovely randy little slave.'

Stella slumped dreamily on the seat as Quincy rolled her over onto her side, her naked rump presented to him. One hand crept round and fondled her breasts, pulling her back against him. His other moved down to the warm wetness between her thighs. Her clitoris was aware, stirring again. She felt naked flesh against her bottom as he curled up to her, and he must have lowered his trousers because his cock pulsed between her buttocks. She waited breathlessly, eager to feel it inside her.

He took it in his fist and introduced it to her slippery entrance. She ground against him encouragingly and the thick, hard length sank in, filling her, stuffing her, driving against her cervix. In one fell swoop all the suspicions, the gut instinct that warned her he was bad, were forgotten and she accepted him gladly. He was rough, but it didn't matter. She liked it; she wanted him to be rough. Quincy growled deep in his chest, holding her in a vice-like hug as he rutted against her, taking his selfish pleasure. His restricted movements became more and more erratic, with a strained grunt he came, and then with detached indifference he withdrew, refastened his trousers and buckled up his belt.

Stella fumbled for her knickers, astonished by her own acceptance of his authority over her. He seemed to have stripped her of any willpower. It was easier to obey, and shamefully exhilarating to play his cruel games.

'No,' Quincy said, stopping her. 'Whenever you're with me you'll be naked beneath your clothes.'

At first sight of Troon Hall, Stella made a pact with it: I'll continue to maintain you in the manner to which you're accustomed, if you'll insure that the ghosts who haunt you don't give me a hard time.

It was comforting to talk to something as solid as this gracious, eighteenth century country house. It grounded her, and dragged her thoughts away from Lazio, and stopped her from seeking the exact location of the monastery, from dropping everything and dashing off to find him. But first she must grapple with the reality of such a manor belonging to her.

Quincy whistled quietly, standing still and running an eye over the place in the distance as if he was an estate agent or auctioneer. 'Well, well,' he opined in a slow, sarcastic manner. 'Who's a lucky girl, then?'

Stella did not reply; too absorbed by the sight of the house. The morning was bright, the rolling landscape a deep moss green, the air fresh and fragrant. As they had covered the remaining miles to Troon Hall, she'd seen the mountains that constantly changed colour according to the light – sometimes blue, or purple, or even grey. Hills and hollows bordered the winding road, and lakes like patches of fallen sky, and streams that inched between the turf and tobacco-brown peat stacked at intervals among the emerald grass.

They were standing before tall wrought iron gates set in a wall that appeared to stretch for miles. Shards of broken glass glittered along the top to keep out intruders. Above the entrance, carved in stone, was the name *Troon Hall*. There was a notice further down, black and white and stark, bearing the warning, *Trespassers will be Prosecuted*. An old man, bent almost double, hobbled from the lodge house and strained on the bolts, then dragged back the gates on their squeaking hinges. He doffed his cap and mumbled a welcome, an aged retainer who appeared to have been in service there for decades, the keeper of the gates, instead of electronically operated mechanism.

The long drive was bordered by sentinel trees and ended in a gravelled area with an ornamental pond in the middle. And at the moment she saw the house close up, Stella bonded with it like a newborn to its mother. The photographs had not done it justice. She had been unprepared for such grandeur.

It comprised a white, central block of Portland stone, with a curving flight of steps leading to the main entrance. There were wings on either side, connected to the house by colonnades, each with a fanciful pavilion at the end. The windows were high and narrow, the façade set with alcoves containing life-size statues of gods and goddesses. Everything was in apple-pie order, and a stocky, greying, elderly man in a sober dark suit greeted Stella at the top of the steps.

'Welcome, Miss Kerrick. This is a happy day indeed. A new mistress for Troon Hall. I'm Caley Rogan, the caretaker, and this is my wife, Maureen.'

A thin woman with a sharp nose and inquisitive birdlike eyes stepped forward and bobbed, saying, 'Pleased to meet you, I'm sure, miss. This would please old Lady Emma no end. She'd be like a dog with two tails, so she would, God rest her soul. I hope you don't mind me saying, but you're the very image of a portrait done of her ladyship when she was young. Darker, of course, but apart from that, you are as alike as two peas in a pod.'

Suddenly Emma Kerrick became a reality to her. This couple had known her, worked for her, cared for her in her declining years. If Stella wanted to know anything about her, all she had to do was ask.

'You knew her… were you with her to the end?' she asked.

'Of course, miss, she left Troon Hall in our charge, till you came to claim it,' Caley said staunchly.

'And I hope you'll carry on, Mr Rogan,' Stella answered earnestly. 'I shall rely on you, both of you, to help me find my way around.'

Just then, the van and the car rattled up the drive and ground to a halt. Everyone piled out and within a short time was ensconced in the entrance hall, which was the size of a ballroom. Their luggage was borne aloft by stalwart male members of staff, and then they were ushered into the drawing room where coffee and shortcake biscuits were promptly served.

'Wow! The high-life, eh?' Kate remarked, appraising the gracious room, where furnishings and décor blended sublimely, forming a harmonious whole where nothing jarred. 'I could get to like this.'

Stella, perched on the edge of a gilded chair, was very aware that Quincy had not returned her panties, and was horrified at the thought of Caley and Maureen finding out. They would probably label her a trollop and hand in their notices. 'I can't believe it,' she murmured.

'I can,' Stephen retorted, prowling around, picking up ornaments and replacing them, and touching the great sheaves of lilies and carnations which a thoughtful Maureen had placed in large Chinese vases in order to make the mistress feel at home.

His sulking turned Stella's stomach and she wanted to order him to leave. He did not fit in here, too much the greedy little weasel, his eye always on the main chance. It was awkward, however, for Quincy seemed to find him amusing, treating him like a lackey there to do his bidding. Besides which, she did not want to spoil her homecoming by having a blazing row with her obnoxious brother.

Caley took them on a guided tour. He led them down hallways and up grand staircases and into reception rooms and saloons, each equalling the other in architectural glory. The conservatory was a jungle filled with hothouse flowers, the library a shrine to reading, the study hung with hunting trophies, the bedchambers palatial apartments complete with en suite bathrooms. Stella was sure that if she lived there for months she would still not be able to find her away around.

The band were delighted with the music saloon, carrying in their instruments and testing the acoustics. 'Man, this is something else,' Jez vouchsafed, as his bongo drum resonated under the crystal chandeliers.

'It's all incredible,' Kat enthused, her eyes dancing. 'Stella, did you notice those hunks who carried the luggage? They're your servants, babe, ready to do your every bidding. Doesn't that float your boat?'

Stella shook her head in bewilderment. 'I just can't get used to it,' she replied.

It was even stranger when a little later, Maureen conducted her to the master bedchamber, which was now to be hers. As Stella entered she could feel the spirit of Emma all around her. It was a wonderful room, the best in the house.

'I've kept it as madam liked it,' Maureen said with pride. 'This is where she died in nineteen-eighty, still a grand, lively lady. I've opened it up every day, kept it spotless. It's full of rare and lovely things, for madam travelled widely when her husband, Lord Clive, was alive.'

'Were these her things?' Stella asked in awed wonderment as she gazed at the rails of garments.

'Yes, madam didn't like to get rid of anything,' Maureen said, and pulled open drawers filled with silken underwear and stockings, and racks containing shoes.

'But they are all outdated.' Stella was astonished and rather repulsed. It was as if fingers from the past were reaching out from the grave to touch her.

'And made all the more valuable for that,' Maureen assured her. 'Wait till you see her jewellery. It's in a safe behind one of the pictures. Did Mr Jarvis give you the combination?'

'Yes, I think so; he gave me lots of information,' Stella

blundered on. 'I'll look for it later.'

'What about the bed?' Maureen said, leading her to it. 'This is where she slept for years, and Lord Clive, too, though she outlived him by a quarter of a century. This is where her children were born, and where she died.'

'And this is where I shall sleep?' Stella felt a shiver running through her, though it was the most magnificent bed she had ever seen, a six-foot wide four-poster, with slim rosewood posts and curtains of antique white lace.

'If you wish, miss. The choice is yours.' Maureen smiled, then moved to where an easel stood, a black velvet cloth covering the canvas it supported. 'Here is your ancestor, Lady Emma Kerrick,' and she whipped the cloth away.

Stella had to acknowledge that Maureen had been right when she said there was a likeness. It was more than that. They could have been identical twins. Over a hundred years between them, and yet Emma's characteristics were repeated in Stella's face and figure. Only the high-dressed chestnut hair was different. Emma was wearing an evening gown, she was self-possessed and exquisitely groomed, gazing out of the canvas at her descendent, her smile seeming to deepen, her eyes to glow, and Stella could almost hear her saying, 'I'm so glad you're here. I need you. Despite my confident appearance, all is not as it seems.'

Just at that moment there came a knock on the bedroom door. 'Come in,' Stella said, and Caley came in. He was bearing a silver salver on which lay a cream envelope. It was addressed to her. She picked it up and examined it. The envelope was made of quality paper, thick as parchment, the edge of the stuck down flap slightly deckled. Maureen handed her a letter opener shaped like a rapier from the dainty walnut escritoire. It took but a second to open it and draw out the card it contained. This matched the envelope, also deckled but with gilding, too. There was a message on it, handwritten in a flowing, flamboyant hand, which said:

Prince Dimitri and Princess Candice, cordially invite Miss Stella Kerrick and friends to a party to be held at St Cuthbert's Monastery, Derforgal Bay, tomorrow evening at 7:30. R.S.V.P.

Chapter Six

'Oh Kate, I'm so muddled,' Stella cried, rushing into Kate's room. She was clutching the card, and thrust it at her friend. 'Look, Dimitri has asked us to visit him.'

'So?' Kate asked. 'That'll be a gas; he's a hunk! Why are you so uptight about it?'

She had changed out of her travelling clothes and was now showered, wrapped in a green silk kimono embroidered with yellow chrysanthemums, her hair in a towel. She stared at Stella, having realised days ago there was something wrong, something she was keeping from her. Was it men? Or rather, one man – Quincy Dubois? Or maybe Conlan? Certainly, Stephen was a pain in the butt and it would be great when they could lose the creep somewhere along the way; he was the type who clung like a limpet, leeching off everyone and trying to bleed them dry.

Stella plumped down on the bed. Kate and Jez had already tested it, having a quickie. It had bounced well and did not shake – solid as a rock. There was something romantic about a tester bed – all those drapes and that feeling of luxurious naughtiness. She'd promised Jez a repeat performance later, then she sent him on his way, wanting to acclimatised herself to her new surroundings, easing here, testing there, as a cat will. So far so good.

She sat beside Stella and put an arm round her shoulders. 'Tell your old Auntie Kate all about it,' she said encouragingly, enjoying the feel of that pliable body next to hers, and wondering how best she could help her.

'It's Lazio,' Stella began, and closed her fingers around

Kate's.

'Ah, the dark-haired dish who was with Dimitri and his wife. What about him?'

'I've seen him before… and the first time it was in a dream. Then he turned up at a gig, and later at my party.'

'I didn't see him,' Kate said sharply, convinced she would have spotted such an attractive stranger.

'I know, that's what is so weird about it,' Stella said, her eyes wide with fear and excitement. 'I was at my party, but he took me on a journey, somewhere remote and cold. There were wolves and a castle and I saw Dimitri and Candice, though I didn't know their names then. I wanted Lazio, like I did in the dream, and he made love to me. His cock was freezing cold, but I was hot… so hot… and I climaxed. It was terrible and wonderful all at the same time. He promised we would be united physically very soon, and he gave me this. It was one of my tears but he turned it into a diamond.'

She opened her hand and there, on her palm, lay a sparkling gem. It could have been glass or crystal or, indeed, a diamond. But a tear?

Kate was nonplussed. Had she not known Stella so well she would have thought she'd been taking drugs. She patted the hand that now rested on her silk covered knee, the jewel put away again, and said consolingly, at a complete loss, 'Well, there you are then; Lazio is it? I thought you were starry-eyed over Quincy.'

'I am – I mean, I was,' Stella answered, shifting restlessly. 'It's so hard to explain. He's cruel. He's even paddled my bottom, and it hurt, but I enjoyed it! I can't understand what's happening to me, Kate. You can still see the marks, if you look closely.'

She stood in front of Kate and hitched up her skirt, then eased down her knickers and turned to display the rounded globes of her bottom. Kate saw the faint pink patches, and could not resist running her hands over them, and then pressing a kiss into the small of Stella's back, pleased when she did not draw away.

'He's into dominance, is he?' she said, and her pussy spasmed as she imagined Stella tied up and helpless, submitting to the cane or the flat of a hand – hers perhaps.

'Oh, yes,' Stella dropped her skirt and sat down again. 'He calls himself my master, and I want him to be. I know it sounds mad, but it makes me feel proud, as if he's chosen me above others. And today, on the way here, he...' she dropped her eyes, and a blush spread into her cheeks.

'Yes?' Kate encouraged, eager to help her, but unable to deny the arousal that was making her wet. 'What did he do?'

'He ordered me to take off my panties, then screwed me on the back seat of his car. He's said I'm not to wear knickers if I'm with him.'

'Could lead to a chill on the kidneys,' Kate replied dryly, but was storing away this information about Quincy's personal preferences. 'So, he fucked you in the car. Did you enjoy it?'

'Well, yes; for some strange reason I like him being rough with me,' Stella sighed. 'But it's not like that when I'm with Lazio.'

'Darling, are you quite sure this *Lazio* exists?' Kate asked, and let the back of her hand pass over Stella's breasts, just where the nipples made little pointed bumps under the T-shirt.

'He does,' Stella insisted defensively. 'I know he does. You saw him yourself in *O'Donoghue's*.'

'But can you be sure you've met him before? He might have been a dream, and then when you were introduced to this man in the pub, you fancied he was the same. The mind plays weird tricks.'

Stella shook her head mulishly. 'No, that's not it. He's real.'

113

'Well then, all will be revealed tomorrow evening,' Kate said, trying to lighten Stella's mood. 'Meanwhile, I'm going to look after you. First, you need a shower. Let me do the honours. I'll pretend you're a harem lady and I'm your odalisque. But don't tell Quincy. It will only turn him on and I'm not sure if I want to take part in his games.'

Stella undressed rather shyly as the two girls, although sharing a house, were unaccustomed to seeing one another naked. Kate handed her a towel, and then took her into the en suite bathroom. It was as sleekly decorated and well appointed as everywhere else in Troon Hall, recently modernised like all the others. Someone had carried out orders that the manor should be in perfect order for the arrival of the new mistress.

'You know, you're so lucky,' Kate said. 'Fancy owning all this.'

'Yeah, but what am I going to do with it? I can't possibly live here, not on my own, and there's the band to think about now.'

'It was all right for years before you arrived,' Kate said, gabbling on in an attempt to control her arousal and handle this situation right. If Stella was a virgin with regard to lesbian love, then the last thing Kate wanted to do was blow it. 'I should imagine it'll go on the same when you're away. I bet you'll get used to this being your base, and coming home to it between touring. Who knows? *Zero700* may bomb. You never can tell in the music industry.'

She took Stella's towel and hung it on the back of the door, her silk kimono beside it. Her skin crept deliciously, goose bumps rising. This was a dream come true, one she had secretly harboured for months. She turned on the tap, and warm water cascaded over them as they stood in the shower stall, then she took up a tube of chestnut gel and squeezed it into her hand. She applied it to Stella's back and hips, then, greatly daring, spread it over her breasts, her nipples standing encouragingly. She heard a faint intake of breath, and Stella leaned into her touch.

'I'll wash your hair,' Kate said, deciding to make her wait a little, stoke her fires slowly but surely.

She adjusted the jets and guided them over Stella's head, working up a lather with her free hand. The mellow, spicy odour of their favourite shampoo rose with the steam. Kate massaged Stella's scalp, strong fingers digging and pummelling, setting the blood coursing. She was wet again, having already showered away the essences left by her coupling with Jez.

Rinsing the hair clean, she set aside the shampoo and reduced the force of the water, facing Stella under the gentle trickle. She looked into her eyes and smiled. 'We've both suffered because of men,' she whispered. 'They are all very well, but there's nothing quite as sweetly satisfying as two women pleasuring on another. Will you let me show you?'

Stella nodded almost imperceptibly, and Kate kissed her, enjoying the feel of soft lips after Jez's harsher technique. Slowly, eyes closed, she ran her tongue across Stella's mouth, and it yielded, permitting entrance. It was so exciting to feel an answering flicker that Kate was aware of the beginnings of an orgasm. Just a spasm, not the real thing, but it showed how close she was.

She ended the kiss and traced her tongue over Stella's nipples, sucking first one, then the other, satisfied to hear Stella moan. She kissed and mouthed her way down the slim, lissom body, then knelt, circling the rounded dimple of her navel and down to her soaking wet pubic hair. Pausing, Kate waited for a refusal. It did not come. Instead she felt Stella's hands on her head, urging her on. She did not need telling twice.

Kate found the hidden jewel rising from its sheltering labial wings. She touched it with her tongue. Stella quivered and Kate was aware that she was holding her breasts in both hands, teasing the nipples into peaks and rubbing them to augment her pleasure. Kate massaged the hard nubbin in slow circles, then dipped into Stella's vulva, feeling where her juices met the shower water, thicker and more slippery and highly scented.

Kate eased her free hand under Stella's pudenda, her middle digit finding her vagina. It closed round her finger when she pushed it inside. She moved in and out very gently, while still massaging the clitoris. Stella moaned and arched against the pleasure, increasing it by playing with her nipples. Kate speeded up, but never allowing her touch to become routine, varying it, sometimes hard, sometimes feather light over that hard bud. Stella stiffened and cried out. Her clitoris throbbed and her inner muscles convulsed as she shuddered in violent orgasm.

'Oh, that was so good,' she whispered, collapsing into Kate's arms as she rose and held her. Then she looked at her and said, almost apologetically, 'But what of you? Would you like me to pleasure you in the same way? I've never done so before, but I'm willing to learn.'

Kate laughed huskily, ablaze but wanting to hold on to this fire, just for the moment. 'Later,' she said. 'We'll share a bed tonight, though I have promised Jez, sort of, but I'll join you after he's asleep. Do you feel better about your troublesome lovers now? Have I shown you that men aren't the be all and end all?'

'Yes, you have, and thank you,' Stella said, as they stepped out of the shower and enveloped themselves in the thick white fluffy towels. 'But I can't wait to see if Lazio is at St Cuthbert's tomorrow.'

'Is everything ready?' Dimitri demanded from the large carved chair that had once belonged to an abbot.

Though from outside St Cuthbert's looked the archetypal dilapidated monastery, he had bought it with the express purpose of being close to Troon Hall. He had hired an architect and builders and within weeks it was ready for him to move in, refurbished and filled with costly antiques. Even the chapel had been repaired. The only places he left in their original state were a few remote rooms, surplus to requirement, and the vaults.

'All is ready, master,' Carl replied, rubbing a bony hand over his ivory smooth, shaven head. 'Party fare, just like you ordered.'

He fussed with the buffet tables, smoothing imaginary creases from the sparkling napery, rearranging the bowls of fruit, the flowers, the canapés and dishes of olives, the large gold platters where whole salmon rested on beds of vine leaves, and all the other delicacies he'd prepared or had a caterer deliver. Red wine was left to breathe. White wine put in ice buckets to chill, likewise champagne.

He was an invaluable servant and had been with the family for decades. He provided them with sustenance if necessary, offering his own blood and, to the witch sisters, his seminal fluids. In return he'd been granted immortality, though without becoming a vampire. He was their emissary, braving the outside world during daylight hours, carrying out business transactions and generally acting as their factotum and ambassador. It was he who had liased with the architect and workmen, not Dimitri – he merely paid the bills, so promptly that no one queried his absence.

'It must all seem perfectly normal, Carl,' Candice said, nervously driving her fist into her palm as she paced the floor of the fan vaulted hall, her long purple skirt swishing. 'I don't want Stella frightened.'

'I understand, milady,' Carl replied, the semblance of a smile crossing his cadaverous features.

'If I find you've made any mistakes, no matter how minor, then you shall be flogged,' she stated flatly.

It had seemed like a miracle when she saw Stella in the

stuffy interior of *O'Donoghue's*. It could have been Emma standing there – slightly changed, but still closely resembling the dear friend she had known so many years ago, when she was a human, not a blood drinker. It confirmed everything Dimitri had told her; though he did not permit her to become involved till he was ninety-nine percent sure she wouldn't be disappointed. He could not bear to see her shed red-tinged vampire tears, his aim to keep her happy and content. No one could have asked for a better spouse, and she loved him with all the passion and sexuality of her tempestuous nature. This had no way abated since first he wooed and won her.

Stella, poor child, she reflected, soon to become closely associated with monsters like them. But she and Dimitri had given strict instructions that she was not to be harmed, on pain of the most severe punishment. Dimitri's temper was renowned in the far-reaching Undead circles, godlike in his awesome fury. She once witnessed him chastising his sisters, reducing them to near madness by having them tormented by creatures from the netherworld, aroused sexually but never satisfied, their preternatural powers stripped from them. No one cared to risk his wrath. Even she, his best beloved, knew the kiss of the lash if she displeased him.

But the time had come for action and Lazio, their surrogate son, had been despatched to make contact with Stella. Young, handsome and charming, Candice's heart swelled with almost maternal pride as she looked at him. The girl would be unable to resist him, surely? Yet it was not her intention to have her make the ultimate sacrifice for him, as she had done for Dimitri.

She had struggled to see into the future, even enlisted Belphegor's aid, though he was not her favourite fiend, but the dimensions between worlds were clouded, her vision blocked. Even that most cunning and Machiavellian of vampires, had confessed to being baffled. There were several alternatives, he had said, diverse pathways open to Stella. Only the Three Fates knew what was in store for her and they, malicious old hags who shared one eye between them, refused to divulge it, cackling gleefully and telling him to go screw himself.

'Am I being selfish?' Candice murmured, no sooner thinking it than being coiled on Dimitri's lap, her arms wound round his neck, her face raised to his.

'You? You're the most selfless being I know,' he said, caressing her breasts through the clinging silk of her gown, his thumbs revolving on her nipples.

She sighed and wished it was still dusk or that dawn was approaching when they could couple as man and woman. It was neither of these, and they had already slaked their appetites, both for sex and for sustenance. After making love they had left their black-canopied funereal bed and, swiftly and silently, passed through space to visit Dublin again. It was a rich feeding ground – so many bars and public houses, crowded and cosmopolitan, home of artists and poets and playwrights. Dimitri preferred to sup off intellectuals. Candice, who had once found it hard to drink from her victims, had become selective, too. She disliked swaggering bullies and coarse women in life, and it was the same now she inhabited the half world of the *nosferatu*. She chose those who would not be affected by a little bloodletting; the young, strong and healthy, and there were so many of these to choose from nowadays.

'Huh, you go for fitness fanatics,' Madelon said scornfully, with a toss of her platinum blonde curls, leaning over Dimitri's shoulder possessively. The sisters had always been jealous of his devotion to Candice. 'All those muscles and training and aerobics. My dear, give me something more blue-blooded and effete… a dilettante member of royalty, perhaps.'

'You always were a snob,' Medea mocked, giving her a

black-eyed stare. 'Blood is blood, whether it's blue or not…
rats, cats, kings, movie stars… I don't give a flying fuck!'

'It doesn't matter; this is a capital place,' put in Allegra.
'And we have disciples, too. Not only our own kind drawn
here because of us, but people from the big houses, students
from the university, and those we bring in from the clubs.
We fascinate them. They can't decide if we are real or
charlatans. It's fabulous fun, and they all taste divine.'

Candice had never got used to their ability to read her
mind. It still embarrassed her. Nothing was sacred. She could
do it, of course, but was shy about prying into other people's
private thoughts. Dimitri never hesitated. As for Belphegor?
He always had been nosy, even when a mortal.

Lazio was reticent, she knew, keeping a little in reserve,
but his feelings for Stella were too powerful to hide. The
boy was in love, and Candice worried about him. This had
not been part of the plan, and she did not fancy having a pair
of star-crossed lovers on her conscience for eternity.

Now she and Dimitri were about to play host and hostess,
drawing Stella and her friends into their web. She was not
concerned about the wisdom of this, for with their hypnotic
skills the vampires could manipulate humans, using them
for pleasure or to quench their thirst, but insuring that they
remembered nothing.

'I'm not too certain about Quincy Dubois… or rather,
Costache Giugaru,' Dimitri said, his green eyes hooded. 'He
is from a remote Rumanian village. He knows about us. I
shared his memories when we met in the bar. He was a child
again, with his grandmother. She was warning him, speaking
of the erl-king and the *nosferatu*. He could be dangerous.'

'We can't stop now,' Candice whispered in his ear,
breathing in the special scent of him, a combination of
perfume and spices and the vital fluid he ingested in order to
survive. 'I already feel her presence.'

'Stella?' he asked, with his sardonic smile.

'No, Emma,' she said, and extended her tongue, running the tip along his full scarlet lips. He was so extraordinarily handsome that she did not regret denying salvation in order to be his bride. The bone structure of his face was perfect, his profile hawk-like, his skin as pale as a shroud. He had been twenty-six when Belphegor changed him, an athletic duellist and horseman without an inch of spare fat anywhere on his body. Respected as a medical student and dabbler in alchemy, he had also been feared for his fiery temper and reputation with the rapier. Above average height, with those pronounced features and slightly slanting eyes that proclaimed his Slavic ancestry, he wore his hair long, a mane of black ringlets that fell across his shoulders and halfway down his back. Caught in his prime, his appearance had been frozen and he had not changed since that fatal night when he joined the ranks of the Undead.

'I love you,' Candice whispered, and her fingers explored his sex, passing through the fabric of his black evening trousers. She fondled his balls and stimulated the cock that lifted to meet her phantom caresses.

'And I adore you,' he answered. 'I want to give you your heart's desire – contact with your dead friend who has passed to the Elysian Fields where you are forbidden to go.'

'That poser, the Archangel Michael, stands guard at the entrance with his flaming sword, so I understand. How theatrical,' snapped Belphegor, tousling his luxuriant curls with his fingers, having decided to go tawny blond for the night. 'This is the one and only time I wish I was alive,' he added pettishly. 'I long to be able to see myself reflected in an ordinary mirror. Lend me your scrying-glass, Medea, there's a pet. At least I can squint in that and see if I'm at my best.'

The guests started to arrive, each announced by Carl, acting as master of ceremonies. They had seized the opportunity to dress up. The ladies wore designer evening gowns, some conservative, some startlingly revealing. Their escorts sported tuxedos, and there were a few in uniforms. Those who were of Dimitri's faith came in quietly and black was favourite among the males. The other visitors thought they were in masquerade costumes, so pale and red-lipped, the female vampires affecting white nightgowns or trailing shrouds, their talons long and crimson, their wild hair, their eyes glowing like embers. They hovered in a group close to Dimitri and Candice, till Allegra roused them, and dragged them onto the dance floor.

Pretty maidservants in cerise basques and fishnet stockings sashayed around on their stilt heels, handing out drinks. They were big-busted, and their firm nipples poked over the low-cut corsets. Their ballet skirts were made of crisp tulle, which, though of several layers, did not hide the nakedness of their buttocks or the angry-looking stripes of recent lashings. The tutus lifted in front, giving tantalising glimpses of furry or depilated mons. The waiters were dashing and personable, attractive to women and men alike in this liberal group who took their pleasures where they willed, enjoying Dimitri's hospitality and admiring his hedonistic lifestyle, ignorant of his true nature.

The servants made no objection when they were handled familiarly. Indeed, their attire encouraged this. Not only the females' private parts were available; the waiters, too, were provocative in black trousers cut so tight that their balls and cock-stems were clearly outlined. Several were unzipped, flies open, ramrod stiff phalli protruding in order to be fondled by anyone who felt inclined. Others had slits in their back seams, amber bottom cracks tempting those who admired the arse above all. Their shirts were skimpy, nipples as exposed as the girls' and equally sensitive and alluring.

But Candice was already bored. 'This is tedious,' she complained, wishing she had the nerve to leap into the fray like Madelon, Medea and Allegra, only too eager to lure their prey, male or female, tease and mock them, use them like sex toys, then feed on them.

'But necessary, my love,' he assured her. 'A smokescreen, as it were. Though I doubt it will deceive Quincy.'

Alithea phoned Conlan on his mobile while he was preparing to go out. He talked to her as he was slipping on his loafers and wondering if he should have packed something more formal.

'How are rehearsals going?' he asked, wishing he had not given her his number. It wasn't that he didn't like her. He did – quite a lot in actual fact, but not with the gut churning passion he felt for Stella.

'Okay,' she said, and he sensed that she wanted him to say something like, 'I miss you,' but he couldn't bring himself to do it. 'And the opera?'

'I haven't done anything to it since I left. There's too much going on, and now we're staying at Stella's house in the depths of the country. It's like a film set... a remake of a Jane Austen story, perhaps. Very grand.'

'Lucky you. Can you let me have the number?'

'I don't know it yet,' he said honestly.

'Oh?' It sounded as if she didn't believe him. 'When are you coming home?'

'I've no idea,' he answered, and it was true.

'Phone me back, Conlan.'

'All right, but it won't be tonight.'

'Why?'

'I've been invited to a do at St Cuthbert's monastery.'

'Sounds intriguing. You and who else?'

'The band and their manager-cum-agent. I've written some songs for them.'

'Sacred ones?' she asked with a chuckle.

'Christ, no! The monastery belongs to a Prince Dimitri, who looks like an exiled Russian aristocrat. It's all grist to the composer's mill.'

'And have you screwed Stella yet?'

'No.'

'You're slipping. Wish I was there to bonk you.'

'I wish you were, too,' he said, his cock coming erect at her words. All right, so he might be falling for Stella, but it didn't stop him responding to Alithea.

'I could fly over at the weekend,' she suggested, with a catch in her voice that made him instantly suspicious.

'What are you doing?' he asked, and dropped his hand down to hold his cock.

'I've got my finger on my clit, and I'm giving it a little rub.'

'What are you wearing?'

'A short black skirt and a red satin waistcoat.'

'Any underwear? Describe it.'

'No bra, a lace suspender belt and open-crotch knickers.'

'And your finger is in your sex?'

'Yes.'

'Leave it for a moment and tweak your nipples,' Conlan said, and unfastened his trousers, taking out his erection. He rolled his foreskin down till it formed a ridge round his wet, reddish helm. The feeling was exquisite, and he could not resist moving his hand along its length, then back up to the glans, spreading the pre-come over it.

'But…'

'No argument; do it.'

'All right. My fingers are coated with love juice, and I've transferred this to my nipples. They're so hard. Oh, it's wonderful.'

'Squeeze your tits together so you can flick both nipples at the same time,' he instructed.

'I'm doing it… squashing them and rubbing one with the heel of my hand while scratching the other with my nails. But please, please, let me rub my clitty.'

Excitement crawled over Conlan as he visualised her. He grasped his slippery shaft, thumb circling the helm, two fingers enclosing the ridge. His arousal rose quickly. He had to back off, lightening his strokes, and saying down the phone held between his cheek and his raised shoulder, 'D'you want to come very badly?'

'Oh yes, I do,' she whimpered.

'Shall I let you?' he gasped, and it was as if he was giving himself permission to start masturbating again.

'Yes… yes…' Alithea sobbed.

'All right, but tell me everything, make me visualise you doing it as clearly as if I was there, watching you.' Thoughts of her made control doubly difficult, but it was an exquisite torture; her generous mouth, her darting tongue, her big breasts crowned by nipples like ripe strawberries – her willingness, her sheer animal exuberance when it came to sex.

Soon, he promised his rampant cock. He knew he couldn't hang on much longer and grabbed up a bath towel, holding it ready to catch the spurting come. No point in ruining his one decent pair of trousers.

'I've left my breasts and pushed my finger into my panties,' Alithea murmured, drawing him back into her own crisis that was about to take place miles away in London. 'The silk's wet with my juices.'

'Can you smell it?' He gave his helm the frigging it demanded, enclosing it at the top of each pull at his stem.

'Yes.'

'Describe it to me,' he said, his attention focused on the lust boiling like lava in his balls.

'It smells like the beach on a summer day… salty, piscine. It's always different when I'm horny… stronger than normal.'

'If I were to sniff your knickers, would I smell it?' Conlan asked shakily, his cock hot and slick, his semen ready to

125

explode. He squeezed the base, stopping it. But it was good; he ached for it, one more stroke, his climax a heartbeat away. Somehow he held off.

'Oh, yes,' she whispered haltingly, and he guessed that she, too, was right on the edge.

'Don't wash them, and bring them with you next time we meet,' he said, and gave his cock a pump. 'Now, push a finger into your pussy and pretend it's my prick. I've a huge hard-on, and I'm playing with it. Tell me what your finger feels like.'

'Listen,' she said, and there was a movement the other end of the line, and then a wet, squashy sound. 'Can you hear it? That's my fingers in my quim. It's soft, like velvet, and it's clenching round my fingers. I wish it was you inside me.'

'It will be soon, I promise.' Conlan had reached his limit. The first spasm fluttered. He pressed down with his thumb, hung on in there for a moment more.

'My clit's hard and wet and swollen,' she chanted, her voice low and dreamy. 'My heart's thumping and I'm hot all over.' Then she cried loudly, 'It's coming! Up and up! I'm peaking. Ah… ah… I'm there! Oh, oh…'

This was the last straw. Conlan's tribute shot from him in steady spurts, hard throbs of sensation that went on and on. His semen hit the towel, then dribbled back down his shaft. There was a further jet, but with less power. His thighs jerked. He gasped for breath and heard Alithea saying, 'Are you all right, Conlan? Have you come?'

'Too right I have,' he managed to get out, weak at the knees and wanting to sit. He found the edge of the bed and collapsed on it.

'So did I,' she purred, as contented as cat on heat who has just been speared by a randy old Tom. 'Have a nice party, darling.'

'I will,' he answered, and heard the receiver go dead.

Lazio sat on the top of the tower, inhaling the scents borne on the breeze and watching the sun go down over the mountains. They were gentle and rolling, nothing like the fearsome crags of Dimitri's home in the Carpathians. Lazio had appreciated the wild beauty of Transylvania, and enjoyed visiting his maker's other properties – in Venice, in Spain, and in New Orleans – but he sometimes yearned for the soft landscape of Devon where he had been raised.

There was nothing to stop him materialising there any night he liked, and he had done so once or twice, but now the family mansion had been razed to the ground and a housing estate developed on the land. He had flown over the spot where once he lived, a pampered member of the upper class, sheltered from everything unpleasant, until he went to war. Now he could not bear to go there any more, aware of the stark loneliness of his existence.

He rose and stood on the balustrade that circled the tower, then left it momentarily to find companionship among the bats that swooped and squeaked, his supernatural hearing picking up their radar signals. The freedom of flight enchanted him; to become small enough to creep into belfries and the hollows of great oaks, then out again hunting for insects. Some nights he would spend hours as one of them, or perhaps an owl.

The sisters chided him, calling him chicken. They liked to change shape to svelte cats and prowl on rooftops under a bright, humpbacked moon. He ignored them, tormented like Candice by their spite and jealousy, their resentment of anyone who captured Dimitri's attention. They were not even his sisters, though liked to be known as such, no more related to him than Lazio, but as alike in evil as if they had sprung from the same womb. Dimitri had made them, rescuing Medea and Allegra from the witch trials in Paris and later saving Madelon from the mob who had wanted to send her to the guillotine during the French Revolution.

And would this be Stella's fate? Was she, too, destined to become a night stalker, an abomination that drank blood? He wanted that, yet also wished to spare her.

Rage almost blinded him and he shot back into his man shape; a fragile bat form was not enough to contain his anger. He sympathised with Candice's cause, and had gone along with it until he met Stella. Things had changed since then; he had felt her heart pounding, had held her body in his arms and, on the astral level, had brought her to climax and possessed her. At dawn it was his intention to consummate their nuptials physically. But would Dimitri allow it? He *had* to, didn't he? He knew what it was like to love a mortal woman.

Lazio had met Stella in dreams and then seen her playing. He looked into her heart and soul, learning all her secrets. She was lightness and compassion, courage and innocence. There wasn't a nasty bone in her body, unlike the vicious sisters who often used him for copulation, and were now angry because, since Stella, he had refused them.

She would be with him soon. He sniffed the wind and could smell her, the sweet blood pounding in her veins, the warm essence seeping from her secret parts. He knew she had been thinking of him, and her thoughts had been heated, making her mouth dry and her sex wet. Yet Belphegor had shown her with Quincy, and hinted that she would soon couple with Conlan. Pain shot through Lazio like a dozen swords. He wanted to kill – not for food, but in sheer, blind anger that any other man should dare to touch her.

The soirée was in full swing and he left, needing to be alone. The hectic gaiety of those who followed the prince meant nothing to him, as did the rapacious enjoyment of the sisters or Belphegor. He waited for Stella, longed for her, fire gathering in his loins, his phallus stiffening, though not yet attaining its full length and girth. She would make this happen when he held her, smelt her, ran his teeth over the

128

blue veins throbbing in her throat, and finally, just before daybreak, thrust himself into her velvety depths.

Unable to contain his impatience, he raised his arms and travelled through the indigo, star-spangled sky, invisible as he looked down on the winding, hilly road that linked St Cuthbert's and Troon Hall. He picked out headlights, and entered Quincy's car. Stella started, sitting in the rear beside Kate. Quincy glanced back from the driving seat, uneasy, as if he sensed another presence. And Lazio slipped into and around Stella, wrapping her in a protective shell, making do with this until the moment when he could appear to her again and, later, possess her as a man.

Chapter Seven

'Miss Stella Kerrick of Troon Hall,' announced the gaunt, black clad usher as she passed under a stone arch and into an impressive reception room.

She was aware of him announcing Kate's name in stentorian tones as she followed her in, and knew that Quincy was waiting to be heralded. So far there was no sign of Conlan. He had elected to bring his own car. Jez and Tommy had declined the invitation, declaring their intention of trawling the local hostelries in search of secret locations where poteen was illegally distilled. Stephen had also refused, giving the excuse of a migraine, though Stella knew he intended to poke around the house during her absence. She had taken the precaution of warning Caley Rogan and Maureen to keep an eye on him, and not let him have any keys.

The main room of the monastery building was large, lofty and overpowering. The atmosphere was eerie, with the sulphurous luminosity and smell associated with the approach of an electrical storm. Stella felt the cold hand of death crawling down her spine and was filled with apprehension and the dark stirrings of arousal. Guests had arrived and it was an oddly formal gathering, despite the risqué costumes worn by the waiters and maids. She averted her eyes from their naked parts, yet wanted to peep. Other than this it resembled a function held by royalty, and there stood Prince Dimitri and his lady, waiting to greet her.

'Miss Kerrick… Stella, if I may be so bold… welcome to my home,' he said seductively. 'I think you have already met Lazio.'

And there he was. No mirage, but a man. And such a one, with movie star looks and a charisma to take the breath away. She felt the colour flush her cheeks.

'Stella,' he whispered, and his voice was as she remembered, deep, cultured and as English as her own.

'You may kiss his hand,' Dimitri ordered, while Candice looked on, smiling faintly.

What? Stella thought, exasperated. Who the hell did they think they were? Was Lazio a prince, too? Nevertheless, she could not help bending over the hand he extended, taking it in her own.

It was large with long, artistic fingers and beautifully kept nails. But oh, so cold. Had he been plunging his fingers into the champagne buckets? Then she remembered that self-same chill permeating her on the other occasions when she had imagined herself to be in his company. Was she still imagining it? His hand was perfect, the skin white and smooth and coated with a sprinkling of hair. It sprang from the pristine cuff that divided it from the lower edge of his black velvet jacket. Unable to stop herself, Stella kissed it. Just for an instant she feared her lips would stick there, frozen solid, but they came away easily, making her ache with longing and filled with the sad, desperate need to cry.

She looked at him and his face was grave, his head surrounded by a golden glow that fragmented into rainbow hues as the tears welled up in her eyes. She blinked them away and was lost in the glacial blue depths of his irises. The pull between them was so strong she could not think straight. She burned, wanted, desired. And, as yet, he had only touched her with his mind. The contact was rooted in some deep, elemental process that she did not understand, only knowing she could not get enough of him, admiring his spectacular looks, elegance and charm. She instinctively recognised that he possessed knowledge and abilities she would give much to share.

He placed a hand under her elbow and said, 'Shall we dance?'

She became conscious of music, the sensual beat of the bossa nova. The tempo was exact, the sound sweet but with an underlying melancholy. A piano, African drums, a saxophone and a man with a guttural voice singing in Spanish. Stella had never leaned Latino dances, but this did not matter. Lazio took her to the centre of the floor and put his arm round her waist. She placed one hand in his, the other on his shoulder, and he led her through the steps, bending her to his will.

Dipping, swaying, sliding the feet, then back to first base, Lazio was a superb dancer, and she kept her knees slightly relaxed, flexible yet firm. She felt his cheek on hers, her breasts pressed to his chest, and the hard baton of his cock brushing her belly. Her heart was thumping. Her juices flowed, wetting her sex, and she was wantonly glad that she had obeyed Quincy's edict against wearing panties when she was with him. He wasn't exactly her escort, but had given her and Kate a lift, so she guessed this counted.

Her skirt swirled up as Lazio's feet formed rhythmic patterns round hers. The music spiralled, and so did her desires. At the conclusion she lifted her leg and wrapped it round his thigh, bringing pressure to bear on her clitoris. Staring down at her, his eyes heavy with passion, he continued to hold her even when the music had stopped.

She was aware of people clapping, Dimitri and Candice, and Quincy, too. Conlan was there, and his face was bleak, but Kate was smiling and applauding enthusiastically, saying to her, when Lazio brought her back, 'So you didn't dream him up. He's real, all right. What a babe!'

But Stella was hardly conscious of anyone except Lazio, clinging to his hand as if fearing he might melt like snow in sunshine. She felt removed from reality, accepting everything about the party as normal, the master of ceremonies with his skull-like face, the servants displaying their private parts, and the guests who were dancing and drinking – more than that, inhibitions cast to the winds, they were fornicating.

She saw a couple lying on a divan, clothing awry as they joined in sexual congress. The woman was flat on her back, her legs hitched high, while her lover drove his cock into her. His bare bottom flashed as his hips pumped up and down, and a golden-haired youth stood behind him, working his phallus into the proffered anus. Further on, a fat man with a sagging paunch was on his knees, head bent to the floor, while a tall, leather-clad girl flogged him with a cat-o'-nine-tails. Three other women, and Stella recognised them as Dimitri's sisters, drifted across and wound themselves around Quincy.

'Come with us,' they purred, exotic figures in the most fantastic garments, jewel-studded, yet diaphanous, their perfect bodies on show.

'Yes, go with them, my friend,' Dimitri nodded, huge and dominating, overshadowing the proceedings. 'Enjoy what we have on offer and forget your past, and all you might have learned there.'

'I know we're going to be friends, Stella.' Candice whispered, her breath wafting flower perfumes and cinnamon. 'I want you to tell me everything you can about your ancestress, Lady Emma.'

Even this statement did not penetrate the hypnotic haze in which Stella now existed, though she managed to reply, 'I didn't know her. She died the year I was born. I've seen her portrait at Troon Hall and Mrs Rogan has spoken of her.'

'Don't worry about it,' Candice cooed. 'You two children go off and enjoy yourselves,' and she placed her lips on the side of Stella's cheek in a salivating, almost hungry caress that Stella found disturbing and rather unpleasant.

'Conlan Henny, isn't it?' said a thirty-something dandy who suddenly appeared beside him, resplendent in a sparkling lurex suit, cut in the last extreme of fashion. 'My name is Belphegor, and I've been wanting to meet you for some time, having heard your music and been impressed.'

'Really?' Conlan replied sceptically, sitting on a carved bench in an alcove, working his way through a plate of delicacies provided by a buxom maidservant. He would have liked a glass of beer, but he was driving.

The waitress had let it be known that he could have anything else he fancied, her breasts bulging over the top of her basque, her slit skirt exposing her pussy, and showing hindquarters that bore the marks of slavery; flaming stripes and purple bruises left by the cane and whip. Conlan had been intrigued. Was Dimitri into sadomasochism? Suddenly, the scenes from his opera seemed to come alive, acted out before him. He sent the girl away, even though the sight of her made his cock swell, and now this overdressed buffoon was accosting him.

'Oh, yes, your pieces for the ballet are so fresh and original,' Belphegor continued. 'And I hear down the grapevine that you have an opera in preparation.'

'Who told you that?' Conlan said angrily. He was superstitious about his work and rarely discussed it with anyone before it was ready.

Belphegor tapped the side of his nose mysteriously, and inched along the bench beside him. 'Shall we say "a little bird"? Though actually she's not so little, rather well developed in the bust area. A real handful, as you should know,' he added archly.

'Alithea,' Conlan muttered, and felt her betrayal keenly.

'Don't be cross with her,' Belphegor said, and rested a hand on Conlan's knee. 'I'm very interested and not without influence in the right circles. I was looking for a venture, and would be prepared to back *Persephone*, all other things being equal.'

Conlan couldn't believe his ears. A backer! An *angel*, as such benefactors were known in theatrical circles. 'Tell me more,' he said, and temporarily forgot to be hurt and worried because Stella had gone off with Lazio, or even alarmed when Belphegor squeezed his knee.

'Hi there, what are you guys up to?' asked Kate, wandering across to join them, gorgeous in a studded and ruched off-the-shoulder dress that displayed the upper curves of her breasts and her long, shapely legs in sheer red stockings.

'Talking music and staging an opera,' Conlan answered. 'Kate, meet Belphegor. He's offered to put money into my show.'

'Wow! Seems that Lady Luck is smiling on you, too,' she opined, crossing her knees with a faint hiss of silk that made the hair stand up at the back of Conlan's neck. He found legs in stockings the ultimate turn on – that and breasts, of course. But then, everything about women, those marvellous creatures, filled him with awe and made him horny.

'Yep,' he managed to say, 'Quincy Dubois for *Zero700*, and Belphegor for me.'

'You have attracted the attention of important beings,' Belphegor vouchsafed, waving away the glass a waiter offered. Only Kate accepted one, her eyes fixed on the young man's tightly muscled bottom.

'This isn't the kind of party I expected at all,' she said, lingering on the waiter's retreating rear. 'Gosh, held by a rich dude in a monastery. Can you wonder I'm surprised?'

'But not shocked?' Belphegor questioned, and Conlan noticed his teeth as he smiled; they were very white and long, especially the incisors.

'What me?' Kate thumped her breastbone with a closed fist. 'It would take more than a few couples having it away in public. I'm just a tad thrown, that's all. And meeting Lazio was another weird thing.'

'How so?' Belphegor asked, his eyes lynx keen, though he continued to smile. 'You saw him in the Dublin bar, didn't you?'

'Yes, I suppose so, though it's vague, but when Stella told me she'd already met him a couple of times before, or rather *thought* she had, I put it down to her imagination, or a dream. So I'm relieved to find he's real, after all. She's my best friend, and I wouldn't like to see her hurt. It's bad enough that she's carrying a torch for Quincy,' Kate said firmly, and fumbled for a cigarette in her bag.

Conlan fished a pack from his shirt pocket, drew one out and lit it for her. He was disturbed, for she was voicing his fears. 'Quincy isn't good enough for her,' he blurted, afraid to show too much emotion.

Kate nodded. 'I agree, but we can't afford to offend him yet. Get the band up and running and we'll see.'

'Why don't we go for a wander?' Belphegor suggested and, almost imperceptibly, passed a hand over their faces.

At once Conlan found this idea appealing, though he had enough sense left to ask, 'But is this allowed? Shouldn't our host be consulted?'

Belphegor laughed lightly and rose, saying, 'Dimitri and I are old friends. I'm almost one of the family,' and, with an arm linked with each, he conducted them from the room.

Conlan wished he had thought to bring a sketchbook with him, for the ancient building was all he might have hoped for when it came to scenery for his opera. Grey stone walls, broken pediments, a gloomy magnificence that stunned the eye and bewitched the senses, some parts like mazes that led down into darkness, others with staircases that looked as if they needed scaling ladders. There was no hope that they might explore the place entirely. There were too many doors that had swollen shut decades ago, too many gangrenous cellars and cobwebbed passages that the builders had not bothered with.

'Does the prince live here permanently?' he asked, as Belphegor switched on a naked light bulb and began the descent into the bowels of the building, via a set of corkscrew stone steps.

'No, he has many properties dotted all over the world,' he replied, the light forming planes on his face and casting the spiky shadows of his lashes against his eye sockets. 'But this suits him very well.'

'He seems to have a lot of acquaintances,' Kate said, and Conlan felt her fingers tightening on his arm as they ventured down the slippery steps.

'He attracts people wherever he goes. Some might say it is a fatal attraction.'

'Why?' Conlan wished he could shake off that feeling of doom.

Belphegor looked up at him from the bottom step. He was smiling, and it wasn't reassuring. 'I jest. That was just a figure of speech,' he said, but Conlan wondered.

They came to a stone-flagged passage and sound drifted from somewhere at the end, the rolling chords played on a church organ. Bach, Conlan thought, a mighty fugue. Was it being performed for his benefit? He wished he could think clearly, but felt intoxicated though not a single drink had passed his lips that evening.

The light grew stronger as they entered an underground chamber, the music louder now, making the floor shake. Conlan's ears were ringing, and then the stereo was turned down, the fugue becoming no more than a background noise. More people, more of Dimitri's guests, watching or taking part, but the games were of an unusual nature.

'What is this, a fetish club?' Kate asked sharply.

Belphegor laughed. 'Call it that if you wish.'

'*Dante's Inferno* or a pervert's delight,' Conlan observed sarcastically, trying to keep cool. Though he might have occasionally thought of spanking Alithea or pondered the rights and wrongs of pleasure through pain, he had never put it into practise. Now, on each side of him was evidence it appealed to some in a big way.

There were benches with holes in strategic places, a contraption that resembled stocks, a vaulting horse and a whipping post set in the middle of the floor, and racks of instruments; whips and paddles, canes and tawse, rods and birches. Iron rings had been hammered into the damp stone walls and several young women hung from them, chained by their wrists. Their loosened hair fell over their faces, and their heads were bowed. One had a gag fastened across her mouth and another was blindfolded. They were naked, apart from one who still wore a few tattered strips left when her dress was ripped off. A man in top boots and riding breeches was moving among them, his crop landing on their thighs, bellies and breasts. Their moans and sighs augmented the organ toccata.

Some of the spectators masturbated as they watched. Some laid wagers as to who among the contestants in the show would win the prize. There were several entries. A woman in an evening gown was bound to a block, her bodice pushed down and small weights hanging from the rings in her nipples. Her skirt had been lifted to expose her pussy from which another weight was attached to a chain and ball that had been inserted into her vagina. A man cuffed to a rack, cried out as a dominatrix in a red PVC cat suit, tortured his exposed cock.

'That's a fine entry!' Belphegor exclaimed, and went over to where a girl was tied with her arms above her head and the ropes passed through rings in the ceiling. She was naked to the waist, further chains snapped on to nipple clamps.

He kissed her lips, then lowered his face to her throat, pausing for a moment, holding her as she began to slump, supporting her to prevent dislocation of her arms. He lifted his head and stared straight at Conlan who was startled by the feral look in his eyes and the wet redness smearing his lips. Then Belphegor stood the woman on her feet again, and went across to the man who was taking the bets.

Conlan saw one of the prince's sisters on the other side of the dungeon. She was the fiery-headed one, beautiful and barbaric. He wanted to cast her as Pluto's mistress, the wicked enchantress in *Persephone*, and wondered if she could sing. Bizarre and flamboyant, she occupied a chair, dressed in a gown that resembled a spider's silvery web, her skirt open, jewels glinting in the pierced wings of her depilated pussy. Her bare legs were spread, her feet encased in shoes with spiked heels, and her hands were busy with the phalli and balls of two young men who stood either side of her.

They were splendid examples of physical perfection, tanned and naked apart from leather straps, brass-studded neckbands and chains threaded through rings in their nipples and navels. Even their foreskins were pierced, and Allegra played with the little gold hoops, twisting them as she pulled the wrinkled collars of flesh down over their rampantly erect cocks, then reached between their legs to torment the sensitive area separating the scrotum and anal opening.

'Down; suck me!' she commanded suddenly, and one of the men dropped to his knees between her thighs, spread open her labia and her clitoris protruded. He stuck out his tongue, buried his face in her wet folds and slurped vigorously. She came almost at once, wailing like a banshee.

'Dear God,' Conlan muttered, and the sense of evil persisted as he saw her drag the other slave towards her and bite the blue, knotted vein inside his elbow.

'It's part of the fun,' Belphegor said. 'Don't take it seriously, my dear chap. Come, let us return to the hall. I'm sure Dimitri will want to hear about our plans. He's an avid music lover.'

'I want to stay here,' Kate declared, and Conlan hardly recognised her. She shimmered in the gloom, even her

139

chestnut hair sparked, forming a penumbra around a face that had become hard and cruel, with eyes to match. 'This is bloody fantastic.'

He followed her stare, and his already agitated cock enlarged. He could see she was lusting to join several girls who sprawled on a couch. The sight of so many denuded or neatly trimmed snatches, the fleshy folds and inflamed nubbins, overwhelmed him. It was as if, should he go nearer, he would be smothered in the wealth of breasts and nipples, the sinuous curves of legs and thighs and arms.

Kate drew in a sharp breath and lunged forward, and Conlan let her go. He had not realised until that moment that she was bi-sexual, and this put a new slant on her relationship with Stella. Did she, too, enjoy lesbian love?

Feeling ever more miserable and confused, he allowed Belphegor to lead him away. His last view of Kate was her tearing off her clothes and laying into the girls with a wicked looking whip. They screamed and moaned and prostrated themselves before her, offering their mouths for her pleasure.

'We can be private here,' Lazio said, setting Stella down on her feet. 'This is my room at the top of the tower. I like it up here; it's close to the stars and the bats.'

'Won't anyone come?' she asked, clinging to him, his body the only safe anchor in a stormy sea of emotions.

'They'll try, no doubt, but I shall weave a spell around us, just for a while,' and he dragged her closer against him so she was aware of his erection. 'The night is nearly gone and we shall make love in that mystical hour when the world pauses on the brink of day. I've already waited too long for you.'

'I know, I know,' she said, delirious with joy, yet riven with panic.

The circular room was furnished with items dark with age. Thick damask curtains were drawn across the windows and candles gleamed everywhere – on the mantelpiece and the tops of dressing chest and bureau. They added to the sense of unreality. A fire had been laid in the marble fireplace. He pointed his index finger. Flames leapt into life and shadows danced across the panelled walls. She gave a little shriek, hand pressed to her mouth.

'How did you do that?'

'Never mind. One day you will understand.'

Oh, Kate, I wish you were here! Stella thought. To be alone with Lazio was the answer to her prayers, but she was afraid. Was he a genuine sorcerer, a stage magician skilled in sleight of hand or a clever hypnotist? She doubted it could be the first, for sorcerers didn't exist, did they? But every member of Dimitri's family was eccentric, and she suddenly wanted to leave.

'It's late,' she said, and turned towards the door. 'I must be going.'

'No,' he said firmly, and his shadow reached her before he did. Then she was engulfed in it, and in him. He was so strong, lifting her effortlessly and carrying her across to the canopied bed. All memory of Quincy or any other man she had known carnally vanished. Now there was only Lazio.

Her clothing had gone, and so had his. She saw him in all his naked splendour; broad shoulders and a muscular torso tapering to a narrow waist, taut flanks deeply hollowed, long thighs and sturdy legs. She wished she were a sculptor, able to immortalise him in bronze. Awestruck and hardly daring to meet his dazzlingly blue eyes, her gaze ran over his body again, coming to rest on the thicket of black hair from which sprang his sublime cock. He gasped as she touched it, and this sign of pleasure made her juices flow. She felt herself opening for him, wanting to feel him inside her.

As he knelt over her she kept hold of his hard length, and worked the foreskin back and forth across the glans. She could smell his hunger, salty and dense, and there was

141

something else, too – something she couldn't quite place, but associating it vaguely with the abattoir. His thighs gripped her, each side of her waist, and he braced himself on straight arms. His hair fell forward like a sepia cloud, and his face came closer and closer to hers till it was out of focus. She thought he was going to kiss her, waiting in delicious anticipation for his mouth to close over hers, wild with disappointment when he went lower, pressing his lips into the curve of her breast, making long, lapping motions with his outstretched tongue.

She heard him mutter and caught the words, 'It isn't daybreak yet,' and felt his breath against her skin.

She was hot, lubricious, ready for him, and a sensual languor swept over her, as if her blood was draining away. She knew such a thing could not be, and waited with madly beating heart for him to caress her nipples with his lips, then trail down across her body to her clitoris. But his teeth nipped and his tongue licked, and her fires raged up in an extraordinary manner and she was hurled into an intense orgasm.

'It's time,' he growled, and she came down from the heights to look at him.

He was like an untamed animal, lips drawn back in a snarl. In that light she could have sworn they were bloody, but was held in a sweet lassitude that removed any desire to question. Nothing mattered but him.

She was totally unprepared when he flipped her over. Then she yelled at the unexpected impact of his palm against her bare bottom. *Thwack*! He hit her once, then, giving her no time to recover, did it again.

'Why are you doing that?' she cried, tears soaking into the white linen pillow beneath her head, her buttocks burning, the heat communicating with her pussy. 'What have I done?'

'It's a ritual,' he said huskily. 'If you accept my blows, then you become even more a part of me, suffering as I would suffer for you, if need be.'

'But we love each other, don't we? Isn't that enough?'

'Do you love me, Stella?'

Afraid to look round, she was aware that he had left the bed. She felt bereft, missing his gentleness, his harshness, the paradox of his nature. 'Yes, I love you,' she confessed, and knew this to be true.

'Enough to do anything I ask?'

'Yes, but you haven't told me how you feel about me,' she said, ears straining for any sound that might give a clue to his intentions.

'It goes without saying,' he replied. 'I love you, Stella Kerrick, and shall go on loving you for all time. You are my soul mate. The other half of me. Are you ready to receive chastisement?'

'Yes,' she whispered, and clenched her hands into tight-knuckled fists, determined to endure.

He was behind her again, standing by the side of the bed. He gripped her body and swung her round. She was still face down, but horizontal now, her belly supported by the mattress, her thighs over the edge so that she knelt on the Persian rug. The cool air played over her rump and the deep fissure between where her floss was rendered darker by an abundance of juice.

'I shan't restrain you,' he said softly. 'You will undergo this of your own free will. This is what I shall use.'

He went round to the far side so she could see the plaited leather strap coiled round his hand, its snakelike end tipped with knots. He was so proud, upright and stern that he could have been a cold inquisitor, were it not for the fleshy spear that curved towards his navel, a single drop of dew shining at the slit.

Stella dug her fingers into the quilt and braced herself. He had promised her his cock and she was willing to go to hell and back in order to have him fuck her. He wanted to play

143

games? Very well. She would concede to his wishes. She had done it for Quincy, and enjoyed it. How much greater would be her pleasure if Lazio mastered her?

There was a sudden whistling. A searing bolt of pain winded her. She couldn't even scream. Before she could get her breath that band of agony struck again, and now the air rushed into her lungs and she screeched, bucking and thrashing involuntarily. She grabbed at her bottom but he knocked her hands away, and the lash bit into her mercilessly.

There was a second's respite and she felt Lazio's breath between her cleft and the lap, lap of his tongue, rough as a cat's as he licked. He laid his hands on the burning welts criss-crossing her hindquarters, then stood back and she screamed again at the rush of scalding agony that spread through every nerve of her body and concentrated on her thrumming clitoris.

'Hush! Listen!' He stilled her lamentations, a hand over her mouth, and into the silence she heard the first notes swelling from a blackbird's throat outside the window, a hymn of praise to the sunrise.

He flung the lash down and turned Stella on her back, thrusting between her thighs and drawing up her legs so that they scissored round his shoulders. Then he let himself fall into her, fucking her with fierce strokes until she yelped with the pain and pleasure of his entry. He rose to a kneeling position, raising her hips from the bed and plunging deeper still, holding her bruised bottom to pull her closer. He was above her now, his cock an icy pole penetrating to her epicentre. They rose and fell together, and the root of his freezing weapon grazed her nubbin with every powerful thrust. Her vagina was hot as fire, but it did not melt him into warmth, the smooth purple helm prodding her G-spot, the girth rubbing her clit. Spasms of agony and delight rocked her, bringing on her crisis and, in her extremity, she stared up into his eyes. They were like Dimitri's now – the eyes of

144

a wolf.

He howled and she put her hand up to his mouth. He bit into her thumb and she felt his essence jetting from him, as cold as the Arctic Sea. She was swept away by the triple sensations of climax, the sharp pain in her hand, and his spunk gushing into her body. Screaming, she rolled from under him, their mingled essences coating her inner thighs. He roused, looked at her and then turned his head towards the draped windows.

'Go now,' he ordered, and flung an arm over his eyes.

'But can't I stay here, with you?' she implored, shattered by the experience and appalled by his abrupt dismissal.

'No, I must sleep… alone. I will come to you tonight. Now *go*!'

Blinded by tears, her body stinging from the red marks left by the lash, she struggled to find her clothes, and there they were, laid out neatly over the back of a chair. Someone knocked at the door. She opened it and the ugly manservant stood there.

'I have instructions to take you back to the party,' he said in grave tones. 'My name is Carl, and you are to call on me any time you need help.'

'But I don't understand, Lazio…' she began, glancing back into the chamber. Carl was going round extinguishing every candle, plunging it into darkness.

'I am obeying orders, miss,' he said, and stood back so that she might precede him through the door. Then he closed and locked it securely behind him.

It started to rain when Conlan left the monastery in the small hours. It had been the strangest evening of his life, and try as he might, he couldn't recall much of it, only that persistent sense of something dire that was impossible to shake off.

He had left the others to find their own way back, and there was no sign of Stella. His heart was like a stone in his chest. She had disappeared with Lazio. Though it must be getting on for dawn, blackness closed in on the road to form a tunnel in front of him. The darkness condensed into a peculiar fog that made the trees evanescent. Then, in the headlight's glare, three figures were discernible on the footpath, kit bags on their backs, faces turned towards the approaching car, thumbs lifted hopefully.

Conlan braked and wound down the window. 'Going far?' he asked, having done his fair share of hitching in his student days.

'To Wicklow,' said one of them, a tall girl in a hooded fleece, shorts and trainers.

'Hop in,' Conlan said, and clicked open the rear doors.

They slung in their packs and scrambled after them, though the tall one, who seemed to be their spokesperson, asked, 'Can I sit with you? I get carsick.'

'All right,' he agreed, and set off again in the direction of Wicklow and Troon Hall.

The car was different now, its three new occupants seeming to exude a pungent, almost mesmerising perfume. Conlan glanced at the girl beside him, and she gave him a sultry look, and slid her hand across his knee and into his crotch. Conlan jumped and so did his cock; that supple hand with its oval, blue-painted nails was too tempting to resist.

'Where have you come from?' he asked unsteadily, making an attempt at conversation.

'Oh, here, there and everywhere,' crooned a soft voice from behind as one of the other girls slid her arms round his neck, her breath fanning his skin. And the third was there, too, smoothing his chest between the open neck of his shirt.

He was finding it incredibly difficult to concentrate on driving, and pulled into a lay-by.

'That's better,' said the girl whose hand had left his chest and was working its way through his flies and boxer shorts and clasping his tumescent cock.

'Isn't it, though,' agreed the one behind him, and she tossed off her hat, blonde hair tumbling loose.

'You've been very naughty tonight, Conlan,' pouted her companion, and shook her black hair free. 'You ignored us at the party.'

'Christ!' he exclaimed. 'Medea!'

'And Madelon.'

'And Allegra.'

They fixed him with their shining, vulpine eyes – black, azure and violet, and they were no longer hitchhikers, but Dimitri's weird, voluptuous sisters. Conlan's pulse raced and his penis quivered with need. They were just too seductive. Their shorts and ordinary clothes had gone, replaced by drapes that floated like mist around them, sometimes covering, sometimes flaunting their perfect, corpse-pale limbs. Somehow, and he didn't see how this was possible but no longer cared, they were all over him. Hands cradled his cock and balls, fingers pinched his nipples, mouths supped at his intimate places. His thoughts were disjointed, as if his brain was stuffed with cotton wool. He knew he should rebuff them, but it was beyond him.

Their voices were enticing, cajoling, entreating. 'Give yourself to us, Conlan. We need you, darling.'

Allegra sat astride his lap and lowered herself onto his upright prick, riding him like a demented huntress. He could feel her crop leathering his arse, but lay back in his seat, unable to move, his limbs heavy as lead. She leaned forward, her eyes slits, and stuck her long, scarlet tongue into his mouth.

'Don't be so selfish,' chided Madelon, flirting her silvery-blonde tresses, and plucking Conlan's nipples like harp strings. 'There's plenty for all of us. He's so young, so strong, so well blessed.'

'Isn't Stella a silly girl to prefer Lazio?' commented Medea, lifting Conlan's balls in her hand and pushing a finger passed his anal ring. He felt it penetrate his nether regions, wriggling its way into his rectum.

'What d'you mean?' he managed to gasp. 'Stella and Lazio?'

'He's fucking her right now,' Allegra hissed, gyrating madly, then gripping him with iron-muscled thighs. She screeched as her orgasm reached a crescendo and threw herself across Conlan's chest and sank her teeth into his throat.

Madelon and Medea acted as one, and Conlan felt the life ebbing from him as their soft mouths feasted on his nipples, testes and cock. He gasped for breath and his penis pulsed in the depths of Allegra's cold passage. Then he was drowning in plump breasts and juicy cunts and glorious, svelte buttocks where the anal holes opened like carnivorous flowers, eager to drag him in. The air was rich with perfume and female essences, and incense and a sour, animal rankness. He was drenched in sweat and soaked with his own blood, his throbbing prick about to erupt.

He heard the sisters singing, and his opera burst into life, almost deafening him. It was a dirge, a seductive siren call that drew men to their doom. He craved paper, a pen, anything, lest those magical notes escaped him, never to be recaptured. He started to scream in agony and ecstasy as the sisters brought him to a wrenching, convulsive orgasm. They weren't women now, but savage beasts, with blazing eyes and slavering mouths that dripped blood and semen.

As he lost consciousness he heard them laughing, singing and shouting, 'Forget Stella! Think only of us. We can give you everything. She's of no importance. We shall return. You carry our brand now and can never escape... never!'

When Conlan opened his eyes, he was alone. It was as if nothing had happened, his clothing intact, no trace of blood or spunk. He felt exhausted and kept getting flashes of devil women, but were they real or simply a projection of his creativity that was working overtime? He slipped the car into gear and headed for Troon Hall.

The rain poured down the windscreen in heavy drops and visibility was bad. He shouldn't be driving. Had Belphegor put something into that soft drink he persuaded him to have on leaving? Was he pushing drugs? He certainly was an oddball. They had arranged to meet tomorrow and, if genuine, he could then put his money where his mouth was.

Those women! They haunted him. They had mocked his interest in Stella. Bitches, every one!

The wipers ticked like metronomes, beating out the time of their songs that rang in his brain. The torrent lashed the car and made the tarmac greasy. Thunder rolled and lightning split the heavens and Conlan, straining to see, suddenly cried aloud.

A figure appeared in front of him, stark in the beam of the lights. It was Stella standing there in the middle of the road, arms outspread as if crucified, desperate appeal in every line of her body. Conlan jammed his foot on the brake, but it was too late. There was a sickening thud. Stella spun over the bonnet, the sound of the impact turning him cold. Then her head smashed against the streaming front window, bursting open, brains and blood spurting out to mingle with the downpour.

'My God,' Conlan whispered, clawing frantically at the door and hurling himself into the deluge. 'I've killed her!'

His only thought was to get to Stella. He ran round to the front, expecting to find her broken body and blood running down the metal. Instead, he couldn't believe his eyes, his hands fumbling blindly over the place where he had seen her so vividly. There was nothing there – no blood – no Stella – only the rain.

And then, faint and faraway, he heard savage laughter and that diabolical singing. He was their toy now, and the sisters were having fun, exercising their sadistic sense of humour.

149

Chapter Eight

Stella woke with a start. Someone was calling her name.

'Who is it?' she cried, but appeared to be alone, disoriented and wondering where she was. Then scraps of memory came back, but nothing was clear. 'What do you want?'

The party last night. Little vignettes floated tantalisingly out of reach. She thought she had made passionate love with Lazio, and yes, on slipping her hand between her legs, she found that she was wet, and a little sore, but had he beaten her? She thought he had, but there was no evidence of bruising on her bottom.

She sat up in that grand four-poster which had once belonged to her great-great-grandmother and scanned the room, then reached for a hand mirror on the bedside table. The curtains were as she had left them before she went out, half pulled across the tall casement windows. She could see her reflection clearly in the looking glass – pale cheeks, and blue half circles under her eyes. When she examined her throat to see if Lazio had damaged her, there were no marks to speak of, only the faint bruising that might have been left by a love bite.

Had she indulged in too much champagne?

And where were Kate, Conlan and Quincy?

She didn't remember being driven home, but someone must have brought her, undressed her and tucked her into bed. It was embarrassing, for she was naked. And it was then, while she was pondering the mystery, that she saw her – a faint figure in the early morning light.

There was a feeling in the breeze, a fondness, a timorous

reaching out. She had not even managed to project her image clearly; transparent as a butterfly's wing, a gauzy haze, but Stella knew at once that it was Emma as she had been in her youth. Just the eyes, like those in the portrait of her as a mature woman, but soft now and sad, trying to say something. She smiled. It was a nice smile, wistful perhaps, but nice. She was a shy ghost, not finding it easy to communicate.

Ghosts? Was she losing it completely?

'Don't be afraid,' said Emma, and her voice was the one Stella had heard calling her. 'I mean you no harm.'

'You're dead, aren't you?' Stella gasped, cold all over. But did she believe in ghosts? It was all perfectly ridiculous and yet, in her present state of mind, entirely logical.

Emma's lips moved, and Stella felt rather than heard the words. 'I've been permitted to cross the divide, but only for a short time. My diary; you must find it. The answer lies within its pages, and there's a letter I wrote to you when I heard you had been born.'

'Where is it?' Stella was out of bed in an instant, shrugging her shoulders into her towelling bathrobe.

Emma was beginning to fade. One minute she was standing by a chair, the next only her eyes remained – wide and pleading. Then a fragile hand appeared, and pointed to the window embrasure.

'There… there…' it came like a sigh. 'I hid it before I died. I intended to tell Maureen… then it was too late. I wanted you to have it when you inherited. Help me, please.'

Stella moved towards her – too quickly. Emma faded altogether and she was left standing there on bare feet, completely baffled. Had it really happened? I'll never drink champagne again, she vowed. Yet she went across and tapped the panelling.

'Where is it?' she muttered urgently. 'Where?'

Then she saw a carved rose, one of many decorating the

wooden window seat, but it seemed a little more prominent. She twisted it and was rewarded by a small, satisfying click, able to slide back a panel, revealing an aperture. The dark, long shut place smelt musty, but there was no stench of decay. There would be cobwebs, of course, and spiders, but she gritted her teeth and inserted her hand. Her fingers met dust, not the ordinary household variety, but the accumulation of two decades, soft and thick as fur. Beneath it lay something hard. She grasped it firmly and pulled out a bundle.

She retreated to the bed with it, her heart hammering. Had she really seen Lady Emma's ghost? If so, why wasn't she running screaming from the room? Something very strange was happening to her, and it was all to do with Lazio and Dimitri and Candice, to say nothing of the beautiful, scary sisters.

She was chilled to the marrow and cuddled down into the duvet's warmth. The book, and she assumed that's what it was, had been wrapped in a black silk shawl with long fringes and red embroidered cabbage roses. Stella parted the dusty folds and there laid a leather-bound journal, embossed with a name in gold lettering, *Emma Collingwood*. With it was a brown paper package, and a letter addressed to her. She opened it and spread out the quality notepaper with Troon Hall, Wicklow, in the top right hand corner, and the date, October 19th 1980.

My dear child, it began, in that lovely copperplate hand in which scholars took such pride before the advent of typewriters and computers. *Today, your father phoned me and told me of your birth two days ago. This has delighted me more than you will ever know. Not only with pride at having lived so long and seen so much, but because you are the one I have been waiting for. The last time Candice managed to communicate with me on All Soul's Eve 1900, she told me that one day a girl child of my blood would be*

152

born to aid us.

Candice! Stella's brows drew together in a puzzled frown. What had she to do with it? She read on.

You see, much as we loved one another, and still do as dear friends, we can never be together in life or in death, Candice being what she is, cursed and damned and unable to die and reach heaven. I implore you to read my tale, and trust that you will find it in your heart to help us. This is why I left you everything, knowing that you were our saviour. Do what you must, dear child, and earn the everlasting blessings of Emma Kerrick and Candice Fortesque. That was her maiden name, and she never changed it. Although she thinks of Prince Dimitri as her husband, the church never sanctified their union. They are pariahs. Abominations. Even hell closes its gates to them.

Here the letter ended, and Stella sat there as still as a mouse, while sunshine made golden pools on the parquet floor, and she was surrounded by the normal, everyday noises of a house stirring into life. She could even smell the mouth-watering odour of roasted coffee beans and sizzling bacon. What did Emma mean – Candice and Dimitri, damned and doomed? What crime had they committed, and how could it be that they were still young? And where did Lazio feature in all this?

Just for an instant she comforted herself by believing that Emma had been senile when she wrote the letter. Yet the writing was firm, the prose succinct, and Maureen had said her ladyship was in control of her faculties till the day she died.

Stella returned it to the envelope and opened the diary, feeling that she was somehow invading Emma's privacy, even though invited to do so. It was a pretty book, a present for a young girl, typical of Christmas long ago when the world was less obsessed with consumer goods. At first, it contained nothing of significance, a few jottings about parties and shopping in London's Oxford Street accompanied by her chaperone, Mrs Flora Smythe.

Mama says she's a widow and very respectable, Emma had noted. *I think she's fun, and so does Candice, much better than that stern duenna of hers, Miss Gwenda Turner. She beats Candice sometimes, makes her take her drawers down and belabours her poor buttocks. Candice is my best friend and we spend much time together. We are eighteen and have had our 'coming out' balls, and our parents are seeking suitable husbands for us. We're not sure about this, neither of us conversant with what happens between a man and a woman on their wedding night, though some of the girls at Finishing School whispered about it. One of them said that her brother's friend had opened his trousers and shown her his male equipment. He had wanted her to rub it, but she was too shy, amazed by its size and stiffness and the juice leaking from its tip.*

So, a pair of Victorian maidens riddled with curiosity, Stella thought with a smile, warming to Emma and her friend. January and February were uneventful, according to the diary, and there were many gaps. Obviously Emma had tired of it, though she did record a happening that might have turned her friendship with Candice on its head.

Today she told me that she is formally engaged to Clive, Viscount Kerrick, the son of an earl with a town house in Dublin and an estate in County Wicklow. I asked her if she loved him and she made light of it, dismissing this as of no consequence. 'What use is love and romance?' she asked. 'My parents think Clive is an excellent choice.'

Clive! Stella gasped. Clive Kerrick? But didn't Emma end up marrying him? What was going on here?

She read on, absorbed in the narrative, Emma coming to life through the pages – her opinions, her forthright comments, her lively, inquisitive nature. She had been quite a girl! Obviously she had never expected that anyone else would peruse her diary – it was too frank for that, and she didn't mince her words.

This morning on waking, Candice confided in me that she had dreamed of a tall, dark, handsome man who had penetrated her with his massive, freezing cold tool. I was sharing a bed with her in her father's London house. We often sleep together. She seemed so sure that it had been real, not a dream, but when we put our arms around each other and I played with her between the legs, a game that we have been enjoying for some time, her hymen was still sealed. Nevertheless, we succeeded in pleasuring one another. I adore her blonde beauty and blue eyes, her slender form, pretty breasts and that heavenly garden that yields up its moist fragrance to me. I love to bedew her tiny pearl and fondle it until she cries out as if in pain, then clutches me, caresses me and performs the same service on my own downy parts.

'Good grief!' Stella exclaimed out loud. 'They were into lesbian sex! Wait till I tell Kate about this.'

Unfortunately, this morning we were caught at it by Miss Turner, Emma confessed, *and she reported that Candice had been misbehaving, though I don't think she said what she had been doing, and then Miss Turner caned her. Candice says the woman enjoys beating her. It was on this day, a momentous one, that I first decided to marry her brother, Fabian, as fair-haired as her and with the same colour eyes. He's dashing and has a reputation as a man-about-town. Yes, I think he'll do, then Candice and I can be sisters-in-law and continue to kiss and toy and enjoy our secret games.*

There was more of this, and Emma was outspoken in her views about the injustice of a society where gentlemen could sow their wild oats but genteel young ladies were expected to remain pure and virginal until they were married. She suspected that Fabian visited prostitutes, but was soon betrothed to him. Then it was decided that the engaged couples should visit Venice, thus increasing their knowledge of foreign climes. The young ladies' chaperones, and the gentlemen's valets accompanied them.

There followed descriptions of the journey and their arrival in that fabled city, and then the adventure really started. *We were introduced to a fascinating pair – Comte Henri Merlion and Countess Bianca Renzo.*

Emma and Candice began their education in earnest, but it was a far cry from visiting museums and art galleries. It appeared that Henri and Bianca were into bondage and chastisement. He did not take Candice's maidenhead, but Emma yielded hers without much hesitation, already bored with Fabian.

Henri's so handsome and gallant and utterly charming, she recorded, pen spluttering as if her hand was flying over the paper, driven by sexual longing and pent-up emotion. *I was with him last night at a party at the Palazzo Barbesi. We were alone in his room and he told me to take off my drawers and then tied me to the bed. He showed me his penis. It was huge. I felt sure I'd never be able to take it inside me. The thought of him pushing it into me terrified yet excited me. I was soaking wet. He had positioned me so that my derrière was high in the air and my thighs stretched open. My secrets were on show, my hairy lower lips, the pink furrow between, my virgin hole and my anus. It was so shaming, and yet so wonderful. I wanted to tell Candice, but she was in the ballroom.*

Stella could feel her own sex tingling, and a surge of fresh dew dampening her cleft. Holding the book in one hand, she inserted the other under the bedclothes and stroked her clitoris. Well done, Emma, she thought. Your journal is as arousing a piece of erotic prose as any written by some naughty gentleman in Queen Victoria's reign.

It got even better, and Stella focused her attention on it while slowly, delicately and lingeringly bringing her clit to the boil.

He tethered my ankles, too, the diary continued. *And I wondered what he would do, but to my astonishment he simply tickled my fanny with the end of a quill pen. Then he replaced this with a mock phallus. I'd never seen such a thing before, but he said it was a lingam. It was large and black and carved to look like a male member. He trailed it round my opening and tried to insert it in my fundament, but this was too tight. I've never, ever tampered with that, and neither has Candice, though now I began to wonder how such a forbidden act would feel. It is against the law, even between man and wife, a thing that perverted men practised illegally with one another. An unnatural, animal action. Mrs Smythe has told me it is called sodomy.*

She was eager to learn, Stella thought fondly, her delta slippery with warm honeydew, her clit enlarged.

Henri was speaking of things I didn't understand, saying he would be my teacher and master, and that I should learn the meaning of agony and desire. And as he spoke he tormented my breasts and rubbed my bud until I was near screaming with frustration and ready to agree to anything if he would only bring me to completion. In the end, I called him master. And then he used his riding crop on me. I've never known such agony. It was white-hot, like a branding iron, not a whip. He delivered the strokes at careful intervals, getting the most from each. I clawed at the bedclothes, feeling the agony rise to a peak, and then hearing the whoosh as the crop descended again.

'I know, I know,' Stella whispered, her bottom burning from Lazio's lashing, the heat forming into a dart delivered straight to the heart of her sex.

He went on whipping me and I cried and mewed and jerked and screamed as the waves of atrocious pain were crowned by the next blistering blow. And all the time I was writhing on the bed, pressing my pubis into the quilt, trying to find some way to bring relief to my throbbing bud. He reached

beneath me and pinched my nubbin, bringing me to a roaring,
screaming climax. Then he rolled me over and took my
virginity with brutal, wonderful force. Even to think of it as
I sit here writing on a balcony overlooking the Grand Canal,
makes me quiver with longing, wanting to be fulfilled again.
Henri was magnificent, especially when he came. He plunged
and thrust and spurted his libation into me. I felt so powerful,
like an invincible earth goddess, and wanted to find Candice
and tell her all about it.

Stella laid the diary aside, too aroused to carry on reading
until she had brought about her own orgasm. Emma's words
inflamed her, and she could no longer delay. She used both
hands now, lying flat with her thighs spread, her free hand
holding open her labia, her clit bare of its cowl. She wetted
it with her dew, then rubbed steadily with her favourite finger,
the middle one of her right hand, not pausing until the wild
and glorious flood of feeling broke over her, leaving her
breathing as hard as if she had been running a race, her
heart pumping madly.

She relaxed into that euphoric state brought about by a
thoroughly satisfying climax. Her eyes were heavy, but she
wanted to go on with the diary. She had left a marker in the
page and now plumped up her pillows, settled back against
them and continued reading. The next entries came as a
shock. It was as if she was reliving her own experiences
with Lazio.

We went to the Lido this morning and while we were
walking on the beach, Candice told me that she had met her
dream lover, the man she had told me about. They had danced,
apparently, but it was in the air. They had kissed and he
brought her to pleasure's crisis, and then they had been in
the ballroom and she was being introduced to his sisters. She
said he was a prince and came from Transylvania, which,
translated means – The Land Beyond the Forest. I must admit
to a feeling of premonition when she declared that she loved

him and intended to have him. What of Clive? I reminded her, but she seemed oblivious to everything except this mysterious prince, though we did snatch the opportunity of pleasuring each other while we were changing into our bathing costumes in the beach hut. She was alarmed to see the stripes on my buttocks left by Henri's crop.

Here this piece of narrative ended, but continued next day.

We had been invited to dine at Prince Dimitri's palace, the Palazzo Tassinari, and were conveyed there by an ugly manservant who said his name was Carl. He took us in the prince's black gondola.

Stella almost dropped the book. Could this be the same Carl who had ushered in the guests at the monastery and taken her from Lazio's room at dawn? It was impossible, and yet, *He seemed to be the only servant, acting the butler when we arrived at this gloomy old mansion on the waterfront. And it was then that I met Dimitri. He was everything Candice had described; very handsome and courtly and aristocratic, wearing the national costume of Transylvania. His three sisters were so beautiful that I felt a dowdy frump in comparison. They were called Allegra, Medea and Madelon.*

'I don't believe it,' Stella cried, dropping the journal as if it was red hot. Over a hundred years had passed since Emma met those strangers in Venice, and yet here they were in Ireland, not a day older. 'Either she was mad or I am!'

They must be descendants, she thought, frantically clutching at straws. The alternative was too fantastic and frightening to contemplate seriously, but with a kind of sick, horrified fascination, she went on reading. Emma's account darkened, no longer concerned with the high society of Venice and her own sexual peccadilloes involving Henri and Bianca and several of their servants. She became more and more worried about Candice who seemed utterly besotted with the prince at one moment, and then suddenly avoiding seeing him. She had become pale and wan, and so had Fabian.

I got the truth out of her at last, Emma had recorded. *She came to my room this morning and broke down. Her story was so implausible that it took a while to sink in. She said Dimitri was a vampire.*

It hit Stella with the force of a tidal wave. Her modern thinking refused to accept it. Vampires were only found in novels and movies, but hot on this came the thought that Candice would not have been exposed to any of these. Bram Stoker's *Dracula* was not published until 1897. Sheridan Le Fanu had written *Carmilla* earlier, but this would have been considered unsuitable literature for a delicately reared young girl. So where and how did she get the notion that her prince was a vampire? And if it was true, and this thought sent Stella cold, was the present day Dimitri of the same stock? No – more than this, *was he the same monster*?

The more she read of the diary the worse it became. Emma discussed the situation with Fabian and Clive and it became apparent that the three sisters had visited Fabian. Not once, but twice – stealthily, by night. He said they had sucked his blood and milked him of his semen, leaving him listless. Clive escaped their wiles, having armed himself with garlic and a cross. But despite all their efforts to save Candice, it had been useless.

The last time I was able to see her clearly, she appeared in my room at the hotel in the middle of the night. She had come to say goodbye, and told me that she had accepted Dimitri's dark gift and was already his bride and a vampire, feeding off human blood and possessing supernatural powers, including immortality. I was appalled, but there was nothing I could do. The die was cast. I had decided to finish with Fabian, he was too weak and a womaniser into the bargain, and I had transferred my affections to Clive. Candice gave me her blessing and said that she would come to me if I needed her. Then she stepped onto the balcony into Dimitri's

arms and they vanished, absorbed by the darkness. I never
saw her again.

The entry petered out, as if Emma could not bear to write further of her loss, but, many years later, she had added a footnote.

Candice had thought she would be able to contact me whenever she wanted, but this wasn't allowed. She was Undead, a blood drinker and a night stalker. By sheer force of will she managed to tell me about the future child, but apart from that we were barred from meeting, and I've never got over it. Neither, I believe, has she. So I'm trusting in Stella to perform a miracle. I've no idea what form this will take, but have faith that somehow, somewhere, there will be a place where Candice and I can meet.

Stella closed the book, her brain numb. She unwrapped the brown paper package and found two photographs inside. They were faded, brownish prints, and one was of the young Emma wearing a tight-waisted bridal gown and a veil held in place by a wreath of stephanotis. She had a bouquet in one hand and her other arm linked with that of a stocky, bearded young man in a morning suit and starched collar. Emma and Clive on their wedding day. The next photo made her heart stop and then go racing on. It was Emma again, standing with her friend Candice. And, as Stella stared at the image, she was stunned to see that Candice had in no way altered. She was still the same – the vampire princess who had welcomed her to the monastery last night.

Quincy had gone to the party with his defences firmly in place, but it wasn't long before Allegra and her sisters won him over completely. Their customised dungeon was everything he could have hoped for, far superior to any he had visited in and around 'the scene' he frequented in London. If they were the erl-king's daughters, then so be it. He revered *babushka's* memory, but she could take a running jump. And if they be vampires, along with their haughty brother and his white-faced queen? What the hell? He'd read enough on the subject to protect himself, hadn't he?

What he saw there that night convinced him that Dimitri ran a tight ship, the happenings organised to the last degree of sophistication. The women were superb, the men attractive, and Quincy never had been able to resists congress with either sex. The last thing he expected to find in the depths of the Irish countryside was an orgy. He flung himself into it wholeheartedly. Nubile girls, chained to the thick pillars that upheld the ceiling, were well schooled in submission, and Quincy had been spoilt for choice – the tools of punishment of the finest quality. Their cries were music to his ears, their wet slits and well stretched arseholes his for the taking.

Robed in scarlet, in place of his evening gear, he had felt ten feet tall, his excited tool protruding from the front closure. He was treated like an emperor, conducted to a marble bath set in the floor and surrounded by squat, perfumed candles. Handmaidens disrobed him, entered the bath with him, soaped and sponged and pampered him, while Allegra looked on, Medea nodded and smiled her catlike smile, and Madelon leaned over to tweak his wine-red nipples and trace whorls in his wet chest hair. His cock was teased until it was ready to burst, and a nude Adonis slipped into the water beside him, and pressing against his back persistently, inveigled his stiff weapon into Quincy's anus.

So many delights all at once had forced a groan from his lips, and this was quickly stifled by Allegra's mouth feeding off his. He could taste his own blood on his tongue, and faint and faraway, heard *babushka* calling to him in her cracked ancient voice.

'Don't listen to her,' Allegra insisted, and her fiery hair tumbled over his face like a veil, blinding and deafening him to everything except the witchery of her caresses. He even forgot to wonder how she knew about his grandmother.

'You know Stella in every way, including the biblical,' said Madelon, with a sneer.

Quincy freed his lips but not his cock. Allegra was under the water now and he could feel her sucking it, milking it, dragging him along the road to ecstasy.

'Yes, of course I know her,' he replied, though his voice was strangled.

'Then you'll control her. Dimitri and Candice have a task for her. It concerns Lady Emma. If she refuses, then she'll incur their wrath and maybe you as well, as you call yourself her master.'

'I don't understand,' Quincy groaned, his balls aching and tight, Allegra's fingers pressing down at the base of his cock, stopping him from coming.

He was too far gone to bother about the question of how she managed to stay under water for so long. His lust intensified when other arms and silken limbs wrapped around him and he felt teeth nipping him all over. Black hair and blonde now joined red to bind him in a perfumed net. He was unable to move, their helpless victim, and even as they crawled all over him like slippery mermaids, so he felt his strength leaking from him, in his blood and in the great flood of semen that Allegra swallowed with the avidity of an infant gorging on breast milk.

He slid down in the bath until his head rested back against the tiled rim. He had climaxed, yet still burned with lust, his cock hard again. Allegra surfaced and straddled him, gripping his head between her iron thighs and sitting on his face, her large clitoris rubbing against his lips till he parted them and took it inside. He was smothered by scented water and Allegra's own pungent essences, her dark pink labia stretched and her hole gaping, her clitoris pulsing as he sucked it. Her spine was arched, her face contorted, lips drawn back over long, bloody teeth, eyes screwed shut as she reached

Nirvana, yelling as she came.

Madelon tumbled her off, both hissing and yowling like cats in season. Quincy was hardly given time to draw breath before the blonde settled over him, back to him this time, her tight buttocks spread, the cleft slicing through her from anus to clit fully exposed, her mouth diving down to fasten on his militantly upright cock. He licked her crack and fastened on her bud and she humped up and down on his face. At the same time the Adonis's place had been taken by Medea, fingers wriggling into his arsehole, while she masturbated against his thigh clenched tightly between her own.

He couldn't see much, his view blocked by Madelon's haunches, but it seemed that the water had turned to blood. Even the soap bubbles held a ghastly hue. He knew fear and exaltation. If they were vampires, then did this mean they had fed on him and he would become one of them, living forever? The idea appealed to him enormously. Immortality! The women and men he could screw. The money he could make.

'Don't even think of it, Costache,' said Dimitri, watching him from the side of the bath, arms folded across his chest. He was speaking in Rumanian and, though he had not used the language for years, it came flooding back to Quincy.

'How do you know what I'm thinking?' Quincy spluttered, as the women were suddenly snatched from him, although he had not noticed Dimitri move. They now sat huddled on the tiles, glowering at their lord and master.

A look of supreme pride settled on Dimitri's distinguished face. 'I am as you suspected,' he said coldly.

'I don't believe you,' Quincy spluttered, refusing to accept what his genes, his birth, his ancestry dictated was true.

Dimitri shrugged. 'It doesn't matter what you believe, and you're lying anyway. We come from the same background, almost the same country, and understand the old traditions

164

and superstitions that are firmly rooted in the truth. As these hellcats have just said, I need Stella, and you will help me to get what I want.'

Quincy looked up into those deep, hypnotic eyes and saw the pine forests and mountains of his homeland, his heart yearning till he thought it would break. It had been so, so long...

'Will you make me as you are?' he asked anxiously. '*Nosferatu*?'

Dimitri smiled thinly. 'No, my friend.'

'But why not? I want to be like you.'

Dimitri turned away. 'One has to have very special qualities to be selected for this terrible yet marvellous condition.'

'Spawn of the devil!' Quincy spat, enraged by this rejection.

Dimitri half-turned and somehow Quincy felt himself held by the throat high over the bath, helpless as a landed fish. 'This is not true,' his captor snarled, as dangerous as a wild animal at bay. 'We are part of creation, too, but then so is Satan. Each and every one of us have a place in the scheme of things.'

'I'm sorry,' Quincy croaked, the pressure unbearable. 'I'll do whatever you say, master.'

He was dumped down unceremoniously, winded and bruised and fearing for his life. In the next moment he was fully clothed again and rounding up his companions, ready to transport them back to Troon Hall. He was stunned, but conscious that time had no meaning here at St Cuthbert's. It was dawn, and Carl brought Stella to him – a dazed, wide-eyed and bewildered Stella. Kate was not available, and Conlan travelled independently.

'Was it you who brought me home, undressed me and put me to bed?' Stella asked when Quincy strode into her bedroom. She was dressed now, and Emma's diary still lay where she had dropped it on the bed, though she had intended returning it to its hiding place.

'It was,' he answered, and he was looking so remarkably handsome that her mixed feelings were hard to comprehend. She loved Lazio, yet this man fulfilled her need to have someone with the ability to defeat, surprise and even bully her.

'I hope you didn't take unfair advantage of me.'

'Would I?' he asked, hand on heart.

'I'm not sure,' she said, wondering whether to confide in him, in an agitated state far worse than any she had known.

'What happened last night?' he asked, his hard blue eyes boring into hers. 'Were you a naughty girl? Did you do rude things with Lazio?'

Her chin tipped up mulishly, gamin and delectable in her tight jeans and crop-top, her hair screwed up on the crown of her head, with little fronds wispy around her neck, cheeks and forehead. 'I feel an empathy with him that I've never known with anyone else. It's as if we've known each other before, in past lives.'

'Oh my, how very cosmic!' he mocked 'You'll be telling me next that he's your soul mate.'

'I think he is,' she averred, out-staring him, and her pussy clenched at her defiance; it gave him a splendid reason for punishing her, not that he needed one. And she wanted to be chastised, feeling tainted, unclean, a debased creature who had been associating with vampires.

'Then why aren't you ecstatic?'

'If only it was as simple as that,' she sighed, and sat down in the edge of the bed.

'Come along, tell me all about it,' he coaxed, and put an arm round her.

'I can't; you'll never believe me,' she said, close to tears.

'Relax… masturbate for me,' he commanded, and his fingers dug into her shoulder. 'Do it slowly, and then tell me what's troubling you.'

She was shocked, but wriggled her bottom into the mattress, aware of the wetness of the tight seam that penetrated her slit. If she did as he commanded it would take her mind off her major problem, for a while at least. He moved back, swung his legs up on the bed and rested against the pillows, smoking a cigarette and watching her.

She unfastened her jeans and squirmed out of them. Now she wore only her panties and crop-top.

'I thought I told you never to wear knickers in my presence,' Quincy said.

'But I didn't know—'

'Take them off, and leave them off.'

Stella did as he told her, and then positioned herself on the bed so he could enjoy an uninterrupted view. Holding his eyes with hers, she began to fondle her nipples through the tight, white cotton. She wore no bra, and two points soon appeared, rising eagerly under her fingers, darkening the fabric. She could not suppress a moan. Still rolling those hard teats she let her other hand idle down, and her thighs fell open.

She let her gaze wander from Quincy's face to his crotch. The material of his trousers was distorted by his massive erection. Stella let go of her breasts, using her left hand to hold her sex lips apart as she started to masturbate. Her nubbin was already stiff and she circled it carefully, wanting to make this last. She daydreamed, summoning up one of her favourite fantasies. In it she stood with her legs spread wide, in front of a vibrator that was glued to a wall at just the right height to reach her clit. It was buzzing, and she angled her hips so that the tip touched her bud. As she now inserted a finger in her vulva and drew it out coated in honeydew, then applied it to her little pleasure-dome, so she imagined the vibrator humming, thrumming, buzzing – its inexorable force taking her higher and higher.

She closed her eyes, her moist lips parted and soft cries

sighing from her throat. Her finger moved over her engorged clit. The imaginary dildo vibrated and she stood before it, legs braced and wide, lifting her hips towards promised bliss. She was almost there, bringing herself to climax.

Quincy leaned over, grabbing her hands and hauling her up. 'That's enough,' he grated harshly.

'But I haven't come,' she protested, struggling in his grip.

'I know,' he replied. 'I'll say when you may.'

Stella felt frustrated and humiliated. She snatched one hand free and slapped him across the face. He paled dangerously, his eyes sparking, and then returned her blow with a force that set her ears ringing.

'First, you'll tell me what's wrong,' he threatened.

She had never been hit like that, and such aggression was alien to everything she believed in. It was different to when he used it as part of a sex ritual. This was violence for its own sake, and she clung to the bedpost as she recovered, frightened of the heavily built man. She started to snivel, unable to stop herself. Today had started badly from the off, and she trembled to think how it might end. 'Why did you do that?' she sobbed.

'Time for the truth, Stella,' he said grimly.

Hesitantly she pointed to the journal near her pillow. 'Read it,' she sniffed. 'It's Lady Emma's diary and a letter to me. You'll think I'm barking, but I saw her early this morning and she told me where she'd hidden it.'

'You saw her ghost?' He didn't sound so incredulous as she had expected.

'That's right. It's all to do with her and Candice. She says Dimitri is a vampire, and his sisters, and that Candice became one to stay with him. But she can't reach her friend, that's Candice, and wants me to help them. I can only assume that Lazio is one of their diabolical breed, and was ordered to entrap me. He doesn't love me at all, and wants to use me.'

To her astonishment Quincy did not laugh. He simply sat

168

there very quietly reading until he had come to the end of the weird narrative. Then he looked at the photographs and read the letter. Stella watched and waited, her clit burning with unsatisfied desire, and her fingers itching to caress it to completion. But she was afraid to move.

When Quincy put the book down at last, he looked across at her and said, 'This is all true. I know. I've been speaking to Dimitri. I don't know about Lazio's feelings for you, but you must do as they wish.'

Stella sprang up, seized her jeans and hurriedly put them on. 'I can't!' she cried, zipping up and snagging a fingernail on the top button. 'They're fiends! Monsters who feed on blood!'

'Oh yes you can, my dear,' Quincy said calmly, and she wanted to cry on his shoulder and be held and comforted like a little girl.

'No,' she insisted. 'It's madness.'

'But you want to make Lady Emma's ghost happy, don't you? And after you've done it, I'll make you a superstar. I'll lay the world at your feet – Svengali to your Trilby. What do you say?'

She tore herself away from him. 'No,' she repeated. 'I'll have nothing to do with it. Why are you getting involved? What's in it for you?'

'Dimitri fascinates me. I want him to give me the gift of immortality. At the moment he refuses, but if I prove myself to be a loyal servant, he may relent.'

Stella wanted to slap him again; he was even more monstrous than the vampires, actually wanting to become one of them. And his motive was greed, she was sure.

'You disgust me,' she hissed, but he merely sniggered and pulled her into his arms.

'We'll drive to St Cuthbert's,' he said. 'We'll take the journal and show Candice, then we can talk it over.'

But it was Lazio that Stella wanted to see. She needed

some explanations from him, still unable to believe that he could be so insincere. She capitulated, not in her resolve to deny the vampires, but in agreement to at least thrash it out with them.

She picked up her denim jacket and shoulder bag and stalked ahead of Quincy out of the door, her spirits low, but her head as high as a queen's.

Chapter Nine

It had started to rain by the time Quincy and Stella reached St Cuthbert's in the late afternoon. A fine, misty rain, that they were beginning to realise was the reason for Ireland being so green. So far, Stella had not seen a single leprechaun or heard the wail of a banshee, but she had come across a fairy ring in Troon Hall's grounds. As she had now been shunted into believing in ghosts and vampires, then all else must follow. This included fairies at the bottom of the garden and flying saucers from outer space, to say nothing of aliens landing and abducting earthlings.

And, as the wheels turned and the lush countryside flashed by the car's windows, so lyrics formed in her head, and she wanted Conlan or Kate to put them to music.

'What are you thinking?' Quincy asked, one hand resting lightly on the steering wheel, the other draped high on her thigh.

'I was thinking that we need to get back to rehearsing,' she said bluntly, unable to refrain from rubbing against his finger, acutely frustrated because he had stopped her achieving fulfilment. 'That is if you're serious about booting *Zero700* to the top.'

'It's all in hand,' he said, calmly reassuring. 'Conlan has brought me two new numbers and we'll be trying them out tomorrow, ready for the gig in Dublin next Saturday. I've heard from Max Golding of *Global Inc*, and he's organising the tour in the States. I've sent Sherry home to deal with the details. All you've got to worry about is placating Dimitri and Candice. Leave the rest to me.'

Oh, I will, when it comes to *Zero700*, but not the rest of it, she thought. Her instincts were against helping Emma and Candice, unless she could be convinced that it would be beneficial to their immortal souls. She brooded on her dilemma as they stopped outside the grey, monastic building. Rainwater trickled from the mouths of gargoyles on the guttering. She supposed that in many ways she had been blessed, allowed to peep beyond the veil that separated human beings from the mysteries. Now she had absolute proof of life after death – normal death like Emma's, and also of the existence of those who were Undead. She'd even fucked one of them, for God's sake! The memory of Lazio's cold cock buried inside her made her shudder with disgust, superstitious terror and rampaging lust.

Quincy switched off the ignition and grimaced at the view. 'Blimey, I could do with a spell in the Bahamas,' he complained, then flung open the door and got out. He went round and opened the one on the passenger side, and Stella stepped gingerly into the penetrating drizzle. Her sandals were not designed for this and her feet were soaked instantly.

St Cuthbert's was silent as the grave. 'I suppose they're asleep,' she said, and tried to turn it into a joke. 'That's what vampires do, isn't it – sleep during the day, afraid of being reduced to a cinder by the sun's rays? What about garlic and crosses and holy water? And shouldn't we have brought stakes and a hammer? Oh, but I forgot; they're your friends, aren't they?'

'Yes, and yes again; all these things apply,' he replied, unfazed by her sarcasm. 'We can wait inside till dusk. There's plenty I want to show you.'

'How are we going to get in?' She disliked this venture more and more, and it became worse when they reached the top of the steps and stood beneath the stone portico, where she received her answer. Bolts were drawn back, grinding and squealing. The heavy door opened ponderously on protesting hinges and Carl was there, unsmiling and grimfaced. 'The master is not available,' he said, in his deep, hollow voice.

'I know, but he's given me permission to wait his return to the land of the living,' Quincy replied, with a trace of irony. 'And I've brought Stella Kerrick, as he ordered.'

'Very well, sir, come in.'

It was as gloomy and desolate inside as out. Gas flares gave a reddish light, and their footsteps echoed in the great assembly hall. Apart from this, there was a deathly hush. 'The dungeons,' Quincy commanded.

Carl led them along a corridor to the rear of the lower floor, then down winding steps that seemed to go on forever, penetrating the very foundations of the monastery. He flicked a switch, and the dungeons began to glow faintly. Stella followed Carl with mounting trepidation. The subterranean vaults seemed endless. They were not exactly cold, though draughty in some places, as if air was coming in through hidden crevices in the arched brick ceiling. But Stella was frozen, clinging to Quincy's hand.

'What is this?' she asked shakily. 'Catacombs? Are there bodies of long dead monks down here?'

'My master and mistress take their rest in the crypt a little further on, and the princesses sleep too,' Carl answered, with a ghoulish twist of his lips. 'But the rest of it is for entertainment, you might say.'

'What do you mean, entertainment?' she demanded, revolted by the gruesome creature. Was he a vampire too? Then how come he was about in the day? Where did he fit into the scheme of things?

'It's like theatre,' he went on, a little spittle spraying. 'We even have a small stage here. The prince and his lady enjoy the show, and so do their disciples. You're wondering how I come to survive amongst them? How much do you know, Miss Kerrick?'

'Most of it,' she returned smartly. 'I've read Lady Emma's diary.'

'Ah well, have you now? I remember Lady Emma.' He led them into an enormous chamber where the flickering light illumined a crosspiece, and various pieces of equipment the use of which baffled Stella. Some of it was like that furnishing a gymnasium, but fitted with iron bolts and chains, and she saw the stage at the far end, with its crimson curtains closed. The implements hanging on hooks around the walls were instantly and painfully familiar.

'You were alive that summer in Venice?' she faltered, trying to pull back but encouraged forward by Quincy.

Carl gave a wheezy laugh. 'Oh yes, that summer and a hundred summers before and since. He gives me life, you see. He's my saviour, my master... my king. I'm almost mortal, but not quite. I don't drink blood and can digest food, but I serve the family in every way. I cook, clean and organise for them. They drink of me if other sustenance isn't available. The ladies also suck my cock and ingest my spunk. I like it when they do that.'

Stella shuddered violently, the idea of getting anywhere near the repulsive creature making her feel sick, and she hoped desperately she would never have to endure fellating him.

'Come along,' Quincy said, and guided her towards the stage. It was raised several feet from the floor and there were footlights and spotlights and everything needed for a theatrical performance.

'Have I to get up there?' she asked nervously. 'What do you want me to do? Sing?'

He chuckled wickedly. 'I don't think so, my dear. I doubt that singing is what Dimitri has in mind. It all rather depends on your co-operation.'

'I've told you I have no intention of aiding him and Candice,' she said stubbornly.

'And what about the unhappy Lady Emma?' he asked slyly. 'Why did you bring her diary along if you weren't ready to discuss it with Candice?'

She had it in her shoulder bag. 'I don't know, I'm not sure. Perhaps I thought it only fair that she should see it and realised that Emma had not forgotten her.'

'Poor Candice,' he continued persuasively. 'I think your heart might melt if you were to see her as she is at this moment.' He turned to Carl. 'Will you take us to where she sleeps?' he asked.

'The master didn't give me instructions,' Carl muttered sullenly.

'He told me to do anything in order to convince Stella that her task is absolutely vital.'

'Very well, sir,' Carl said, lifting his bowed shoulders in a shrug.

He led them down a narrow passage away from the main vault, and then entered a crypt. It was pitch-black and had a damp, musty odour that made Stella's nose wrinkle. 'What is that smell?' she asked, hanging back.

'Earth brought from the foundations of his castle in the Carpathian Mountains,' Carl grunted, lifting the torch he carried, the smoky flare casting a weird light over the interior. 'The master needs to place some wherever he decides to sleep. It keeps him safe.'

There was nothing in the tomb except a catafalque, draped in purple and black. Carl beckoned Stella over and held aside one of the curtains. Hardly daring to breathe, she peered in.

There lay Dimitri, stretched out on his back, attired in a frilled white shirt with bell sleeves, his raven locks curling round his shoulders, his sculptured cheekbones and patrician nose giving him the appearance of a slumbering aristocrat. He was so handsome that she longed to touch him, to run her fingers over that chalk-white face. Then she saw his mouth, blood-red lips parted over uncannily long teeth, and

175

his eyes glinted beneath those semi-transparent lowered lids. He seemed to be watching her.

She gasped, shivered and wanted to run from that place of death, but Candice was on his far side. Candice, clad in flowing white, corpse-pale and lovely, but like her husband, held in a trance-like sleep. As Stella watched in awe she saw a pink-tinted tear appear between those curling eyelashes and course down the ashen cheek. She remembered her own tear that Lazio had turned into a diamond drop. She wanted to break down and sob, sensing Candice's longing to be with Emma. But she couldn't – she just *couldn't* offer her aid to this terrible, beautiful woman.

'Where is Lazio?' she whispered to Carl.

'Close by, in the next cell,' he replied. 'And the princesses have their own.'

She turned away, and was thankful to feel Quincy's arms around her, a real, solid, mortal man. She must forget Lazio, forget the diary, Emma and Candice, and return to sunshine, life and laughter and song, away from these dank, cold environs, away from the dark temptations they offered.

'We must leave, *now*,' she urged, releasing herself from his embrace and tugging at his arm.

'Oh, no,' he said grimly, then glanced towards the catafalque. 'In any case, it's too late.'

Stella spun round. Dimitri stood there, with Candice at his side. Their clothes had vanished and they were both naked, two perfect beings. He was tall and muscular, with wide shoulders and a narrow waist, tapering hips and strong thighs, his erect phallus springing from an ebony thicket. Candice was a head shorter, as lovely as a Greek goddess, her skin like alabaster, her breasts tipped with coral, ready to be kissed, her tiny waist and flaring hips curving deliciously to shapely thighs and dimpled knees and feet that would have graced a dancer. Her golden curls flowed over her breasts and down her back.

Oblivious to everything save their need for one another, she dropped to her hands and knees and Dimitri mounted her from behind. He snarled as he plunged his ramrod stiff phallus into her, lifting her to meet his thrusts. He pumped in and out vigorously, and reached under her to rub her clitoris. It was a brief, animal mating, and he barked as he fucked, while Candice moaned and they both howled as they reached their mutual apogee.

The next moment they were fully dressed again, and he was glaring at Carl. 'What are they doing here?' he demanded.

Carl prostrated himself, flat on the stone floor. 'The man said you gave him permission to enter, master,' he gabbled. 'He has brought the girl, the one who will make our queen happy.'

Stella was scrutinised by those green, lupine eyes and, just for a moment, watched Dimitri's tongue lick hungrily over his sensual crimson lips, then he said, 'So, you've obeyed me, have you, Costache?'

She couldn't understand the language and wondered who Costache might be. Then Quincy answered in English. 'I have, master,' he said. 'She has read Lady Emma's journal.'

Candice was at Stella's side, an arm around her as she turned her luminous gaze to her. 'You will help us?' she asked eagerly.

Stella inched away, though Candice's perfume was enticing and her manner soft and seductive. 'I can't,' she replied.

'You will!' Dimitri roared, and he was everywhere in that small chamber, filling it with his force and fury.

'You can't make me,' she said defiantly. 'I don't wish to be unkind, Candice, but I find you and your kind abhorrent.'

'Won't you do it to make Emma happy?' Candice pleaded, her pale hands fluttering as if she would pluck a solution out of the air.

'No, I'm truly sorry, but no.'

'That's it!' Dimitri roared, his face working with rage.

'Take her to the torture room. Put her on display on the stage. Keep her there till I get back. I'm hungry and must feed. Come, Candice.'

He seized her hand and they became a single whirling pillar of light, then it disappeared, and they were gone.

'Where's Stella?' Conlan demanded, finding Stephen in the conservatory, drinking coffee, smoking, and staring discontentedly at the rainy garden.

'I don't know,' he answered, and it didn't sound as if he cared. 'Haven't seen her since last night, just before she went off to that do at the monastery. She's a bitch, you know. Going around like Lady Muck, giving old Rogan and his missus instructions to keep tabs on me.'

Conlan was not surprised. There was nothing trustworthy about Stephen. It wasn't anything he said or did particularly, just an emanation that hinted at dirty dealings and trickery. 'I'll go find Kate and see if she's seen her today,' he said.

'Can I come?' Stephen said, already on his feet. 'I'm bloody bored.'

Conlan would have preferred not, but the man was Stella's brother, after all, dislikeable rogue though he was. He set off in the direction of the salon, drawn by the sound of musicians practising.

They were playing one of his new pieces, and his critical ear was tuned to the mix. He could have done better, was his first thought, never satisfied with his work. There was a grand piano conveniently installed there, fifty years old and all the better for it. Kate had set up her keyboards and Jez his drum kit, while Tommy was taking up the refrain on the fiddle in the places where Stella would have filled in with the lyrics, had she been there.

'Hi,' Kate said, waving to Conlan as he appeared. Everyone stopped playing, welcoming a break.

'Have you seen Stella today?' he asked, attempting to keep

the anxiety from his voice.

'As a matter of fact, I haven't,' Kate said, swinging her legs as she sat on a stool before her instrument. 'But she slept in her bed, so Maureen says. Then she and Quincy went out this afternoon. I wasn't around, still recovering. Made quite a night of it at St Cuthbert's. Dimitri and company certainly know how to party. I don't remember getting home. Why, what's up, Conlan?'

'I'm worried about her,' he said, getting vivid flashes of the hitchhikers and Stella being flung across his windscreen.

'Didn't you enjoy yourself?' Kate questioned. 'I must confess I can't recall much of what happened, but it seems like I had a ball.'

'I enjoyed meeting Belphegor. Let's hope he feels as generous today as he did then. He offered to back my opera. In fact, I think I'll drive over later and find him. Maybe Stella's there already.'

'Maybe she is. I'll come with you.'

'So will I; seems like I missed out,' put in Stephen, and Conlan's heart sank; the man was a complete pillock. How on earth could he be Stella's brother?

'Maybe I'll come along, too,' said Jez, eyeing Kate suspiciously, who grinned back cheekily, keeping him dangling. Conlan had already deduced that Jez was fonder of her than he liked to admit. Did he know about her interest in women?

'And me,' added Tommy. 'We didn't get far on the poteen search. The locals are as close as a gnat's arsehole.'

A gaggle of them then, Conlan thought. They should be able to ensure that Stella comes to no harm. Yet those weird sisters, like something from *Macbeth*. Were they Satanists? Was Dimitri the leader of a cult – even a coven? And how could they have made him see Stella, broken and fatally injured? Thinking about it made his head ache, and heightened his fear that he had somehow lost the plot. But music wise he was awash with ideas, his brain almost overloaded.

'We'll have dinner first,' he said, unwittingly assuming the mantle of leader.

'And then go to the pub?' suggested Tommy.

'No pub,' Conlan insisted. 'I'll take my car with Kate and Stephen and you can bring the van,' he said, needing to feel free in case he had to make a quick getaway, though from what he wasn't quite sure.

'Strip,' Quincy commanded, a cold, unfeeling master once they entered the punishment chamber.

'I won't,' Stella rejoined fiercely, though she was trembling inside.

'I said strip. If you don't do it willingly, then I'll order Carl to assist you.'

This galvanised her into action, horrified at the thought of being touched by those gnarled hands, the curving talons underlined by half-moons of dirt. Cursing loudly, she pulled off her jacket and her white top, naked to the waist. The sandals came next, then her jeans. She folded one arm over her naked breasts, and cupped her mound with the other, but Quincy would have none of that, striking her smartly and dragging her arms behind her. She felt a rope being passed tightly around her wrists.

Close to tears, she hoped against all hope that Lazio might appear. If Dimitri was awake and hunting, then her vampire lover would be doing likewise, and the three harpies. Perhaps he would return before them, appetite sated, ready to defend her against all comers.

Carl and two male slaves were busy preparing the stage. They were twins, as alike as two peas in a pod, handsome in a bright, blond way, with hair the colour of butterscotch. They looked as if they worked out regularly and spent much time under solar lamps, their skin a deep coppery hue. They were comfortingly human, and seemed to embrace their slavery with zest, naked apart from bondage straps and nipple rings, their cocks partially erect. They obeyed Carl without demur; encouraged by the short handled whip he applied to their backsides with relish.

Under his direction they manoeuvred a piece of equipment into place. It was a large wooden frame. Chains clinked and swung, and when it was firmly fixed centre stage, Quincy shackled Stella's wrists to the top corners and her ankles to the bottom ones. She was spread-eagled, arms strained above her head and out, feet resting on a rung, her legs straight and wide open. In this position her sex was fully exposed and vulnerable. There was no way she could stop anyone from touching her intimately, not even that ugly brute, Carl.

Full-length mirrors hung on the walls and she looked into the one opposite, seeing herself hanging, a naked young woman, completely helpless and a plaything for all. It was lewd and exciting, and she was almost ready to come, the juice seeping from her cleft. She longed for Quincy to caress her breasts and explore her vagina and the tight rosebud of her anus. Above all, she burned for him to rub her clitoris, which was still in a highly aroused state from her own earlier ministrations.

The contraption to which she was bound had its base set on a turntable. At the moment she faced the proscenium. Had there been an audience, she would have presented full frontal nudity. As it was the only eyes that gloated on her were of the twins, Carl, and Quincy. The latter seemed to be deliberating, rubbing his chin thoughtfully, then he went over to the rack of instruments and selected a whip with a triangular tip. He swished it through the air experimentally, then replaced it and balanced a cane in his hand. This did not seem to suit either, so he lifted down a flogger, a nasty device with nine tails. He flicked it and it sang for him. Stella's tethered legs started to shake.

Quincy strolled over and snapped his fingers at the twins

who obediently turned the frame. Stella now faced painted scenery depicting a mythical landscape complete with a ruined temple where a plump Venus sported with a well-endowed shepherd, while chubby, winged cupids frolicked among cottony clouds.

Stella braced herself for what she feared was to come. She felt Quincy behind her, and then jumped as, with a lazy flick of his wrist, he dropped the flogger across her shoulders. It didn't hurt, not then. In a leisurely manner he drew the tails down her spine, then pulled it back and let it land across her right buttock with considerable force. Stella yelped, bucking against her shackles, sweat breaking out all over her. He repeated the motion, but swiped those vicious lashes over her left side this time. It stung unbearably, and she imagined red stripes marking her soft rounded bottom.

'Are you prepared to aid Candice?' he said in a mild, fatherly voice.

She could taste blood where she had bitten her lip, but refused to give in. 'No,' she gasped.

He sighed, more in disappointment than annoyance. 'Oh dear, such foolishness. You know we'll win in the end.'

The frame rotated and he stood in front of her. She watched the flogger in fascinated terror. It was black, with a plaited handle, and her backside burned from its caress. He smiled, and had never seemed more devastatingly attractive.

'Untie me,' she begged. 'I want to make love to you.'

'Do you, indeed? Well, it's up to you, darling. Do as they want, and you shall have all the sex you can take. Continue to be defiant, and pain will outweigh pleasure. This is only the beginning.' He lifted his arm and she flinched, but he merely tickled the tails over her breasts, lingering on the hard nipples and continuing across her belly and down to her cleft. Stella writhed in an agony of desire as he worked the whip handle into her vulva, drawing it out, shiny with her juices, then working it back in again. At the same time he palpated her clitoris and she was on the screaming edge of completion, tears of disappointment filling her eyes when he roughly withdrew both whip and finger, leaving her throbbing but unsatisfied.

'You're too cruel,' she whimpered, but he made no reply, walking round and round the frame ensuring that the flogger left no part of her unattended. With an occasional movement of his wrist he varied the blows; sometimes they were caresses, at others stinging darts that set her on fire. Slowly, his gentleness faded and the tails descended with more force. Stella whined, unable to control herself. He paused, and his hands glided gracefully over the flesh he had marked with the flogger. She waited, hoped, sobbed and prayed that he might fondle her clit, enter her pussy, and give her the relief she craved.

Every aspect of her torment was reflected in the mirrors, and she saw how he moved his hand round to her bottom, smoothing the reddened globes that had taken so much punishment. He ran his hand low, into the deep valley to her wet sex and the anal hole and wonderful sensations soared within them.

'Do you give in?' he whispered, bending close, the male smell of him driving her crazy.

'No,' she whimpered, her mental defences cracking.

He stepped away and the leather extension of his arm landed mercilessly on her breasts, its numerous tails leaving a trail of destruction on the smooth globes. He lowered it, measured it, then struck her between her spread legs, and she couldn't stand any more, crying and screaming, but still shaking her head in denial.

He hung up the flogger and took up a cane. It hit her bottom like a streak of lightning. Then he struck her again on either cheek and she went out of control, pulling against her bonds desperately. He put his hands on her breasts and crouched low, his face level with her pussy. Orgasm was a heartbeat away, and then Quincy was hauled from her and flung into a far corner of the vault.

'You remain obdurate,' Dimitri shouted, his eyes boring into hers, filling her mind with pictures of hell and its fearful tortures. 'You shall be punished further.'

'Stop, set her free!' demanded Lazio, rounding fiercely on the older vampire. 'You lied to me, Dimitri. You didn't tell me you would treat her like this if she refused you.'

'And I didn't expect you to fall in love with her,' Dimitri stated flatly.

'I had no idea I would,' Lazio said, leaning across the frame and running the back of his hand down Stella's tearstained cheek.

'What is to be done?' mourned Candice, her eyes blue wells of pity as she looked at Stella.

'Beat her, torture her, give her to us and our demons,' chorused the sisters, licking their bloody chops, having fed deeply and well.

'No, no, I want to talk to her,' Candice insisted, and she stroked Stella's sweat-soaked hair and stared into her face. 'I've read Emma's diary, and oh, it brings her vividly to life.'

'But it was in my bag,' Stella blurted, hanging limply by her wrists, her head lowered, her body aching and sore.

'I read it without even opening it,' Candice replied, and her hands skimmed over Stella's breasts with a feather light touch. 'There are advantages to being as I am.'

'Emma disapproved of you going with Dimitri; she thought, as I do, that you were mad to love a vampire,' Stella said, but by some alchemy of her own Candice transformed the wall into a screen and projected moving pictures of herself and Emma when they were eighteen year olds.

'Look how innocent we were,' she urged. 'Did you ever see two more lovely young women? And here we are in Venice. See the gondolas and our chaperones and Henri and

Bianca. Fate can't mean to keep us apart forever. We did no harm.'

'Emma didn't, perhaps, but you threw in your lot with a blood-drinker,' Stella reminded wearily, tugging at her wrists, shoulders aching from the strained position of her arms.

'Dimitri, set her free,' Candice said.

'As you wish, my love,' he replied and Stella, suddenly released, would have fallen had not Lazio been there to steady her.

He held her close, pressing her against his erection. He kissed her, his tongue sliding between her lips, moving with hers in a dance of pure magic, but although his breath was cinnamon scented, she caught an undertone – the taste of blood. But he was healing her, the pain of her flogging receding like a fiery tide, replaced by relief and sensual pleasure. He released her mouth and took her hand and, as she watched, the raw marks of the manacles faded, leaving her wrists unblemished. Then he pushed her hand down to the bulge in his velvet trousers and rubbed her palm slowly over it. Her fingers burned with the heat, need and energy in his cock.

'Agree to help Candice,' he whispered fiercely. 'Then we can be together always. I've never wanted a woman as I want you. Even when I was a mortal I had few experiences with the opposite sex. I was a young man when Dimitri saved me, and there had been little time for love – a servant girl or two – a prostitute in the French town where I was stationed. Since then I have been a loner, as most of us are unless we find a soul mate. Dimitri found his in Candice, and I feel that you are the one for me.'

'He's a liar,' commented Madelon, shimmering in a gold lurex mini-dress, her hands cupping her breasts and lifting them coquettishly. 'He's coupled with me at many a dawning.'

'And with me at dusk,' Medea added, winding her arms

round his neck and smiling spitefully at Stella.

'It was only physical relief, nothing to do with love,' he retaliated. 'This is different. More like the bond between Dimitri and Candice. We must have known each other in a former life.'

'Balls!' Madelon snapped, and flounced off to tease Carl and the twins.

'Will you aid Candice, then stay with me and be mine for all time? Without you, I have nothing.'

His words thrilled her, heart, body and soul, but she managed to say, 'What nonsense! If the stories about vampires are true you have enormous powers, riches beyond imagining, the whole world and its recourses at your command.'

His hands were in her hair, holding her head steady as his blue eyes bored into hers. 'All this is worthless without you. I feel so alone and cold. But if you give yourself to me, then I shall be happy always. Say you will, please, my love.' His lips were on hers again, as if he could brand her with his kiss, and his cock swelled, pressing into her palm.

He was silver-tongued and very persuasive and Stella burned with desire, her nipples so stiff they hurt, her clitoris protruding from her swollen labial wings. There was nothing she wanted so much as to be alone with him in his romantic tower room. She yearned to know every inch of his body and explore the convolutions of his supple mind, and pick his brain concerning the events of the past one hundred years. She no longer doubted that he was a vampire – that they all were. The signs were there, as well as Emma's corroboration; although the chamber was hung with mirrors, not a single one of them was reflected in the glass – only herself, Quincy, the male slaves and Carl.

Lazio was hammering at her passions and her emotions. Part of her wanted to help Emma and Candice, but that other, rational, clean living and well brought up girl balked against having anything to do with fiends who consorted with wolves and bats, hunted like predators every night and glutted themselves with the blood of their victims.

'Come with me. Come,' he repeated, and with a whirlwind rush and a molecular shift, she was transported to his room. Her naked feet encountered the soft plush of the priceless Persian carpet.

Lazio caressed the back of her neck and murmured, 'Don't leave me, Stella. Stay with me. All you have to do is agree, and no one can make you do anything you don't want to do, but what harm is there in bringing two friends together? Supposing it happened to us, wouldn't we leave no stone unturned to be reunited?'

Stella didn't want to think about it further, bedazzled by him. His clothing had gone from his body and his penis rose like a lance, free and unfettered. He was upon her like a hungry wild beast, carrying her to the bed and plunging down onto it with her. His hands were on her breasts, her nipples, her wet and welcoming delta. He knelt between her thighs and she hooked her legs round his waist, drawing him to her. She stared up into his eyes as he lowered himself and inserted his tool into her vulva. She could feel herself stretching to take him and heard his savage grunt of satisfaction as he finally lodged the last inch inside her, his helm nudging her cervix. It was blissful, but there was something missing, and Stella slipped her hand down between their bodies and rubbed her clitoris. It needed more stimulation than could be achieved by contact with his cock root.

Within seconds she was riding the roller coaster to orgasm, bucking against him and crying out. Lazio pressed down, letting her inner muscles spasm round his girth. Then, when she lay quiet, breathing deeply and enjoying the final climactic ripples, he withdrew and rolled her over and dragged her hips back towards him.

She knew instinctively what he wanted to do, and her

anus clenched momentarily, then she felt his finger there, applying a sweet-scented oil and paving the way for his massive tool. He kissed her bottom cheeks, making a wide circle to end up in her cleft, and running his tongue round her quivering ring.

'Don't tense up,' he said, in that deep, cultured voice that thrilled her to the core.

'I've never done it that way,' she panted.

'I know, I shall possess your virgin arse,' he answered, and stood between her spread thighs and she felt the tip of his cock at the entrance to her forbidden hole. He placed his hands either side of her hips, and started to ease himself in.

She gasped, one part of her wanting to draw away, and another, wanton part backing up to assist him in his endeavours. He slid in, inch by inch, until she was certain that narrow passage would split asunder. Stella dug her fingers into the mattress beneath her. She couldn't scream. She could hardly breathe as his huge member gradually entered her anus. His jism and the oil he had applied earlier greased it, but even so it was as if a monstrous pole was impaling her. They struggled, and finally he prevailed, his cock penetrating her until she could feel the brush of his wiry pubic hair against her bum cheeks.

She screamed, writhing under the onslaught, but even then she felt powerful as his weapon was imprisoned inside her. She wanted to keep it there, her captive, and clenched her rectal muscles round it, hoping he would fear that he'd never be able to withdraw. She clenched and clung, wanting to own it, twist it, and he started to pull out, then thrust in again, the conflict bringing on his crisis. He was jerking, coming, swamping her in ice-cold semen.

'Ahh…' he cried, and slumped over her back, his hands reaching up to claw at her hair.

Stella gloried in his possession of her and that strange way of taking, wanting to give herself to him entirely. He moved round, holding her with an arm under her shoulder as he stared up into the shadowy recesses of the tester.

'Next time, we'll perform the joining ritual, and we shall be one for all eternity,' he said quietly, but with implacable resolution. 'You'll do what Dimitri asks, and they will plan a vampire wedding for us.'

Chapter Ten

Kate followed Conlan up the steps of St Cuthbert's and through the half-opened front door that looked as if it could withstand a battering ram. Carl stood just inside. 'Christ!' she shouted, nervous and jittery. 'Why are you lurking about? You scared the living daylights out of me.'

'I have orders to vet those who wish to enter,' Carl said solemnly. 'Would you care to state your business?'

'I'm looking for Miss Kerrick,' Kate snapped, brushing past him. 'Have you seen her recently?'

'Yes, miss…?'

'Barnes. Kate Barnes.'

'Ah, yes, Miss Barnes. Miss Kerrick is here. She arrived not long ago with Mr Dubois.'

'Take me to her.' There was dirty work afoot, Kate thought. She could feel it in her water.

Carl shook his bald head, and said, 'Sorry, Miss Barnes, but she's gone off with Mr Lazio.'

Kate exchanged a glance with Conlan, sorry that the poor idiot was allowing himself to get hurt, not by Stella but by his feelings for her. She was thankful that she didn't do emotion. Sex, yes. Matters that smacked of love, no.

'What the fuck's going on?' Stephen shouted, glaring at Carl. 'Who's this Lazio geezer? She's my sister, and I want some answers.'

'I can assure you she is perfectly safe, sir,' Carl returned, his contemptuous stare indicating that he considered Stephen undeserving of that title. 'Mr Lazio is a gentleman.'

Jez and Tommy were behind Kate, eyes wide and mouths

open. 'Watch out for flies,' she said caustically.

'Eh?' Jez said, shaking his head as if waking from a trance. 'What?'

'Your mouth; you look like a fish.'

'It's this place,' he mumbled. 'What a pad. But I could get real spooked if I was here on my own.'

'You always were a yellow-belly,' teased Tommy, but even he shifted uncomfortably, looking over his shoulder as if sensing an unseen presence.

'Prince Dimitri is in residence, Carl informed them. 'Shall I tell him you're here?'

'Don't bother – just take us to him,' Kate demanded firmly.

'And is Mr Belphegor about?' Conlan asked.

'Good evening,' answered the man himself, though Conlan could have sworn he wasn't there a second ago.

Kate was intrigued, as she had been last night. Belphegor was the epitome of elegance, reminding her of a matinée idol in a silent, black and white movie of the nineteen-twenties. Tall and slim, with a knack for wearing clothes superbly, he had panache, and even a trace of bravura.

'Miss Barnes,' he said, bending from his sinuous waist, raising her hand to his lips and kissing the back of it. 'We didn't get a chance to talk last night. You were swept away by the princesses and their slaves.'

If Kate had been of a more retiring nature she might have blushed, for as far as she could remember her behaviour had been indiscreet, to say the least. 'Are they here at the moment?' she asked lightly as they followed Carl into a sombre, candlelit room that resembled a chapel. Organ music played as it had done on their first visit, but the source was invisible.

'Of course,' he replied. 'They are expecting you.'

The impression of churchlike grandeur was increased by the golden chalices and incense burners, the icons and paintings that, on first sight appeared to be religious, but on closer inspection proved to be extremely erotic. Kate saw pictures of nuns, eyes turned to heaven as if in prayer, while they raised their black gowns and exposed their lily-white buttocks to monks who inserted large phalli into their vaginas and rectums, or beat them ruthlessly. There were others of white robed novices on their knees before priests as if at confessional, but their ruby lips were fastened round the portly prelates' cocks.

'Fuck me, will you take a look at those?' Stephen cried, going closer to peer at them in detail. He shot Kate a suspicious glance. 'What is this place? A knocking-shop?'

'Ah, there you are,' chorused the princesses, and Kate felt them all around her, pressing close, their tapering fingers touching her breasts and her sex as if clothing was no barrier.

'Where's Stella?' Kate asked.

The bizarre trio laughed. 'Don't worry about her,' advised Medea.

'You've brought young men along, too,' Allegra carolled joyously, glittering serpent-like, her flimsy gown undulating, sometimes there, and sometimes drifting away from her magnificent naked body. She homed in on Jez, and Kate did not feel the slightest twinge of jealousy. There was too much taking place within her own sexual parts, her clit throbbing, her juices flowing like a spring tide.

'This is what you want, isn't it?' Medea said to Tommy, and signalled to a gorgeous slave girl, who crawled across the floor, a bottle clasped to her large bare breasts. 'The potent firewater of Ireland. The magic poteen.'

A glass appeared in his hand and the slave knelt before him, pouring a generous libation. Then she crouched at his feet, her manacled hands creeping up the inner thigh of his tattered jeans and palming the bulge behind his flies.

'Wicked!' he exclaimed, and lifted the drink to his lips while rocking his hips against the girl's expert manipulation.

'What about me – don't I get any special treatment?' said

Stephen, and the princesses descended on him, tormenting, kissing, working him into a frenzy of lust. He was turned over to a gaggle of slave girls who bore him away to the jacuzzi situated in an antechamber.

Madelon approached Conlan, as enchanting as a naughty fairy. 'I've wanted you from the start,' she cooed, and her soft red lips parted over teeth that were small but pointed.

'Go away,' he snapped, and Kate was startled from her sensual haze by the vehemence in his voice. 'You're not human. You tormented me in my car last night. You pretended that I'd run Stella down and killed her.'

'A joke, that's all,' she said, lifting her slender white shoulders and attempting to worm her way round his body.

'I didn't find it funny,' he growled, and pushed her away. 'How did you do it?'

'You don't want to know, my friend,' put in Belphegor, and rounded on Madelon who retreated, hissing and spitting with fury. 'Leave him alone, she-devil. He's mine.'

Kate wanted to ask questions, but nothing seemed important, not even finding Stella, as she was led towards a bench upholstered in sumptuous crimson plush. Slaves stood around it, including identical twins who might have featured in a fashion magazine or been male strippers. They were utterly gorgeous, and she lusted to handle their naked, leather bound cocks, and weigh their tight balls in her hand, and delight her fingertips by caressing their golden-brown skin and honey-blond hair.

Small, impudent, female fingers removed her clothes, and she was powerless to resist, trembling in anticipation of what was to come. Then a black silk scarf was slipped over her eyes and knotted at the back of her head, reducing her senses to hearing, smell, taste and, above all touch, or being touched. Hands gripped her arms and guided her faltering feet. Then her fingers encountered the texture of velvet and her body was eased down, presumably onto the couch. She felt the material all along her spine and at the backs of her legs, and a pillow supported her head.

It was so comfortable that she might have slept, had not a collection of objects been drawn around her breasts, across her belly and into her cleft. They seemed to be attached to a hasp wielded by someone, probably one of the princesses. It had several tails, each different; one felt like leather, the next silk, a third metal, a fourth rope, and others Kate could not define. She enjoyed it, yet was apprehensive, knowing that whoever plied this instrument was a master of subtlety, and that the gentle, almost tickling administration would soon be replaced by something harsher.

Prepared though she was, she jumped as the flail smacked down across her, each thong holding its own particular sting. Her wrists and ankles were held firmly and fingers began to explore her vulva and anus, mouths licking her nipples and clitoris. A cock was brushed across her lips. She could taste its salty dew and sucked it into the cavity of her mouth. Another was thrust into one of her hands, and her palm and fingers responded to the size and heat of it, rubbing the foreskin over the glans and back until it suddenly gushed its tribute of warm, creamy rain. The one in her mouth shot in unison and she swallowed it, guessing these ardent weapons belonged to the twins.

Her clitoris was in such a sensitive state that she came herself, and felt a tongue at her anus, pushing past her ring. Then she was turned and someone was whipping her, and she screamed and struggled but to no avail. Tears soaked the silk blindfold, but she had never been more aroused. It was a relief to be so helpless, for it was usually she who was the organiser and, in sexual relationship, often the dominatrix. Now she was at the mercy of her persistent, knowledgeable tormentors, and despite the pain and the fear, enjoying every moment of it.

A rubber covered cock penetrated her vagina, pumping

until it spurted semen, then another entered her forbidden hole, making her jerk and squeal while waves of pleasure buffeted her, and she howled with delight. Sweet women's breasts and their clefts pressed to her face, then the whip, then male attention. She wanted it to go on forever, and it seemed it would, till at last she lay there half fainting, mind whirling, her body exhausted by multiple orgasms, completely forgetting the purpose of her visit – that of finding Stella.

Conlan stood in a large drawing room in an elegant Regency house in London. He recognised the area when Belphegor and he arrived; it was just off the Chelsea Embankment, a stone's throw from the River Thames.

'I'll take you to my town abode,' Belphegor had said when Kate left them to play amorous games with the princesses.

'Okay,' he recalled answering, and the next thing he knew they were there, and Belphegor had poured him a drink and urged him to make himself at home.

'You like this?' Belphegor said casually, and Conlan noticed he did not have a glass of wine himself, neither did he smoke, though he offered a silver cigarette box and used a gold lighter to ignite one for him. 'You can have it as your base, if you want. I'm not here a great deal.'

Conlan was nonplussed. 'That's a most generous offer,' he began, leaning forward with his elbows on his knees. 'But I don't understand. How did we get here? And why should you want to help me? The rent on this place would be well out of my league.'

Belphegor waved a delicate, limp-wristed hand. 'No rent, my boy,' he said. 'I own the property, among others. It suits me when I'm staying in London. It has a wonderful, dark, dry cellar. I need this to sleep in. As for the rest of it, including how we got here from Dublin with no apparent means of transport, well, you'll understand when you've read this,' and he placed a leather bound book in Conlan's hands. 'I borrowed it from Stella,' he added. 'The dear girl won't miss it and I'll replace it in a trice.'

At first Conlan hesitated. It was private property. Then his curiosity got the better of him and he read the letter first. That grabbed him, and he carried on reading Emma's diary, not stopping till he had absorbed every word, and the postscript.

'Good God!' he exclaimed, when he had finished. He raised his eyes to Belphegor, and his voice rose an octave. 'Does this mean what I think it means? Are you a vampire, too?'

'Naturally,' Belphegor replied, carefully buffing his nails in his sleeve.

'And you want to help me without feeding off me? Why?'

'Believe it or not, I revere talent, and you have been given a great gift. Music is one of my passions, and I've assisted more than one struggling composer to achieve recognition. I don't ask for much in return, certainly not your blood, but to be there and share in your glory, perhaps, when you receive your first standing ovation.'

'And you'll let me use this house?' Conlan was stunned, both by the contents of the diary, Belphegor's involvement, and the fact that he really liked the creature.

'For as long as you need it. I'm fully prepared to advance you a very large sum of money and use my considerable influence to find a theatre for *Persephone's* debut. You'd be surprised at the number of people in significant positions of power who know me and what I am and admire me for it.'

'The vampire is accepted? I'm gob-smacked.'

Belphegor clapped his hands with glee. 'The street speak of the twenty-first century is so expressive. Gob-smacked! I must remember that one. Yes, vampires are accepted in certain quarters, but we still keep ourselves to ourselves. We have had a lot of bad press down the years. Now, what do you make of Emma's request?'

Conlan thrust his hands through his unruly brown hair,

deeply troubled. 'I don't know.'

'Stella was against having any part in it,' Belphegor continued. 'Quincy knows about it and he is trying to persuade her, but Lazio has the greatest influence, and I think she'll agree and also become his bride and a vampire, like Candice did.'

'No!' Conlan leapt to his feet and started pacing the carpet. 'She can't. I won't let her. What are we going to do?'

Belphegor was considering him through narrowed eyes. 'I think I may be able to arrange that she meets a very powerful personage indeed, who may suggest a way out of this dilemma,' he said. Then he added with a touch of pride, 'Dimitri may be the leader of the Undead, but I have been around far longer and I'm sure I can swing an interview with the Archangel Micha-el.'

'You what?' Conlan was convinced he had lost the plot. He wondered if Belphegor had slipped an acid tab into his drink. Was this a bad trip?

'I'm talking of Michael, the chief angel, though I was using his proper title. There's an EL at the end of every angel's name – it means 'shining one',' Belphegor said, smiling at Conlan's bewilderment. 'Besides being adopted by the Christians, Michael was once a Chaldean deity. His name can be translated as 'who is as God', so he's pretty big in the pantheon. Like Anubis, the jackal-headed god of the Egyptians, he's a psychopomp, a conductor of souls to the other world, and there he weighs a mortal's heart in the balance, against a feather. In plain English, he arranges for one's next incarnation. Not that of a vampire, of course, as we are condemned to remain *nosferatu* till Judgement Day.'

Conlan had to sit down, suddenly weakened by this rush of information. Did he believe it, or was it so much crap? But there was the evidence of the diary and the uncanny things he had already experienced. He loathed the idea of Stella marrying Lazio and disappearing from human sight.

He wanted her for himself.

'Will she be in any danger?' he asked, filled with dread. It was all too much like his opera, Stella becoming Persephone entering the underworld.

'I think not,' Belphegor answered, crossing one slim, white-trousered leg over the other. 'Her innocence will prevail.'

'And who is going to put this proposition to her?'

'I will.'

The doorbell rang and Conlan jumped. 'Who is that? Not her, surely?'

'No, it's another friend of yours, the beautiful Alithea. Don't keep her waiting,' Belphegor advised.

'But how did she know I was here?' This was becoming more and more surreal.

'She thinks you phoned her, but actually I put the thought in her mind.'

'And the address?'

'Of course.'

'There are distinct advantages in being a vampire, aren't there?'

'It has its pluses,' said Belphegor, smiling widely, as smug as a Cheshire cat. 'Now hurry, let her in.'

Conlan crossed the hall and opened the door. Alithea beamed at him, then flung her arms round his neck, like a breath of fresh air in a hothouse. She was delightfully earthy and normal, and he responded enthusiastically, so relieved to see her that his cock rose sharply and he felt no disloyalty towards Stella because of it.

He kept an arm round her as they entered the drawing room, and she was obviously impressed.

'My!' she gasped. 'So you've moved, have you? Left your flat and the randy Mrs Loftus?'

'Not exactly – not yet. I'll explain later. Meet Belphegor.' Conlan was curious to see how she would react to him. 'He's very kindly offered me this house for as long as I want, and. what's more, he's backing my opera.'

'Charmed, I'm sure,' Belphegor said, standing up.

'Pleased to meet you,' and she gave him her hand. 'A backer. How splendid. Just what Conlan needs.'

Conlan could see she was brimful of questions and decided to pre-empt them. 'We flew over for a few hours,' he said. 'Things to organise, people to see.'

'Then we mustn't waste time, must we?' she suggested archly, and he could think of nothing except opening her chiffon blouse and caressing those upstanding breasts cradled in a black bra.

'Go ahead, my dears,' Belphegor said. 'Don't mind me.'

It was as if he had made himself invisible, and Conlan no longer attempted to control his urges. He pulled her hard against him and swooped towards her mouth. Her lips parted, welcoming his tongue. As he probed, explored and tasted, she ground her pubis against the line of his stiff cock, and shoved her breasts upwards, begging him to fondle the rock-hard nipples. He fumbled with the pearl buttons and the blouse fell open. He pushed down the black lace cups and her breasts protruded, the nipples and areolae bright with scarlet lip-gloss. He bent his head and sucked them, tasting the perfumed cosmetic and the nutty flavour of her skin.

'Over the back of the sofa,' he ordered.

She tottered across on her high-heeled mules, her hair coming unpinned, a tangle of curls the colour of crystallised ginger. Her blouse was hanging off her, the black bra straps emphasising her fair skin, and her miniskirt was wrinkled so high that the vertical line of her black panties showed, barely covering the fullness of her pudenda. Suspenders scored the generous buttocks, clipped to the lacy welts of sheer, seamed stockings. It was enough to lure a saint to sin.

Conlan chased after her, his belt dangling, his flies undone, his cock jouncing as he moved. He caught her and she leaned across the couch. It was firm and hard and straight. He paused to prepare himself, covering his tool with a silvery film of latex. Alithea bent over, her belly supported by the settee back, and he gripped her hips, getting a purchase. He used one hand to reach under her and pull at those large breasts, hearing her moan and feeling her arch her bottom, as if searching for his cock. He released her tits and dived a hand between her thighs, wetting his fingers in her copious juice and applying them to her clit.

She was writhing on his fingers, and he judged her climax to be close. His cock was more than ready to discharge and he thrust it deep into her. 'I'm coming, now!' she yelled.

He heard her and moved hard and fast, so forcefully that she screamed. His orgasm burst then, exploding like fireworks in his brain, and as she collapsed over the sofa he lay against her spine for a moment, breathing as deeply as if he had just run a marathon.

'Darling… that was super,' she vouchsafed, in her upper middle-class accent.

He kissed her cheek and pulled away. He felt a mess, his trousers down round his ankles, a wet condom hanging from his limp prick. He tidied himself up quickly, wiping his cock on a tissue and wrapping the discarded rubber in another, then dropping both into the wastepaper basket. By the time she was adjusting her clothes, he was once again presentable and in control.

'I don't suppose I can stay?' she said wistfully. 'I'll bet there are half a dozen guestrooms here, though I'd want to share your bed.'

'Not this time, sweetie,' he replied, dropping a kiss on the top of her head. 'I'm getting the next flight to Dublin. But my music drama's going ahead, and I want you to audition.'

'Oh, Con, thanks!' she beamed, and hugged him. 'That will be wonderful.'

As once before in his shabby flat, she rang for a cab on her mobile and he was soon kissing her goodbye on the

200

doorstep and promising to get in touch. Then she was lost in the darkness of the taxi, her face a pale blur at the window.

Sex with living, breathing humans was the best, Belphegor decided, and he had joined in Conlan's and Alithea's coupling with gusto. He had used his astral body to take both of them, sharing every passionate moment. He invaded their hearts, bloodstreams and nervous systems, enjoying Alithea's female parts and entering Conlan's virgin arse. He was like a shadow raping them; they didn't know what was happening, yet were aware of heightened sensation.

As a man, he rammed into Alithea's willing cunt and discharged his spunk. As a woman, he reached a far greater orgasm through the clitoris than a male could ever achieve with his phallus. As a homosexual, he plundered Conlan's fundament, fisting him before using his orifice for the last extreme of pleasure.

Belphegor was convinced there was no harm in this, as much a predator as when he fed at the dark of midnight. As Alithea sank down, replete, he smelt her voluptuous flesh and hunger washed through him. He suckled at her breast and relished the taste of her warm, sweet blood filling his mouth. Before Conlan recovered he sank his teeth into his throat, a phantom hand placed over his lips lest he be aware and cry out. Conlan's blood zinged with youth and energy, and Belphegor gained strength through its infusion with his own.

Satiated, he withdrew and observed the lovers' parting. Both seemed invigorated and the vampire was more than satisfied with his work. He usually made sure that his victims did not suffer – liking to enrich their lives, not destroy them.

'Lazio has asked me to marry him,' Stella burst out as soon as she and Kate walked into the master chamber. She had been waiting for the opportunity to talk to her since daybreak.

This had been impossible in the car with Quincy at the steering wheel.

Kate looked drained, her eyes huge in her wan face. She kicked off her shoes and curled up on Stella's bed, feet tucked under her. 'I could murder a coffee,' she said, as if Stella hadn't just announced mind-boggling news.

'I'll fetch some in a minute; I doubt Maureen's about yet,' Stella said, rather disappointed at this tepid reception. She plumped down beside Kate. 'So? What do you think?'

'What about the band?'

'It won't affect that. I'll still sing with it, but only after dark.'

Kate shot her a puzzled glance. 'Do you love him?'

'Yes, but it's complicated.'

'How so? Has he a wife already?'

Oh dear, Stella thought, and ferreted in her pocket for the journal. She held it out to Kate. 'You'd better read this,' she said.

Kate yawned, snuggling down amongst the pillows. 'Must I?' she grumbled. 'Can't it wait till I've had a coffee injection?'

'It's vitally important,' Stella insisted, so worried that she didn't know where to turn. Kate had always been a staunch ally, so sensible and level-headed. Probably too sensible to believe a far-fetched story like this one.

She went down to the silent kitchen to put on the kettle. This time of the morning was so still and peaceful. She stood at the back door and looked out over the cobbled yard, listening to the birds and seeing the sunlight drying the rain from the ancient slate roof of the stables. Pain pierced her heart like a sword thrust as she realised that if she went through with the ritual and became Lazio's wife, then it would never be possible for her to see daylight again. Other things would be on offer, wild and wonderful things – shape-shifting, time travelling, never to grow old or decay. However,

202

she was still highly confused. She loved him with every part of her being and had never felt so close to anyone, and yet...

Last night she had talked with Candice who had almost convinced her that the sacrifice would be worth it. She said she never regretted becoming one with Dimitri.

'Never?' Stella had asked.

'There are one or two things I miss,' Candice answered truthfully. 'I can never walk abroad with the sun warming my skin. Never linger in a summer garden, only at night.' Then she sobered and the pain on her lovely face brought tears to Stella's eyes. 'The saddest thing of all, is that I can never have children, never give Dimitri an heir, never bring up his sons and daughters.'

'But you have Lazio,' Stella suggested.

'That's not the same as carrying your lover's baby in your womb and giving birth to it and nursing it at your breast,' the vampire queen sighed, and Stella felt such overwhelming pity for her that she had agreed to do what she could to reunite her with Emma.

Now she regretted her impulse. For one thing, she had no idea how she was going to perform this miracle.

'What do you make of it?' she said, pushing the bedroom door open with her hip and carrying the tray across to the bed.

'I don't know what to think,' Kate said, the photographs of Candice and Emma spread out in front of her. 'Was she barking?'

'If she was, then so am I. Maybe it's in the genes. But I saw her, Kate, here in this very room and she guided me to the place where she had hidden these things. Quincy believes in vampires. He hails from Eastern Europe, apparently, where such legends are accepted.'

'I'm stumped,' Kate confessed, pouring coffee into two cups and adding cream. 'But it's the stuff of fairytales, wonderful for our songs. Who else knows? Conlan? Not

Jez and Tommy, surely?'

'Only you and Quincy, unless the vampires have let anyone else into the secret.'

'Belphegor's an oddball. He's a vampire, I suppose, if all this is true.'

'That's right. Lazio has told me everything about him, and the princesses, and how he himself became a vampire.'

Kate finished her coffee and poured some more, then she patted the space beside her and said, 'You look like a ghost yourself. We both need to sleep. Hell, I've come over all goose bumps at the idea that they may have been sucking my blood last night. Can you see any teeth marks?' And she stretched out her long neck.

'I can't see anything,' Stella said, and fingered her own throat. 'It seems they lap over the wounds and heal them at once. The same goes for the bruises and welts from beatings. They are gone in a trice.'

'But they can't banish the tiredness; I've never felt so wrung out,' Kate complained, and her head dropped back on the pillow, her eyelids closed and she was fast asleep.

Stella pulled the duvet over them both, but her thoughts were going round like a hamster on a wheel and it was some time before merciful oblivion claimed her.

They both woke refreshed and, after lunch, got together with the other band members and practised. It was like the old days, with everyone arguing and coming out with ideas and playing magnificently. Conlan sat in on it, listening to the new songs he had provided, and Quincy was alert, making notes, using his mobile and exaggerating down it as only pop group managers can. Much tea was consumed, and chocolate digestive biscuits and Maureen's home baked shortbread. It was an idyllic session, and all seemed set fair in their favour. *Zero700* looked forward to record-breaking success in the biggest concert hall in Dublin next Saturday night.

'And then there's gigs in England and the American tour in the autumn,' commented Quincy, whisky tot in hand. 'Enquiries are coming in from Canada and Australia, and Japan is testing the water.'

Once more Stella's wayward loins clenched as she looked at him and heard the deep, dark timbre of his voice. He had become even more a romantic man of mystery since she had found out that his name wasn't really Quincy and that he hadn't been born in England. If only life was more simple. She longed to turn back the clock to the day before she inherited Emma's estate, wealth and problems. She owned her a debt that she could never adequately repay and, much as she fought against it, she knew that she would do anything for the lost Candice and her dead friend.

During a break she wandered on the terrace. It was sheltered there and the sun was hot. Conlan joined her and they sat on a stone balustrade and drank tall glasses of iced lemonade prepared by Maureen. He told her about his backer, and plans for *Persephone*, and she thought how stress-free and companionable it was to be with him, and was glad they hadn't yet made love. Somehow, once that line was crossed the dynamics changed and friendship was never the same again.

She wondered what he would say if she told him that she was about to marry Lazio and become a vampire. Would his major concern be about her musical career, as Kate's had been? Looking at his clean-cut features, untidy mop of hair, and clear eyes, she thought he would be devastated at the thought of losing her. And the sunny day lost some of its sparkle as she visualised an existence where she'd be unable to communicate with him.

'I suppose we'd better go back in,' she said, hearing Tommy striking up on the drums.

'Just a minute,' Conlan said, and took her hand in his. It was a nice hand, warm and smooth and dry. She liked it, and wanted to feel it on her breast.

'What is it, Con?'

'I want you to know that you can always come to me, if you have any problems or want to talk things over,' he said earnestly, and his hand slid up her arm, his touch that of a lover as well as a friend. 'Don't hesitate to contact me, will you?'

'No, Conlan, thank you.' She awaited the inevitable kiss.

'Stella,' called Kate. 'We're ready to start.'

'I must go,' she said.

'Will you let me take you out tonight?' he ventured, and there was a sudden urgency in his voice that took her by surprise.

She had promised to see Lazio, but that would be later on. 'Yes,' she said. 'We can find a nice village pub and have dinner.' How normal it sounded. How ordinary and sweet. So different to the tempestuous swell of desire and the weirdness of her compulsive relationship with Lazio. She felt suddenly weary beyond utterance, but forced herself back to the music salon and the task of honing and perfecting her art.

By six o'clock they were worn out but jubilant, and decided to call it a day. Quincy was more than just pleased, painting elaborate word pictures of a brilliant future for *Zero700*. Even the super critical Kate was satisfied, cautiously agreeing with him.

'Conlan's taking me out to dinner,' Stella told her on their way up to their rooms. 'And then I'm seeing Lazio. Don't wait up for me.'

'Would I?' Kate said with a grin, and then a shadow crossed her face. 'Be careful,' she added.

'I will,' Stella replied automatically, but a cold chill made her shiver.

'What's the matter?' Kate asked sharply.

'Nothing – someone's just walked over my grave, that's

all,' Stella said, and tried to smile.

It was dark enough to need artificial light, and she switched on the bedside lamps, then undressed and went into the bathroom. She turned on the taps and the tub started to fill with warm water. Naked, and relishing that state, she drizzled perfumed oil on the surface and watched the bubbles form. She stepped into the bath and sank down with a contented sigh, enjoying being alone.

She needed her own space, she concluded. It would be wonderful to be at Troon Hall by herself. Just wandering around and getting acquainted with it. She wished Stephen would sling his hook. He was rapturous about St Cuthbert's on the way back. Free sex and lots of it; his idea of heaven. Little did he know that he probably provided a vampire with its supper.

She began to doze, her head resting back, the frothy water covering her shoulders. Peace, peace, and a vision of a calm pool where swans floated, a cob and his hen and their cygnets. *Swan Lake*, she thought dreamily, and caught strains of the ballet music.

She heard a rustle and opened her eyes a little. At first she thought a cob had stepped right out of her brain. Then someone said, 'Hello, Stella, I'm Belphegor.'

'You're not a swan?' she asked sleepily.

'Alas, no, though you might be deceived by my feathery breeches and the black stripe down my forehead,' he said, a handsome creature with a strong chest, shoulders and arms, his hair slicked back, his eyes outlined with kohl. He could have been a ballet boy.

'Why are you here?' she asked. 'Can't a girl have a bath in peace?'

'My apologies, but the matter is a trifle urgent. You see, I've arranged for you to see someone who will advise you what to do about Emma and Candice. Are you ready to come with me now?'

'Yes, but give me time to dress.'

'No need,' he said, and sure enough she was standing by him clothed in a translucent white robe like a Greek chiton, her body towelled dry, her hair too, and her face as skilfully made-up as if by a cosmetic artist from a film studio.

'Where are we going?' She wasn't afraid, as if she'd been on tranquillisers.

'I'm taking you angel visiting,' he said, and huge feathery wings, glistening like snow, enfolded her, and his arms, and that wonderful feeling of peace and security.

Holding her as carefully as if she was a piece of rare porcelain, he left the bathroom, left Troon Hall and entered starry realms.

Chapter Eleven

The interior of the glistening domed building resembled the
departure lounge of an international airport. It was so vast;
Stella could not see either its end or sides. It was extremely
busy. People waited in line, while others were being
interrogated by white-coated officials who sat behind large
white desks facing row after row of computers.

More were arriving in a ceaseless stream on never-ending
escalators. There were young and old, male and female and
those of crossed gender. Both Caucasian and coloured, smart
and shabby. Priests in robes and soldiers in uniform, airmen,
sailors and mercenaries, nurses, mothers carrying infants,
ladies in evening gowns, glamorous models, prostitutes,
housewives and farmers. Every type was there. Some were
happy, others despairing, some weeping, laughing or
confused. They hung around uncertainly, like passengers
waiting to board the next flight.

It was noisy, voices ringing overhead as if through the
Tannoy system at a railway station. Names were called and
guides ushered those who answered to the desks, while the
persons already interviewed were escorted away in the care
of stewards.

The computers oscillated. People shuffled up the queue,
and Stella turned to Belphegor and said, 'Where are we?'

'In the sorting office, as it were,' he chuckled, though
less bombastic than usual. Even he seemed a mite awestruck.
'This is limbo where all souls go as soon as they've left the
body. Michael will look at how they've done this time round,
and decide where they're going next.'

'So there isn't a heaven?'

'It's what you make it. If you imagine it to be a beautiful country or that you sit on a cloud playing the harp all day, or it's one long wild party, then that's how it will be for you.'

'Can you hook up with friends and relatives?' Stella asked. 'Could I see my mother and father?'

'I'm not sure how the rules will apply to you as you're only visiting.'

An androgynous individual bore down on them. It was very tall and lean and wore an iridescent robe and a high hat like a bishop's mitre. 'Your name and business,' it demanded, plucked brows raised questioningly, a pad in one superbly manicured hand, a pencil in the other.

'I'm Belphegor and I have an appointment with the Recorder,' the vampire answered, and Stella admired his cool.

'Indeed,' replied the tall one dubiously, and consulted the list. 'Ah, yes, so you have, and this must be Stella Kerrick. It's rather irregular, I must say, but if he's agreed to see you, then that's it, though I can't think why he's bothering.'

'You're forgetting something, aren't you?' Belphegor pointed out, albeit respectfully. 'Isn't he the one who intercedes between God and humans?'

'True, Micha-el is the greatest of us all,' the official sniffed, threw him a supercilious glance and consulted the notes again. 'I see that this concerns your brethren, the *nosferatu*. You are to be taken to him immediately.'

The waiting room vanished, replaced by an immaculate office. It was furnished with leather covered couches and had polished parquet flooring and chrome fittings. Bonsai trees were artistically arranged, and rainbows illuminated the walls. There was no apparent ceiling. It just went up and up, forever and forever.

The building was on a hill above a city that shone with marble, porphyry, silver and gold, stretching endlessly

whichever way Stella looked. It seemed boundless; a maze
of palaces, temples and gardens. White villas and monuments
contrasted with the blue-green of cypress groves; flaming
patches of colour and green ribbons of trees showed where
the principal roads intersected the streets and plazas.

Is this heaven, she wondered, as I imagine it?

She hadn't expected the archangel to be lounging behind a
superbly carved desk, like a company director interviewing
clients. He was dressed as an executive too, in a designer
suit consisting of cream tailored trousers and a draped jacket.
She could only manage a peep at him; he was so radiantly
beautiful it hurt. His shoulder-length golden hair was tied
back as a concession to the role he had adopted, and his
vivid blue eyes pierced her to the depths, capable of rooting
out every dark and devious secret. His austere expression
reduced her to jelly.

'Belphegor,' he said, and his voice was like a bell, or a
thunderclap, or sonorous chords of music.

'Micha-el,' the vampire answered, bowing low.

'You have a favour to ask?' the archangel replied and he
seemed faintly amused, elbows on the desk, steepling his
fingers together and regarding him over the top.

'I have, or rather I request your clemency towards the
vampire queen Candice and the spirit of her friend, Emma
Kerrick. This is Stella, Emma's descendent, who wants to
help her.'

'I know all about it,' Michael said as his eyes flashed and
impatience darkened his noble features like a gathering storm.
'I've seen what has taken place both then, now and in the
future.'

He raised his arm and the walls melted. The city disappeared
and a huge arc appeared, spanning the universe. It flashed
ceaselessly, its surface in constant motion, as if lighted
windows were opening up and closing. It reminded Stella of
a fabulous diamond necklace glittering against a black

woman's throat. It was awesome and compelling and she couldn't stop looking at it.

'What are you showing me?' she whispered, and Michael smiled, so compassionately that she could feel herself falling in love with him, aching for him to be a physical being not a celestial one, so that she could achieve the impossible and enjoy sex with him.

'The Akashic Record where everything that has ever happened has been imprinted, from the beginning of the world, the planets and the entire shebang,' he answered, and he stood beside her on what appeared to be nothing, the floor having disappeared. 'I've studied Emma's life and that of Candice and those associated with them, and your own existence, too.'

'You know what the future holds for me? Are there no choices? Is everything preordained?' She was more aware of him than anything else, tingling from the tips of her toes, through her pussy, up her spine to her cortex and down to her clitoris.

The angel's smile was all knowing, and petrifying. 'These are the questions that have puzzled philosophers for ages, along with the alchemists' quest to turn base metal into gold. Few are given answers. If it were common to all, then what would be the purpose of living? Wouldn't all humans commit suicide, if sure of a more pleasant existence in another dimension?'

'I-I don't know,' she stammered, the sacred record shimmering against a void that now changed to indigo, but more intense. 'I suppose so. Let me look.'

'Only I consult the records.'

She felt a hand on her shoulder and looked round into Michael's luminous eyes. She could bear to hold them now, and was sure he had tempered their glow. They betrayed no emotion, neither pity nor desire, or even curiosity. His blond hair was loose, framing his stern, firm-jawed face, and her gaze panned down to below his waist where his cock swayed in front of her. The Akashic Record flashed enticingly, but the angel held her tightly, absorbing her, his aura spreading around them.

'How is it that you're naked now?' she said, reality spinning away like a jewelled ball as she was lifted high in his muscular arms, close to his face, close to those marvellously chiselled lips. 'Why aren't you in armour? That's how I've always thought of you. St Michael the Dragon Slayer, with a drawn sword.'

How would it be, she wondered, to kiss an angel?

'What do you want to see?' he asked, and put her down. 'My war against evil?'

She staggered, regained her balance, and saw him in the full kit of a medieval knight; gilded chain mail and breastplate and a sumptuous tabard. Soaring, peacock feather wings rose from his shoulders. He brandished his sword and demonic hordes screamed, the ether black with their writhing forms as they fled in terror from his vengeance.

Now he was at the head of a shining host that advanced out of a bloody haze, an inexorable, endless wave of horsemen trampling their adversaries beneath their stallions' hooves. Giant paladins in gleaming armour, their faces grim beneath crested helmets, held their lances at the ready as they rode their fierce chargers forward in a blaze of glory.

It was like witnessing creation. Earthquakes tore at the revolving, floating horizons far below. Volcanoes spewed forth fountains of molten rock. Vast magenta pools whirled, and black holes appeared, sucking in the battling entities. Everything spun. There was a last blast of light, then profound darkness and the shrieks of creatures being pulled into unutterable voids in the far reaches of space.

Stella trembled and clung to Michael. She was humbled. He had allowed her to witness events that were shown to few. 'But why?' she whispered. 'Why me?'

'As a reward, perhaps. If Emma and Candice are to be reunited, then you must be prepared to make a sacrifice.'

They were in a villa with a tranquil view of olive groves and mountains. Bright-hued birds chirped and fluttered in ornamental aviaries, and the garden was pied with the vivid colours of anemones, hyacinths and poppies. And roses in profusion too, flaming scarlet and snowy-white, filling the air with perfume. Water gushed from silver pipes into basins of marble so thin that the flowers could be seen through them. It was delightfully warm. From veined alabaster columns hung awnings of purple silk to filter the strong sun and give a subtle, flattering half-light.

Michael reclined on a divan. His armour had been replaced by a short tunic girded at the waist, his feet strapped into sandal-boots. A laurel wreath banded his fair head, bathed in a halo from behind. Stella knelt in front of him, as naked as the moment she was born. Greatly daring, she stroked his coppery thigh, his short kilt riding up as he lay back. His skin felt like silk or cool water. She ached to touch the swollen penis that tented the linen, and reached towards it greedily. But his hand shot out and held her by the wrists, inches above her goal.

'Please,' she whimpered. 'Let me feel it.'

'Not yet,' he grated, but his cock stirred and she knew he wanted her.

But he was an angel!

An *archangel*, to boot!

Then she suddenly remembered a passage from Genesis, one that had always puzzled her, even in the days when she believed in the Old Testament. As she thought about it, so Michael quoted slowly: '"Now it came to pass, when man began to multiply on the face of the earth, and daughters were born to them, that the Sons of God saw the daughters of men, that they were beautiful, and they took wives of all whom they chose."'

'Is it true? Can angels mate with humans?'

'Haven't I just said so?' he answered sharply. 'Don't you read anything at all except rubbishy fiction? Giants existed in the world's early days, the offspring of angels and earth women. We called them Nephilim, and they were great warriors.'

'Are you sure these Sons of God weren't spacemen from another planet?' she ventured. 'There are theories about this.'

The angel shrugged his wide shoulders and there was an explosion of light dancing round them both, turning pink and violet and finally silver. 'Perhaps,' he conceded.

'Is that all you're prepared to say?'

'Yes.'

'I want to go home,' Stella brought out wearily, her mind overloading.

'Without securing a pardon for Candice and her friend?'

'Let me go, please, I'm so tired,' she sobbed. 'I'm only human after all, not an immortal like you.'

'Dear child, you shall return when we've concluded our business,' he said, and his hand rested lightly on her head, while his other dipped down to touch her pert-tipped breast. 'Just for now, you're not going anywhere.'

She was unable to move, chains winding like snakes round her wrists and criss-crossing her body, over her legs and down to her ankles. 'What's this?' she teased, suddenly emboldened. 'One of the perks of the job?'

'You could say that,' he rejoined, and his smile broke over her like a sparkling waterfall and she wanted to bask in it and stay there, indulging in his marvellous presence for aeons. 'You're not unfamiliar with submission. I was under the impression that you welcomed it, along with being chastised.'

'If you're so sure that you know everything, then tell me what to do about Lazio,' she asked, though scared of what he might say.

'He intends to marry you and perform the ritual exchange

215

of blood, making you a vampire,' Michael answered.

'I want it, too.'

'You think you do at the moment, but if Emma is to find peace, then you must give him up.'

'I can't,' she cried, and tugged at the cold metallic chains that stretched her arms painfully over her sides.

'There's no alternative. If you follow in Candice's footsteps, then nothing can be done.' He was behind her and she heard the rush of air and felt the full impact of a many-tailed whip on her buttocks. She screamed and jerked and realised that she was firmly fastened to the floor and escape was impossible.

'But I love him,' she whined, as the whip rose and fell, scorching her buttocks and turning her sex to liquid fire.

'It wouldn't be a sacrifice if you didn't,' Michael said, a Titan balanced on strong legs, arms akimbo, the flail dangling from one fist. 'Your renunciation of him is necessary in order to obtain redemption. In return, Emma and Candice will be allowed to meet on the astral plain, to renew their friendship and talk of days of yore. Emma was fond of Clive, a good wife and devoted mother, but never passionate about him. Candice was the love of her life. They are depending on you.'

'It's so unfair!' she raged, pulling frantically at her bonds. They parted suddenly and melted through her flesh and away.

'Do you agree?' Michael asked, and she was lost in the inky depths of his pupils.

'I… I guess so… but never to see him again!'

He held her by the hair, steadying her as he murmured, 'I can arrange for you to meet him once a year, on All Saints Eve, when the veils between the quick and the dead are thin. How would that suit you?'

'Could you do it?' She ran her fingers round his throat and caressed the nape of his neck under the fall of bright hair.

'Of course,' he said, and the full extent of his power struck her like lightening. Maybe she hadn't really believed that he was who he said he was until that moment. Now there was no doubt.

Pictures flashed against the glowing walls. He was Anubis, the jackal-headed god, who weighed souls in the balance. He was Hermes, the winged messenger. He was Mercury, holding the caduceus, the alchemical and healing symbol. He was the Prince and Commander of the Angels, and he was bothering with an insignificant nobody like her.

He touched her back and her stripes healed, no longer a sea of blistering agony. She sank down and took his huge cock in her hand, kissing it reverently, then drawing it into her mouth and sucking it, tasting the flavour of him; salty, spicy, yet sweet as wild honey. She fondled his balls with her other hand, rejoicing in the weight of those twin plums in their lightly furred sac. She heard him groan and was thrilled to be pleasuring such a superior being. She had shaken his composure, a humble mortal like herself, and the thought sent a moist quiver of anticipation through her. She freed her mouth, but continued to masturbate him.

'Will you promise to arrange this for Lazio and me? And allow Emma and Candice to meet? What can I do for you in return?' She raised herself higher and reached towards his nut-brown nipples. She licked one, and tongued the other with swift wet flicks.

'We angels have a weakness for the daughters of earth, as you already know,' he said, then lifted her and she opened her thighs and received the full force of his organ inside her slippery vagina, settling down on it, winding her legs around his waist.

He held her effortlessly, moving her gently on his mighty member so that the girth and length of it did not tear her. And he lowered his mouth to hers and probed between her lips with his tongue. She had wondered how it would be to

217

kiss an angel; it was everything she hoped for – and more. He was gentle, persuasive, masterful and a touch selfish – a potent mix. And as he kissed, so he jerked his hips a little, his phallus easing deeper into her sex, the purplish head bumping against her womb, the width expanding her walls, the base chafing against her clitoris.

His pace quickened and he hammered into her and she rode him on a surge of passion as his powerful thrusts pierced her so profoundly that she imagined herself impaled. Ecstasy poured through her as she pushed her clit against his cock-stem at every inward stroke, the air filled with the slippery sound of his frenzied intrusion into her core. She screamed and came as the energy poured out of him and into her, his climax having the force of a huge wave formed by a cataclysmic undersea earthquake. He put her down and turned her round and she fell to her knees and stretched out her arms and took her weight on her palms.

Michael held her by the hipbones and slipped his still erect member into her and penetrated deeply, withdrew, then plunged in again. He was so large she felt as if he was driving upwards through her vagina, into her belly, chest and throat. He slipped a hand under her and rubbed her clit. She came before him and he lost control, pushed her to the marble floor and filled her with his gushing tribute again.

He pulled out of her and, still stiff, was about to take her from above when he suddenly tensed. The androgynous clerk stood there, saying, 'I'm sorry to disturb you, sir, but a river has burst its banks in Africa, flooding acres and destroying villages, a jet-plane has crashed in India and there's a blood-bath in Jerusalem. Souls are arriving in their droves.'

'So what's new? It's as I expected,' said the archangel, kissed Stella briefly, and added, 'Remember. Halloween only. Enjoy your life and make the most of it. Be kind, be loyal, be loving and follow your star, but I don't have to tell you this.

You already know. I shall see you again in seventy years of your earth time, when your body dies.'

She was dressed, and Belphegor was waiting, tapping a foot impatiently.

Then there was blackness from which she emerged to find that she was back in Troon Hall, lying in the bath in a froth of scented bubbles. The hands of her wristwatch had not moved.

She sat up, the water cascading from her breasts. Had she dropped off and dreamed the whole thing? If so, then she needed a shrink. The visions were so clear in her mind and she winced as her buttocks grazed the slippery surface of the bath, her sex as sore as if she had been indulging in a week of frenzied lovemaking.

She'd had sex with the chief angel himself. It was incredible, yet she knew it was true. Hot on this came the memory of the promise she had made to give up Lazio. Tears stung her eyes and ran down her cheeks. Lazio, Lazio, her soul mate and love. How could she do it? How could she break it to him?

'He already knows,' said Belphegor, stepping from the bedroom.

'You've told him?'

'Yes.'

'What did he say? How did he take it? You should have let me do it.' She was furious with the meddling vampire that never could keep his nose out of other people's business.

He looked offended, pushing back the quiff that fell over his forehead in contrived negligence. 'You wouldn't have had the guts. Lazio would have persuaded you to change your mind. Anyway, it's done now and Candice is over the moon. She's dashed off to meet Emma.'

'So I shan't see him again?' A great bubble of pain was rising inside her, threatening to burst and drown her in despair.

'On All Saint's Eve, as arranged. Don't try to interfere

with this arrangement. One doesn't mess with angels, my dear.'

The cordless phone trilled, a reassuringly normal sound, and she picked it up. 'You haven't forgotten our dinner date, have you, Stella?' said Conlan.

'Of course not,' she lied. It had completely slipped her mind.

'I'll pick you up around eight. Okay?'

'That will be fine,' she said, and put down the phone.

'He's a thoroughly nice person, and a genius,' commented Belphegor and, though he cast no reflection, he posed in front of the bathroom mirror out of habit. 'Stick with him and you won't be sorry. That lad is going far, with my assistance.'

'We'll see,' she said darkly, not very pleased with him.

'Don't be like that,' he rejoined. 'I've put myself out for you.'

'How exactly did you manage to get an interview with Michael?'

He tapped the side of his nose, grinning at her puckishly 'That's for me to know and you to find out. Let's say that I called in a favour. Goodbye,' and he was gone, leaving a little glow on her retina, like a blown out candle.

'Don't fret, Lazio,' whispered Allegra, drifting round him, all arms and legs and breasts. 'You can see Stella once a year, and there's always me. You know how much I enjoy fucking you. Why do you need anyone else? We're here, darling, in our lair, and it's dusk.'

She was a most experienced enchantress, and no whore could best her when it came to a contest of sexual prowess. Several had tried, even the Roman Empress, Messalina, on Allegra's various visits to the ancient capital, and Messalina was renowned for her staying power, especially if there was money involved.

Lazio remained inconsolable, even while Allegra and her slaves used their expertise to arouse him. Beautiful, big-breasted girls undulated their hips and pressed their clits to his thighs. Hands were everywhere, little teasing, nipping fingers on his nipples and his cock, and testing the heaviness of his balls. Voices chanted, a wordless liturgy, the harmony obscure but tingling along his every nerve and gathering in his groin. Memories of Stella were being stifled. Allegra, her sequinned dress like a snake's scales, crept towards him, and he stood stock-still, trembling in anticipation of her touch.

It was freezing cold, but so was his flesh and he sank to his knees and knelt before her, transfixed by the red sparks in her eyes. She kissed him, fangs meeting fangs, and he tasted the rich, dark scent of blood emanating from her throat. Not fresh blood, but that of yesterday. His hunger raged as hers must do, the longing for enveloping darkness and the sweet, forbidden fruit overriding the need for sex.

'Quickly, quickly,' Allegra panted and pushed him with her vampire strength, removing his will to resist. Kneeling over him, she let her crotch dance over the tip of his cock, then held his arms over his head, binding them together with invisible threads.

Her acolytes sang and laughed, winding their limbs around one another, caressing breasts and mouths and the lush petals of labias that glistened with dew. He stared, twin hungers pounding through him, and Allegra made patterns over his chest with her razor-like claws and licked the trickles of blood.

'Do the same for me,' he begged, and strained against her spider web bonds. 'Let me drink of you. I'm starving.'

She threw back her head and laughed, her teeth stained scarlet. 'Wait. Wait. I promise we'll go hunting together and find rich pickings. But first…'

She moved down and his cock penetrated her folds and entered the icy cavern of her sexual darkness. She worked herself like a machine under full steam and her voice rose, yelling her weird song, and the rasp of her nails was excruciating. Lazio was in torment, but healing even as he suffered. He had the vampire powers of rejuvenation. His spunk was surging against his stem, demanding release, but Allegra pressed down on the base, delaying his orgasm until she had achieved her own.

His breathing was coming in gasps, every muscle stretched like a steel cable. Her wailing drowned his protestations of pain, till she suddenly clamped her thighs round his hips, and sensation rushed over him as she thrashed in the throes of climax. He yelled in anguish and ecstasy, and Allegra tossed and writhed and ground herself onto his ejaculating cock as if she would wrest it from him.

His arms were free and he dragged himself up, so weakened by her excesses that feeding was essential for his survival. Allegra spun in the air above him, crystalline and effervescent. Her draperies swirled, her eyes shone wickedly and, 'Come on!' she ordered, while her slaves applauded.

Visions of blood clouded his eyes and his hunger was appalling. The fragrance of the night broke over him; full night that shrouded everything. And that darkness held the seductive promise of blood. He was a predator intent on striking, and love and Stella was far removed from this primitive urge.

Stella was getting ready for her date with Conlan, trying to concentrate on anything but the terrible loss of Lazio. She felt cheated. She should have been allowed to say goodbye and console him with the promise of a yearly meeting. This was better than nothing, and she thanked Michael for his mercy. But gone were the dreams of being with Lazio for all time, his companion and wife.

She had selected a triangular top in tan suede with a matching skirt. Both were brief but highly fashionable, and she was about to put them on, but paused to stare at her slim shape in the pier-glass, uncompromisingly critical. Despite the ordeal she had just endured, she looked healthy and fit, though her face was a little pale and her eyes blue-shadowed. She cupped her breasts and rolled her thumbs over the nipples. They responded instantly. So did her clit.

This is the body that pleasured the Archangel Michael, she said to herself, and shook her tumbling dark curls in wonder. She intended to wear nothing underneath, except a pair of coffee-coloured panties, and had decided to go out barelegged. It was warm enough for this, and for the high-heeled sandals she already had on. Though she would have rather stayed moping in her room, Conlan interested her, and if she was to believe Belphegor, and she saw no reason not to after the last incident he had orchestrated, then he was going to be important in the music world.

I must get back to work with *Zero700*, she thought. They were gigging on Saturday night and not nearly ready. This made her feel guilty, and she considered putting Conlan off and calling a rehearsal instead, but probably the other members of the group would have made plans for the evening. Her mind wasn't functioning properly and, most of all, she wanted to cry. She sniffed resolutely and leaned towards the mirror, applying her make-up, her bare bottom inviting, the gap between her braced thighs encouraging exploration.

'Superb, my dear,' said Quincy, coming in at the door.

'It's polite to knock,' she observed, watching him in the glass as she dabbed her carmined lips with a tissue.

'A master doesn't have to ask his slave's permission to enter her room,' he reminded, and walked over, placing his hands at her waist, then sliding down till he cradled the under-hang of her cheeks.

She thought of Michael. 'I'm not your slave,' she retorted.

'No?' he said coldly. 'Don't be silly. Nothing has changed.'

'Then you obviously haven't heard the latest. Or has

Belphegor been blabbing?'

'I haven't seen him. Why? What have you been doing, slut? Screwing someone else without my permission?'

'None of your concern,' she snapped. 'Suffice to say that I've given up any right to Lazio, except for one night a year, and Candice and Emma have got their way. They are now free to meet.'

'So Dimitri may now agree to give me the dark gift,' Quincy mused, his eyes shining. 'But you should have consulted me.'

'I couldn't; it was out of my hands.'

'Then you'll have to be punished,' he grated, and his hands gripped her buttocks painfully. 'I can't have you acting on your own initiative. That would never do.'

He shook her roughly and forced her to lie over the dressing table stool, her buttocks raised high. Then he picked up a hairbrush from the lace duchess set standing on the mahogany surface and brought it down across her rump with a whack. He hit her six times on either cheek with the flat of the brush, but she did not yell, refusing to give him the satisfaction.

'Stand up,' he ordered.

She scrambled to her feet, the imprint of the brush burning like a brand, but she stared him in the eye defiantly, and said, 'Can I go now? I'll be late for an appointment.'

'With whom?'

'Conlan Henny.'

'Ah, keeping the composer sweet... then you have my approval, but first, open you legs.'

'What?'

'Open them.'

She parted her thighs slightly and he stared at her exposed slit. 'Beautiful,' he said, 'but I want you to be pierced. I shall arrange it.'

'And if I don't want to?'

'Tough,' he said, and his determined tone thrilled her like

224

a shockwave, making her realise that, despite everything, he was still her master. 'Now rub your tits.'

She couldn't disobey, her hands going to her breasts, fingers brushing over the pointed nipples. 'Oh…' she sighed, and closed her eyes as pleasure spiralled down to her clit.

He inserted a finger into her wet sex, and she wriggled her hips. She looked into his eyes and he smiled. He held back her secret lips and exposed the stiff sliver of flesh topped by its hard bud. He knew precisely how to tantalise it; circling round it, rubbing just above it, flicking the head, then massaging it firmly. Stella could hardly breathe, her anxiety acute. Would he bring her off, or leave her hanging there, mad with frustration?

But no, he was massaging her clit steadily; a slippery, wonderful frottage in just the right place, with her nipples responding and her body bathed in sensation; even her stinging rump added to her lust. Her climax took over, a wrenching, shuddering whirlwind that made her scream and scream again.

Quincy dropped onto the stool, dragging her between his opened thighs, his cock exposed. His hands on each of her shoulders forced her to kneel. She parted her lips, thinking he wanted fellatio, but instead he caught hold of her breasts and squeezed them together, then inserted his penis into the deep cleavage. He used it like a vagina, working himself feverishly, wetting her flesh with his pre-come, his cock-head appearing between her breasts at every thrust. Stella squinted down, watching its progress as is got wetter and shinier, its red hue deepening, flushed and angry looking. His face contorted and he grunted, his spunk shooting upwards like a geyser, hitting her chin, her cheeks, even her eyes, then dropping back to spread over her breasts in a warm, milky tide.

Emma saw her across the moonlit garden and, tears streaming down her face, ran and embraced her, holding on as if she would never let go.

'Candice! Candice! At last…' She was sobbing, and so was the vampire, and she dashed the tears away and held her by that mane of golden hair and looked into her cornflower-blue eyes.

'My darling, this is wonderful. Stella has done well, sacrificing her love so that we may be happy.' Candice sobbed, her pink tears shining against her pale cheeks.

Emma could do nothing except hold her and wonder at the miracle. Candice had not changed and she herself was not a day older than when they parted in Venice all those years ago. This transformation happened as soon as she left the body that had served her faithfully. She had become young again and, for a while, content to revel in this rebirth. She found Clive and her children and grandchildren and friends who had passed over years before her, and knew that she could be with them again whenever she chose. But this was the icing on the cake – this meeting with Candice.

They walked arm in arm through the garden of Candice's father's house in London where they had strolled so often. Whenever either of them mentioned some place in the past where they had been together, they found themselves transported there. Venice featured large, that unforgettable vacation when so much had happened to shape their futures.

'Oh look, there's Countess Bianca, and Comte Henri!' Emma exclaimed as they entered the Palazzo Barbesi and joined the elegant throng. Waiters in knee breeches and white powdered wigs passed among them with silver salvers of champagne and, on a shell-shaped stage, an orchestra played waltzes. 'He's as handsome as ever.'

'And she's as wickedly seductive,' Candice added.

'Do we really want to get involved in their games?'

'I'd rather we were alone on this first occasion,' Candice

whispered, and her hands fluttered at the opening of Emma's low-cut gown. 'I've missed your lovemaking so much.'

'Doesn't Dimitri satisfy you?' Emma asked, thrilling to these words.

'He does. He's a perfect lover, but we were so close, weren't we?'

'And can be again,' Emma said, and thought of the Victorian bedroom they had shared as young women. Immediately, it was there.

They were in bed together, a beautiful tester bed with mahogany posts and lace drapes, a place of intimacy where they could share the secrets of their nubile bodies. Candice appeared to be asleep, but Emma slipped her hand into the opening of her white frilled nightgown and found her voluptuous breasts with their luscious nipples. They hardened at her touch.

Emma's own breasts were awakening, and that delicious bud at the top of her cleft was throbbing demandingly. Candice stirred and flung her arms around her, drawing her closer, her own hands exploring, pushing up their nightdresses, landing unerringly on each of Emma's erogenous zones. They broke away long enough to strip naked, then fell back into the feather mattress, grabbing at one another in a frenzy of passion.

'This is so good,' Emma cried. 'I longed for it for years. I was happy enough with Clive, but no one could take your place. Then he died and I remained and grew old. Ah, Candice, thank God you'll never experience this process, when gradually one's limbs stiffen, one's hearing is not so acute, or one's eyesight. Inside I felt like a young women, but hated looking in a mirror and seeing what the passage of time was doing to me.'

'It won't happen any more, dearest. Now you're in your prime, and will remain so until you reincarnate on earth, or wherever you are destined to continue your search for enlightenment. Even then, with Micha-el's intervention, we should still be able to contact one another, even if you are born a man.' Candice chuckled and added, 'That would be fun, wouldn't it? Emma with a cock.'

Emma met her lips, full on, poignantly recalling their honeyed taste, but now there was a different, even more exciting quality about Candice's kisses. Her saliva filled Emma's mouth and its heat ran through her veins like fire. When Candice trailed her lips over her skin, alighting on her nipples, it was like fever and ice, and Emma's breath caught in her throat. Desire swamped her, and they rolled together, then changed position, so that each could feast at the other's sex.

Emma lay with her head between Candice's thighs, and her hands caressed the golden down that fringed her labia. It was wet and fragrant with the subtle aroma that was entirely personal to Candice. She parted the lips and gazed at the shining pink pearl between, then gently stroked it, rewarded by hearing her lover moan. Lowering her face, intoxicated by her odour, she licked the little organ and then sucked it steadily until she felt Candice buck and heard her plaintive cry and knew she had reached an orgasm.

Candice's mouth travelled down to Emma's luxuriant russet bush. As she burrowed into it and found the sliver of flesh that quivered eagerly, she reached up and caressed the full breasts and pinkish-brown nipples. Spasms of acute pleasure rippled through Emma's entire body. She lifted her pelvis off the mattress, and Candice increased that enticing tonguing, and Emma could feel the waves washing over her, lifting her higher – higher, till she was on the edge of the dazzling cascade – then over into paradise, pierced by a dart of supreme ecstasy.

They were together again! It was true! All her prayers had been answered.

Stella ran down the stairs and Conlan met her in the hall. His expression of joy at seeing her was heart-warming, and she forgot the heat of her punished backside, revelling in being in the company of such an undemanding man.

'Ready?' he enquired unnecessarily, seeming slightly nervous. 'I've booked a table at the *Kicking Donkey*. It has a five star reputation.'

He slipped a hand under her elbow and they went down the wide stone steps to where his car stood. It was dark now, but the outside lights mitigated the gloom. Conlan opened the passenger door for her, and as she was about to get in she suddenly hesitated, aware of a translucence that wavered in the air close by.

She stared, the moment frozen in time, and a hand appeared out of the glow, holding a single red rose. It came nearer, wavering in the breeze, and the petals fell from it, showering Stella in their perfume.

'Lady Emma, is that you?' Stella whispered.

The hand was hazy, and she couldn't be sure if she heard her speak, or if the words were a mere echo in her mind, but, 'Thank you, bless you,' someone said.

The petals drifted to Stella's feet. They grew light, ethereal, then faded altogether.

Chapter Twelve

'There's something wrong,' Conlan said to Stella as he drove away from Troon Hall. 'Do you want to talk about it?'

With a lover's instinct, he knew she was troubled. The revelations made by Belphegor had been shocking and he worried at what might happen to her under pressure from those mysterious influences.

'How much do you know?' she asked dully, and a quick glance at her profile made him want to stop at the roadside and take her in his arms. It was more than simply lust; he felt that for Alithea, but this was different.

'Belphegor took me to London… don't ask me how… we were whisked there in the blink of an eye. I didn't believe in magic, but I do now.' He was still marvelling at the vampire's proposal. It had inspired him to work even harder; every free moment spent labouring at the piano. *Persephone* was shaping up well, but there was still a long way to go before it burst onto the stage. 'He's offered me his house in Chelsea, rent-free. I can move in when I get back, and work on the opera. Apparently he's willing to finance it, and knows at least one impresario who'll stage it.'

'And you trust him?' she replied listlessly. 'What is he getting out of it?'

'He loves music, apparently, and wants to be the force behind the scene that helps bring *Persephone* to life.'

'He's a vampire.'

'I know. They are all vampires.'

'And this doesn't trouble you?'

He thought about it for a second then replied, truthfully,

'No, it doesn't. In fact, I find it rather inspiring. There are far worse monsters in politics and big business, bleeding people dry.'

She fell silent and he drove for a while without speaking. It was a beautiful starry night and the ribbon of road wound before him, tree-shrouded and isolated. He shuddered, unable to forget his recent experience with the hitchhikers that had turned out to be Allegra and her so-called sisters. And Stella smashing into his car.

Involuntarily, his hand reached out and felt for her. He wanted reassurance that she was sitting beside him, unharmed. He felt her start, then relax, permitting his exploration of her thigh beneath the soft suede skirt.

'What is it, Conlan?' she asked, turning to him.

'I'll tell you about it later,' he promised, and withdrew his hand to change gear. 'Belphegor showed me Lady Emma's journal.'

'He did?' She was instantly alert, like a hunted deer.

'He had brought it with him to London. I read it, and now understand everything.'

'But you don't know the latest... that he took me to see the Archangel Michael,' she whispered, and he did not doubt that she was telling the truth.

Concentrating on the road that led to Wicklow and the *Kicking Donkey*, he listened to her account of everything that happened to her on the celestial plane. She omitted nothing, not even her sexual encounter with Michael. Jealousy twisted in Conlan's gut, but he pulled himself up; hadn't he screwed Alithea, blatantly and lustfully?

When she came to the part where she agreed to give up Lazio, his heart lifted and he wanted to sing and shout, though realising that she had reached a compromise with the angel, granted permission to see the vampire once a year, when, presumably, she would enjoy his embraces.

'Candice and Emma have already met, I'm certain of it,'

she concluded, and told him what happened when she was about to get in his car. 'She brought me roses, to say thank you. I know I've done the right thing, but oh, Conlan, it's so hard. I love him more than life itself.'

Conlan cursed to himself; he would always be second best. Could he settle for that?

He decided he could. Half a cake was better than none at all. Besides, he had the advantage of being alive and able to see her frequently. He could offer her a proper marriage and, in the fullness of time, babies to love and care for. So up yours, Lazio, he challenged, sending the message through the ether with such determination and fervour the vampire couldn't miss picking it up.

There remained someone else, however, but he didn't mention Quincy until they were in the public house. It had once been an establishment for the locals but, under new management, had been turned into a meeting place for trendy clientele. Many of the original features had been kept, and it was situated off the high street in an old part of town. The proprietor, an Englishman, was into haute cuisine and the menu was interesting.

Conlan confirmed their booking, and they were shown to a table in an alcove. The smells coming from the kitchen were mouth-watering. A waiter came up to them and Conlan ordered wine. This was brought and by that time they had decided what they wanted to eat. During the lull while their food was being prepared, Conlan took the bull by the horns. 'What about Quincy?' he asked. 'Are you still having a thing with him?'

She looked so lovely sitting opposite him that he really did not want to upset her, and hated mentioning that powerful personality who seemed to have such a hold over her. Desire warred with the longing to shield her from harm, even though pictures of Alithea rose unbidden in his mind. His cock stiffened under his chinos, and he dropped a hand into his lap and gave it a furtive rub.

Stella looked at him across the yellow and white chequered tablecloth. 'Quincy has done a lot for *Zero700*,' she replied.

'More than that,' Conlan persisted, unable to stop staring at the curve of her cheek and the rise of her breasts under that little leather top that revealed more than it concealed. Her nipples lifted it, twin peaks that weren't contained in a bra.

She raised her glass to her lips, then said, 'It seems you know all about me from Belphegor, so there's no use denying that Quincy has taught me a great deal. He is, in fact, my master.'

This statement almost tipped Conlan over the edge, and he squeezed his throbbing cock to stop it spurting. 'Does – does this mean you're his slave?' he asked, when he had recovered enough to speak.

'Sometimes,' she vouchsafed.

The waiter arrived, setting dishes on the table and cutlery wrapped in white napkins. They ate, but Conlan was hardly aware of what passed his lips. It could have been a burger and chips for all the notice he took. Every time he looked at Stella it was to see her tied to a crosspiece while Quincy wielded a whip, embroidering scarlet stripes over her naked bottom.

'When are you going back to London?' he asked, desperate to focus on anything but that inflaming image.

'We've the gig on Saturday and shall head for the ferry next day.'

'And Troon Hall?'

'Will be looked after by Maureen and Caley Rogan, as before. I'll return when I can, but the band is touring England and then Quincy has a hefty itinerary worked out for abroad.'

'And Stephen?'

She sighed. 'I suppose I'll have to bail him out and pay his debts, but that's all he's getting from me. If he causes further trouble I'll ask Quincy to deal with him. What about you?'

'I'll leave at the same time and start moving my things into Belphegor's house, then I'll be working full tilt to complete the opera. We shan't see much of each other.'

Her eyes sparkled in the subdued light as she reached across the table and took his hand in hers. 'I'll miss you,' she said.

He leaned forward and, as he did so, his foot slid across the floor towards her, hidden by the cloth, and touched her ankle. She didn't withdraw it. In fact, he felt a slight returning pressure. He held his breath, as exhilarated as a lovesick boy.

The waiter appeared again, bringing dessert. They broke away and Conlan watched her eating, envying the spoon that entered her lips, to be caressed by her pink tongue. At one point he wiped away a tiny trace of chocolate mousse from the corner of her mouth with his finger, transferring it to his own and licking it.

They talked like friends, but the tension was growing between them, and at last he could bear it no longer. 'Do you want coffee, or shall we go?' he said, but awkwardly, not wishing to rush her in any way. This was too rare, too finely balanced a moment. He could wait a little longer, having fantasised about making love to her so often that a few more wanks wouldn't hurt.

'Let's go,' she said, and picked up her bag.

Almost trembling with anticipation and fear of rejection, he settled the bill and left an over-generous tip for the waiter. Outside he resisted the urge to put his arms round her and kiss her till they were both giddy. Instead, he didn't do or say anything until they were in the car.

'Do you want to go back home?' he asked, the engine idling.

'No,' she said. 'If we're going to become lovers, then I'd like it to happen somewhere different. In the open... in a wood or meadow or by a mountain stream.'

Bemused and a stranger to the terrain, Conlan drove until they came to a gate at the side of a lane near a small copse. Stella got out first, following a slope that led to higher ground, the whole area blue-white by moonlight. Conlan followed, inhaling the heady scent of bruised leaves as he brushed against the tall, feathery grasses. Stella ran ahead and he came out into a clearing. It was dominated by a tumulus, an ancient burial mound left by remote people from prehistory. Carpeted with short, springy turf, it was dotted with dark clumps of heather and the tapering spikes of foxgloves.

Stella scrambled to its crest and lay down, looking up at him. He was hardly able to believe his incredible luck. He lay beside her, at first wanting to take things slowly so as not to frighten her off, but then taking fire from her passion, trying not to be aware of its desperate quality. She held his hands and pushed them under her top, and her warm breasts and ardent nipples made it impossible to delay any longer. He found her mouth, open and willing, her tongue tangling with his. As if hungry to feel his touch on her clit, she gripped his thigh between hers and ground her pubis against it. Then, as if this wasn't good enough, she tore one of his hands from her breasts and rammed it between her legs. He felt the scrap of silk that covered her mound and pushed it to one side, sliding a finger into her. She was slippery as oil, wriggling her hips till he located her clitoris. It pulsed and rippled under his expert fondling.

He wanted to spread her legs and bare her secrets, but it was too dark in the hollow formed by the barrow's ancient rim. All he could see was the contrast between her pale flesh and the shadows. It was enough, and he lowered his head and licked the deeper darkness of her slit. He wanted so much to simply fall on her and plunge his aching cock into that inviting entrance, but he knew he couldn't – not yet. Instead he stood up, took a condom from his back pocket and unbuckled his belt, then let the zip that restrained his penis run down. His trousers started to slide past his hips, and he wriggled to get them lower, impatiently pushing aside his shirt.

Fumbling in his eagerness and haste, he ripped the packet and found the little circle of latex, then started to slip it over his distended cock. Even this action could have precipitated disaster. His helm was so sensitive that the smallest friction made the semen surge but, by a miracle, he managed to hold on. Kneeling over her he rested a hand on her furry mound, then found her centre again, rubbing until she moaned and came.

He pushed against her with his awkward, swollen weapon and she hooked her legs round his waist and took it in. He sank slowly into that warm, wet passage, feeling her fingers between his thighs, cupping his balls. A groan escaped his lips, and he was breathing hard as he moved his prick backwards and forwards, sweat running down his face as he increased his pace. He angled the base of his cock so that it touched her clit, but this was obviously not enough and she worked her hand down there, masturbating herself with her finger.

Conlan was no longer in control. His cock had taken over. His breathing was ragged, his heart pumping. He felt her come again, her vaginal muscles convulsing round his length, and he let go, pumping savagely and shooting his spunk into the rubber.

He collapsed on her, his hands clenched in the short grass, smelling the fresh tang of crushed vegetation. The world righted itself and he opened his eyes, her face a pale blur beneath him as he rolled away slightly, afraid of hurting her. She murmured something indistinguishable, and lay with his arm pillowing her head. He wanted to sleep, promising himself a catnap before starting all over again, if he was lucky.

Stella stood on the top of the tumulus, her arms outstretched, her face uplifted to the moon. It was as if she was making an invocation. She was held in an enchantment. All was unnaturally still. She glanced back and saw Conlan fast asleep, as if he was drugged or bewitched. She heard a woman sighing, and realised it was herself. She saw her hands wringing together in the moonlight, fondling each other in despair, then reaching out as if she would pluck Lazio from space.

He was there, standing in mid-air where the rounded sides of the barrow fell steeply away. His eyes blazed and his face was like marble, frozen into an expression of terrible rage.

'Lazio!' She took a step towards him and her knee met a resistance that was totally impenetrable. She put out a hand but could not break through, her fingers held there as if pressed against a sheet of glass. 'Lazio! Lazio!' She hammered against the invisible barrier with her fists, but it was useless.

She saw his lips move and his voice reached her, but it was muffled. 'You betrayed our love,' he said.

'No! We can meet. Didn't Belphegor tell you? Every year we'll be together on Halloween.'

'Samhain,' he retorted with a sneer. 'All Saint's Eve. It is not enough.'

'But better than nothing,' she pleaded, pounding on the glass wall. 'Oh, let me through, please! I had to help Candice and Emma.'

His handsome face wore a dark, brooding look. 'You don't love me,' he accused.

She was crying now. 'I do! I do! Oh, Lazio, please agree. Meet me on the last day of October.'

'No,' he said sullenly, throwing a fold of his long black cloak over one shoulder.

'Don't abandon me. Say you'll be there.'

'I promise nothing, goodbye,' he said icily, and disappeared

237

from her sight.

Stella fell to her knees, and now there was nothing stopping her reaching out to where he had been. She sat there on the dewy grass, weeping despairingly. That was all she needed: a vampire with attitude.

'Are you happy, my sweet?' Dimitri asked, and Candice nestled her head into his shoulder.

'Completely,' she whispered. 'Seeing Emma was wonderful. Not that this means I love you any less,' she added tactfully.

'I know,' he said gravely, and she looked up into his stern, classically handsome face and blessed Stella for making it possible for her to enjoy both her lovers.

They stood on the tower of St Cuthbert's, under that blood-red moon with its retinue of stars. 'It's time we left,' he added, holding her close to his powerful chest. 'I miss my wolves. It wasn't discreet to bring them to Ireland. As it was, we were lucky to get away with it, the Irish being a fey race who might well have guessed what we are.'

Candice knew they must move on. Vampires were nomads who never stayed long in one place. They broke camp and left before anyone started asking awkward questions about the sudden rise of tired, anaemic people and the occasional unexplained deaths in any given area where they had lodged. There was one place where Dimitri always liked to return, a place where he was accepted by the gypsies who revered him and his kind – Transylvania.

'Do the others know?' she asked.

'Oh, yes,' he rejoined. 'They are restless too, and homesick for the Carpathian Mountains. With the exception of Belphegor, who is a law unto himself. He intends to hang around London, assisting Conlan Henny.'

'And Lazio?'

'Is nursing a broken heart,' Dimitri said acerbically. 'He'll get over it.'

'I'm not so sure,' Candice murmured, sorry that her surrogate son had been made to suffer on her account.

'He's proud,' Dimitri commented.

'Just like you, beloved,' she teased.

'I should have been destroyed if you had refused to marry me and become one of the Undead,' he admitted, and his arm tightened around her painfully. Then he suddenly released her and, standing on the edge of the balustrade, pointed towards the east.

An open carriage drawn by four black horses was bowling across the sky. It stopped and Dimitri helped Candice in, and tucked a sable lap robe about her, then climbed onto the coachman's seat. He flourished a long whip and the steeds leaned into the straps, then leaped forward. The stars flashed and the accompanying wolves howled, loping along beside the vehicle, their fiery eyes gleaming.

Candice looked back once, watching the monastery become smaller and smaller beneath her. 'Goodbye, Stella,' she whispered. 'We shall meet again.'

It was as if her words remained imprinted in the air, and Stella tuned into their wavelength when she made a dismal pilgrimage to St Cuthbert's before leaving for Dublin. Kate went with her, and they stood staring at the closed, barred and shuttered building. It was as if their experiences inside it had been nothing more than a weird and wonderful dream – where their quirky, most perverted fantasies had been played out.

Stella found a message on her return from an exhausting but highly successful tour of the UK. Kate had dumped her bags and gone into the kitchen to put on the kettle while Stella checked out the machine.

She was tired, though the touring bus had been the last word in comfort and they had stayed in the most expensive hotels en route, but there was no place like home, and Kate's house with all its familiar contents seemed to welcome them fondly. She clicked on the recorder and heard Quincy's crisp, cultured voice.

'Hi, Stella. Sounds like you had a major success. Everyone's talking about *Zero700*, and you in particular. I shall expect you at my place at eight tonight. Don't be late.'

'Quincy?' Kate asked, coming in with two mugs of tea and a packet of chocolate digestive biscuits and setting them down on the low table. She had kicked off her shoes in the hall, and padded about bare foot. 'What did he want?'

'I don't know,' Stella said, curling up on the old, saggy settee. 'A résumé of events, I suppose. You know what he's like.'

'I'm surprised he let us go on the road without him,' Kate said ironically. 'He acts as if we're half-witted school kids or something. Doesn't he realise that student bashes, gigs in pubs, and auditoriums that seat thousands are nothing new to us? Well, maybe the last bit; it *was* rather overwhelming to face so many people.'

'We were shepherded by his road crew, and the tour manager who thought he was our nanny,' Stella reminded with a smile, her head still reeling from the experience of being pursued by the press, the fans and all the clamouring attention of the media.

And now, when all she wanted to do was put her feet up and doze by the telly, Quincy had summoned her.

'Did you plan to see Conlan later?' Kate asked, sipping her tea and eyeing Stella shrewdly.

'Not exactly. He's been phoning me, of course, but is frantically busy on his score.'

'When will it be staged?'

'Next year,' Stella replied, but forefront in her mind was the idea that it was now September. Only a few weeks to All Saint's Eve. A hectic gallop round venues in France, Holland

240

and Germany, and the band would be back in time for the solstice.

Would Lazio show up? There had been no telepathic response to the urgent pleas she had sent out to him. It seemed he had withdrawn from her completely. Shortly after she saw him on the top of the tumulus, she had searched for the crystal teardrop in her jewel case, but it had gone, leaving nothing but a small, damp stain.

'Conlan loves you,' Kate stated. 'He's a babe. You couldn't find a better bloke.'

'I know,' Stella mumbled, wishing her friend would drop the subject. 'But I'm not ready for commitment yet.'

'And you won't be while you're still mooning about hoping that Lazio will return,' Kate said crossly. 'Why don't you drop it? He's history.'

'I know, I know,' Stella replied, and buried her head in her hands.

'All right, hon, don't get stressed,' Kate said kindly, and hugged her. 'Men are nothing but a drag… living or Undead, they're all ruled by their cocks. And you be careful of Quincy. He's too fond of bossing you about. Master? My arse!'

Stella remembered her friend's words when Quincy welcomed her into his apartment, always the perfect gentleman. He approached her, arms outstretched, and his smoothly shaven cheek brushed against hers as he kissed her. Stella yielded to his charm and sophistication. He made her feel protected, this commander of underlings who had but to snap his fingers for his every whim to be catered for.

'The reports coming back to me from all quarters have been highly satisfactory,' he began, and gently stroked her face and throat, and dipped into the opening of her silk blouse. 'And now, you are going to please me further.'

She stiffened, instantly wary. 'How?' she demanded.

He tapped her on the bottom, not hard but threateningly. 'I

said I wanted you shaved and pierced. But first, we'll put on the nipple clamps. Undress.'

Mal, Quincy's chauffeur and general dogs-body, appeared, carrying a small leather case. Flipping back the lid he displayed several pairs of what at first Stella thought were earrings, until Quincy lifted one and she saw the clamp with its sharp teeth.

She shook her head and backed away, but Quincy seized the blouse and tore it open, ruining the expensive garment. She struggled but to no avail, and was soon stripped to the waist. Mal was waiting for his chance to pounce, but Quincy managed without his help.

He gave her a shake, then handcuffed her, pulling her arms behind her back.

Knowing that one word from Quincy would bring Mal into the fray, she held herself upright, chin lifted, challenging him to do his worst. And to her eternal shame, she was quivering, not with fear but with excitement. Quincy took one of her breasts in his hand, opened a clamp and fitted it round the deep pink teat, then let the diabolical invention spring back.

Stella yelped as fire stabbed through her breast and into her clit. Before she had time to recover he treated the other in the same cruel fashion. The teeth bit spitefully, and the blood throbbed in her tightly pinched nipples. She shivered and sweated, and was consumed with lust. Would Quincy condescend to thrust his cock into her? It had been so long since she'd had a man. Conlan obliged the night before she left for the opening concert in Edinburgh, but she had kept herself to herself during the tour.

Quincy stood back and admired her. 'That looks so sweet,' he remarked, and it pleased her to have this swarthy, craggily handsome man complimenting her. Then he took her hand and walked her towards the area that accommodated his gym.

The clamps stung. The little silver bells dangling from them jingled. Stella's insides quaked. What was he going to do now?

The round spots in the ceiling lit the accoutrements of the polished room. It reminded Stella of an operating theatre. Her gaze became riveted on a high couch covered by a white towel.

A young man stood beside it. He was wearing a spotless loincloth that bulged interestingly at the front, and had a perfectly proportioned body, the lines of his tanned torso sculptured and hard. Quincy urged her towards him and, when she came to a halt, her thighs resting against the couch, he undid her skirt and let it fall in a bundle at her feet. She heard him tut and sigh.

'Oh dear, I'm disappointed in you, slave,' he said. 'What have I told you about wearing knickers when you're with me?'

She jumped at the cold prick of steel at her hip as his flick-knife sliced through the side of the offending garment. The silky triangle dropped away, and she was completely naked. The young man did not even spare her a glance, his eyes fixed straight ahead, like a sentry on duty.

'Right, Raoul, get to work,' Quincy barked, and lifted Stella onto the couch, making her lie full length. He shackled her wrists tightly to the head of the couch and then had her bend her knees so that her thighs were parted. He manacled her ankles to iron rings on either side, and she felt like a trussed chicken with nowhere to run and nowhere to hide.

Raoul positioned himself on a high stool at the foot of the couch, and she knew he had an uninterrupted view of her nakedness.

When he touched her she almost screamed, but he did nothing more than spread white paste over her mound. It was soft and soothing and smelt of sandalwood. It warmed her pubis and made her bud swell. She wished his finger

243

would slip and land on that eager tyrant. But he knew his job to perfection and, when the cream had been on for a few moments, he picked up a spatula and drew the flat edge over her, from mons to anus, scraping away the fronds of pubic hair. He was very thorough, as precise and impersonal as a surgeon. He rinsed the wooden tool clean of dark curls and cream, then applied it afresh, till her pudenda was as bare as a newborn infant's.

She lifted her head and squinted down her length, seeing the astonishing spectacle of her denuded pubis, rosy and fresh and smooth. Quincy touched the labial wings. They parted easily and her clitoris rose, ultra-sensitive, quivering at every breath of air that passed over its pearly surface.

Raoul wheeled across a trolley where small instruments lay on a spotless cloth. Quincy unclipped the clamps and feeling rushed back painfully into Stella's nipples. She watched Raoul with wide, scared eyes as he wiped her breasts with surgical spirit and then applied his pincers, piercing both so quickly and skilfully that she scarcely felt it. But the numbness disappeared and pain rushed in as he did the same to her navel. She squirmed and protested as he parted her labia and prepared her clit hood.

'No!' she pleaded. 'Tell him to stop! Please, Quincy!'

'Hush,' he soothed. 'I'll let you look in a moment. I'm sure you'll agree that the little gold rings look charming, and as soon as you've healed, we'll think about adding jewels, a few diamonds perhaps.'

Diverted by his voice, she was hardly aware that Raoul had succeeded in inserting his instrument between the inside of the little cowl and the fleshy button it protected. Then a sharp pain lanced her delta and groin. She wanted to curl up and protect her poor, abused genitals, but Quincy unlocked her manacles and ordered her to stay still.

When she was allowed to sit up, she was aware of the rings with each movement. The antiseptic stung, the piercings were sore, but the rings enhanced her feelings, never letting her forget her nipples and clit, their chafing a constant reminder. Although she couldn't bear to be touched, her clitoris thrummed and she needed to desperately climax.

Quincy opened his trousers, made her stand by the couch and turned her around, his hand at her neck forcing her to bend. He inserted his cock between her buttocks. He held her by her waist, and though her breasts swayed as he pushed in and out of her vagina, he did not attempt to touch them. After several deep strokes, he moved out of her and positioned his helm at her anal mouth.

'What is it you want, slave?' he muttered.

'I want you to fuck me,' she replied, bearing down on his tool.

'And who are you addressing?' he asked. 'What's my name?'

'Master. You are my master.'

He hesitated no more, and Stella screamed as he rammed into her rectum and began to bugger her frantically. The couch shook and she shook too, as he used all the force available in his strong body.

Halloween came and went, and Lazio stayed away. Stella had rushed back to England. There were parties everywhere; Trick or Treat, children dressing up as witches and goblins and even, vampires, but although she waited and watched, the night passed, the next day soon dawned. Lazio never materialised.

The iron entered her soul and she buried herself in her work. She was a star now, always in demand, appearing on TV chat shows, giving interviews to the papers, and there was always the next performance or recording session to look forward to. She took time out to visit Devon where Lazio told her his family were once lords of the manor and owned a village. There was no trace of the house, or of them, but in the small square-towered Norman church, she came across a wall plaque carved with the names of local men who had died in the Great War. A ray of sunlight struck across it and she read the words, *The Honourable Jeremy Farquarson, aged 24. Missing, presumed dead.*

But he wasn't dead, she sobbed quietly. He was Undead, but for all the good it did her, he might as well have perished completely at Mons.

She saw Belphegor occasionally and always asked him the same question. 'How is Lazio?'

He gave her the same reply every time. 'As well as can be expected. He likes to get his own way, that one.'

She became much closer to Conlan. The birth throes of *Persephone* were almost over. He was coming out of it, thinner, paler, even more intense, but the rehearsals were underway, the theatre booked, the cast selected, with Alithea in the lead as the heroine. Stella might have been jealous of her and the huge amounts of time she and Conlan spent incarcerated together with only a piano as a chaperone, was it not glaringly apparent that she was having a passionate affair with the principal baritone.

'We're colleagues,' Conlan explained, when surfacing briefly from a heap of manuscripts, scribbled notes and an ink-blotched score. 'It's you I love, Stella. Marry me.'

'I'll think about it,' she promised, and jetted off to the States where *Zero700* was booked to appear in New York, San Francisco, Los Angeles and Salt Lake City, taking in a few minor towns on the way.

Canada followed and then Japan, where wildly enthusiastic fans greeted them. By the time Stella returned to England it was autumn again, and as it transpired, the opening night of the opera was booked for All Saint's Eve. She had promised Conlan to be there.

He was conducting, and she was more nervous than he was, trembling as she entered the foyer of the grand old theatre that had retained all the pomp and ceremony of a bygone age. It had recently been lovingly restored, with floral paper and dark panelling, much gold leaf, bevelled mirrors, crystal chandeliers and deep pile crimson carpet. Stella took the opportunity to go backstage before the curtain rose, grabbing Conlan who, evening-suited and dapper, was giving last minute instructions to the chorus master.

'Stella, I'm so glad you could make it,' he broke off to say. 'I love the dress. There's something I wanted to say, but it'll have to wait. No, fuck it; I'm going to say it anyway. Are you going to marry me? What's to stop us announcing our engagement at the first night party when this is all over?'

'Oh, Conlan, have you forgotten that it's Halloween?' she answered, while all around them people rushed about, costumed, bewigged and made-up, and the orchestra in the pit were starting to tune their instruments. The excitement was electrifying.

His brow darkened and he gripped her under both elbows, dragging her close to him. 'And you're hoping that Lazio will come? Is that it?'

'Yes,' she whispered, on the edge of tears.

He let her go, and answered the call as someone shouted, 'Overture and beginners, please!'

'I'll see you after it's over,' she cried at his retreating back, and he waved without turning round.

Conlan had acquired the best seats in the house for them, in the middle of the front row of the royal circle. The theatre was packed; Belphegor and his team had gone to great lengths to secure the maximum amount of media coverage. A wave of applause rippled round as Conlan took his place on the conductor's rostrum. The house lights dimmed. He raised his baton and the first, low, ominous chords of act one rolled out.

Stella was spellbound. She was familiar with the music, having heard Conlan playing it often, but even so was totally

247

unprepared for the scope and scale of his composition. She sat in a daze during the interval, while Jez and Tommy went off to get drinks and it was then that something made her glance across to one of the stage boxes. Framed within its swagged opening, she saw the pale faces of Dimitri and Candice. Not only them: Allegra, Madelon and Medea were there too, showing off and behaving badly as human aristocratic harpies might do at the opera. Belphegor was encouraging them, foppish and elegant as ever in a midnight-blue satin suit, with lace at the cuffs and edging the Byronic shirt collar.

Behind them, almost obscured by the gloom, stood Lazio.

Stella met his eyes and their blaze scorched right through her. He moved, and so did she. They met in the car park at the side of the theatre.

'I couldn't stay away,' he said, his broad hands spread wide in appeal and explanation. 'I tried. Oh, so hard, but I love you, Stella, and I must see you, even if it's only once a year. If I don't do this, then I may as well stand in the glare of the sun until I shrivel and perish.'

'I'm so glad you came,' she whispered. 'I hoped for it. Prayed for it. I can't live without our tryst.'

'But you will marry Conlan, and enjoy your physical life to the full, continue to be successful and, darling, I'm proud of you. Oh, yes, I'm there when you're singing in concert, but you never see me.'

'I'm not allowed. Only on Samhain.'

'I know. I've been a fool. Will you forgive me? I'm grateful for any chance of being with you, though Conlan will be your husband, and you'll have his children and grow old with him. But on this one magical night every year, you'll be with me, no older than you are now.'

'And perhaps the Recorder will show clemency and let us continue to meet once I'm no longer in the body.'

Headlights blinded them as a car wheeled into the parking

area. The music of act two of *Persephone* swelled from the auditorium. Stella shivered in awe. Conlan's genius had captured it all – the demon women, the lost souls, the heroine's fear and fascination with the dark side, and the powerful master, the Overlord of Hell.

Lazio wrapped Stella in his cloak and said, 'Come with me. We need somewhere private.'

He kissed her and she tasted blood on his lips; he had fed before going to the theatre. She was torn between desire and a soul-wrenching revulsion. Had she stayed with him, she too would have been a predator, supping deeply of vital, life-giving fluid. Yet excitement surged through her, and anticipation. His eyes held so much hunger, so much possession. He knew, despite everything, that she was, and always would be, his.

In the next moment they were in her bedroom in Highgate. During their absence, the painters and decorators had moved in to refurbish the house. They had put it back to how it was in Edwardian times, though adding advanced technology to the kitchen, central heating and security system. Kate had employed landscape architects to revamp the garden and the whole place looked like something out of a television DIY programme.

Stella loved her bedroom, and had left instructions with the interior designer that she wanted it to be supremely feminine. Lazio smiled as he looked round it. 'It reminds me of my boyhood,' he said. 'Mama's bedchamber was like this.'

'I can afford luxuries now,' she said, though wanted nothing but to stand in the circle of his arms, never to part.

'I could have bought you anything,' he growled, that dark, passionate anger returning. 'I'm rich. I have castles, houses, properties all over the world, just like Dimitri.'

'Not possible,' she whispered, and felt herself teetering on the brink of despair, the sting of tears behind her eyelids.

He showed her anyway. Disembodied, they travelled across the miles but always where it was dark. He took her into treasure chambers and bank vaults, dazzling her with caskets of gems, heaps of gold and coins and rooms filled with priceless antiques. He draped her in silks, and covered her in jewels, then stood her in front of mirrors. She looked like an empress, but he cast no reflection, reminding her that this was only a mirage.

The light was changing and they were back in Highgate. 'I've missed the end of the show and the party,' she said, sinking into bed with him. It was like a vast shell, and she dreamed of sharing it with her vampire, though at one time that dream seemed unlikely to be realised.

'We haven't long,' he said, his mouth against her throat, his hands sliding along her spine, and kneading her buttocks. 'Who has been abusing you?' he added, his voice angry as he pushed down the sheet and saw Quincy's rings in her nipples.

'I didn't mind, I wanted him to do it,' she answered. The sheet slid lower and Lazio's eyes widened. 'Yes, he did my navel, too, and my clit-hood. I like it, don't you? It feels so sexy.'

'I would have done it,' he grumbled. 'You didn't have to make yourself a slave to Quincy.'

'Oh, forget about it – fuck me,' she insisted, digging her nails into his flesh.

His face was between her thighs; tongue examining the ringed clit-hood, then lapping at her so firmly that her orgasm broke abruptly. She urged him to cover her then, her legs wrapped round his waist as he knelt over her. His cock was every inch as long and wide as she remembered, and just as cold, yet no man's penis had ever heated and aroused her so much. He took her to places she had never been before – gardens of sexual enchantment where the tropical flowers had magical stamens, miles of snowy wastes where phallus-shaped icicles penetrated her like diamond studded lingams. Then back to his own chilly, alabaster flesh, scarlet lips, teeth that nipped and pleasured her, and a mighty cock to die for.

He thrashed and lunged inside her and she took him to the hilt, a second climax making her scream. He came, and it was as if the force of his discharge passed into her and they shared the same experience. She came again and again, then took his semen-tasting cock into her mouth, bringing him off, worshipping at the strange altar of his sex, and dedicating herself, body and soul, to this god who would be there for her through eternity.

'I must go,' he said, rousing at last from the welter of sex and emotion that had enthralled them.

At once he was dressed again, and Stella wore her high-fashion evening dress, all chiffon and flimsy straps and showing a great deal of cleavage, back and thigh. She glanced at the crumpled sheets of her bed, fortifying herself against that great void – that empty well of loneliness that she must face for another twelve months. She looked up into Lazio's face, wanting to carve every detail into her memory. Her body came alive at his touch. She had trembled at the solid, undeniable reality of him. Now the terrible hunger would start again all too soon – the wanting, the needing, the ache. Oh, Quincy would be there. He'd flown over to see her when she was abroad, but it wasn't the same.

Conlan would come through for her, and she took comfort from this. He was so tolerant and understanding, never critical. He even admired her piercings, finding the sight of them arousing. Dear Conlan, she would go back to him now, and grovel a bit because she'd missed the rapturous applause and after-show party. She hoped Alithea hadn't jumped in there.

Outside the sky was paling, the rising sun driving away the serpent that had swallowed up the light. The birds rejoiced, and all living things started to stir and wake and begin another day. Not so Lazio; he must find an earthy, underground tomb in which to sleep till dusk held the land again.

He pressed her to his wide chest and she clung to him for one more time. Then she was in Conlan's room in Chelsea, and Lazio had gone, though she still felt his cold kiss on her brow.

Conlan was asleep, his clothes strewn over the floor as if he had staggered to bed, worn out by all the adulation. She made a resolve to get down to the newsagents and pick up copies of all the daily papers where his opera would be reviewed.

But first, she slid out of her dress and crept into bed with him, curling up against his back, relishing flesh that was warm and alive. 'Eh? What?' he muttered sleepily. 'Is that you, Stella? Finished fucking your vampire, have you?'

He wasn't really awake, but turned to haul her into his arms, one leg thrown across her thighs, his cock already semi-erect. She smiled and coiled her body closer to his. He wasn't angry or possessive, leaving it to her to decide what she wanted to do and with whom.

'Yes, I saw Lazio.'

'The others were at the show, along with Belphegor,' he said, kissing her lightly and twiddling the ring in one of her nipples. 'They came to the party. You going to meet him again?'

'Yes, next year, same time,' she said, and found that suddenly it wasn't such a big deal. 'Conlan,' she continued, cradling his cock in her hand. 'D'you still want to marry me?'

'Yes,' he answered without hesitation.

'Good,' she said, and meant it. 'Let's do it soon. Before Quincy organises another tour... to the moon or the outer rings of Saturn or somewhere.'

'Right on,' Conlan agreed. 'We'll have a proper do...

flowers, reception, church... the whole works. We can even ask Quincy to be best man, if you like.'

'I don't think so,' she answered, smiling. 'You're only wanting to rub his nose in it, aren't you? If you do that, then I might as well invite Alithea to be a bridesmaid.'

Both laughed at the absurdity of this suggestion and, as Stella sobered under his kisses and caresses, her bodily responses taking over, she knew she had been extremely lucky to find him. Lucky too, to have experienced magic and beauty and the means of fulfilling a duty. She was a whole person now, with a human male who wanted her as his lifelong partner, and a vampire who would love her forever.

More exciting titles available from Chimera

* * *